EXODUS OF THE PHOENIX

EXODUS SERIES
BOOK ONE

ROBERT STADNIK

ISBN: 978-1-953865-03-8 (Paperback)
ISBN: 978-1-953865-04-5(eBook)

Library of Congress Control Number: 2020922613

Any references to historical events, real people, or real places are used fictitiously. Names, characters, and places are products of the author's imagination.

Books Fluent
3014 Dauphine Street
New Orleans, LA
70117

CHRONOLOGY OF EVENTS

FEBRUARY **2018** – Relations between Pakistan and India deteriorate after years of hostilities between the two nations. They recall their ambassadors and urge all foreign visitors to leave. In a dangerous game of brinkmanship, they aim their nuclear weapons at each other. United Nations negotiations break down as participating members bicker about how to resolve the crisis.

By the end of the month, the Russian Confederation has aimed its nuclear missiles at India and Pakistan to quell the latter's mutual aggression. The United States formally protests Russia's actions and breaks off diplomatic relations.

APRIL **2, 2018** – India launches its nuclear missiles at Pakistan. Forty-three seconds later, Pakistan launches its arsenal at India. In less than an hour the major cities of both nations—including their capitals—are destroyed.

APRIL **3, 2018** – Syria and Iran, now both nuclear-capable, blame the United States for inflaming the situation between Pakistan and India. Each nation launches their single nuclear missile at the United States in retaliation. The NATO satellite defense network destroys both missiles and the U.S. responds by launching warheads at the attacking nations. Both Syria and Iran are obliterated. Outraged by the United States's actions, Russia and the European Union formally break ties with the U.S. and withdraw from the United Nations. The European Union also leaves NATO.

SEPTEMBER 2018 – Millions of civilians have fallen ill from the nuclear clouds drifting from both Syria and Iran. A large nuclear cloud has also spread from the India/Pakistan region throughout much of the continent. Massive relief efforts to help those suffering begin. The entire Middle East becomes uninhabitable and the population migrates to the continent of Africa. The governments of several African nations collapse, unable to handle the influx of refugees crossing their borders. Global media outlets state that humanity is at its end.

NOVEMBER 2021 – The radiation clouds dissipate in the atmosphere. Final tally puts the death toll at nearly one and a half billion people with millions more afflicted with radiation sickness. Shock from the enormous loss of life and the collapse of so many governments convince the nations of the world to meet and discuss how to prevent such an atrocity from occurring again.

DECEMBER 25, 2021 – The Accord of India is signed. All nations agree to dismantle their nuclear arsenals immediately. The United States is the only country that refuses to sign, citing its right to defend itself from aggressors. Rioting erupts as U.S. citizens respond violently to their government's refusal to sign the treaty.

DECEMBER 29, 2021 – A civilian coup backed by the military and supported by state governments overthrows the federal government. Congress is dismantled, and the president is removed from office. A new interim government is installed by civilian leaders. Their first and only act is to sign the Accord of India.

FEBRUARY 2022–MARCH 2028 – The world's nations pool their

resources to clean up the nuclear waste left by what's become known as the 'Nuclear Holocaust.' As they work to make radiation-afflicted regions habitable once again, they begin to address other social issues.

JULY **4, 2029** – With nations feeling more united from their efforts to improve world conditions, the historic Paris Gathering takes place. A new world government, the Global Republic of Nations, is formed and leaders from their respective nations become representatives of the new government. The headquarters of the new government is located in Sydney, Australia.

MAY **2031** – With Earth entering a new age of peace, the world government focuses its attention on space exploration and colonization. The International Space Agency (ISA) is established. The agency's first directive is to begin preparation to colonize both the moon and Mars.

SEPTEMBER **2032** – The first colony ship, the ISA India, establishes a colony on the moon. The moon is officially renamed Luna.

APRIL **2036** – The first Martian colony is established by the ISA Pakistan. The Global Republic of Nations passes a directive prohibiting individuals with genetic disorders created from exposure to nuclear radiation, as well as any of their offspring, from becoming colonists on Luna and Mars. This is done to prevent the need for additional medical resources in the colonies and to ensure these individuals receive the best medical care on Earth.

NOVEMBER **2037** – Voters on Earth and the colonies approve legislation making the world government the sole governing body of Earth, Luna, and Mars. The Global Republic of Nations becomes the Interstellar Republic Alliance. Luna and Mars are given equal powers as provincial regions and elect representatives to speak for them.

2032–2061 – Through the efforts of the ISA, new technologies rapidly develop. Ship designs are tested and refined, and environmental systems are improved. These advancements allow the rapid growth of the Luna and Mars colonies. On Earth, technologies are developed that improve the lives of civilians. New techniques in recycling permit the re-use and conversion of all manufactured materials. The biggest accomplishment is the development of technology that quickly breaks down nuclear matter and radiation. Scarred regions of Earth are cleaned up, allowing people to inhabit these areas once again. Near the end of this period, spaceships regularly travel between Earth, Luna, and Mars. Probes are sent throughout the solar system, establishing a network of sensors that scientists use to explore the other planets and moons from the comfort of their labs.

FEBRUARY **2062** – Francis DuBois successfully creates a computational equation that allows the properties of mass to be displaced from normal space. A secondary effect of displacement is the hyper-energizing of the surrounding spatial matter, allowing an object to be hurled faster than the speed of light. Work to create technology that utilizes this new theory immediately begins.

FEBRUARY **21, 2068** – A miniature prototype jumpgate successfully hurls satellite Voyager IV outside the solar system. The ISA orders construction of an exploration starship at the Luna shipyard while construction begins on a large-scale jumpgate in Indonesia on Earth.

JUNE **15, 2073** – ISA HORIZON is officially commissioned, and the ship is deployed from the Luna shipyard. Two months later, the jumpgate is delivered to the HORIZON from Earth.

DECEMBER **1, 2073** – ISA HORIZON reaches orbit around Pluto. The public's last visual of the ship on the broadcast networks is watching it deploy three cargo containers housing the jumpgate.

DECEMBER 7, 2073 – Contact is lost with the HORIZON. The ISA remains tight-lipped about the ship's status. They release a brief public announcement stating, "The mission has encountered some difficulties."

JANUARY 1, 2074 – The ETS RENAULT is secretly hired by the ISA to travel to Pluto and confirm the HORIZON's status.

MARCH 30, 2074 – Several ISA associates, working in conjunction with computer scientists on Mars, hack into ISA's solar system sensor array. The goal is to patch the array's tracking of the RENAULT into the public airways.

APRIL 20, 2074 – ETS RENAULT is lost near the ring formation of Saturn. The public watches in horror on the broadcast channels as the RENAULT is destroyed by a green, triangular alien ship.

APRIL 20–22, 2074 – Panic hits Earth, Luna, and Mars as people fear an imminent invasion. It takes two days for the regional military divisions to restore order.

APRIL 26, 2074 – The government assumes direct control of ISA and discloses the fate of the HORIZON to the public. The ship was attacked and destroyed by the same type of alien craft that destroyed the RENAULT.

MAY 2074–MARCH 2084 – For the next decade, human vessels are attacked and destroyed by the same green triangular ships. All attempts to communicate with the aliens fail and no one can determine if one ship is conducting the attacks or if it's multiple ships of the same class. New defenses developed to counter the attacks fail.

JULY 2085 – TERRA (Tactical Earth Reconnaissance and Recovery Authority) is officially established. The remaining divisions of the ISA and all global military divisions are merged into this new institution. TERRA designates the hostile aliens as 'the Screen.'

OCTOBER **2085** – An analysis of Screen attacks reveal that no human-operated ships are harmed within the sphere of Mars's orbit around the sun. The government orders a ban on all travel to the outer solar system. TERRA begins regular patrols around Mars to prevent any ship from attempting travel to the outer solar system. A moratorium is instituted prohibiting the installation of hyper-drive engines on space vessels.

SEPTEMBER **11, 2114** – The last recorded Screen attack occurs, destroying the ES DARK REBEL. Finally seeing the futility of trying to pass beyond Mars, no one attempts to travel to the outer parts of the solar system. The Screen attacks cease.

DECEMBER **2121** – The EXODUS Project is initiated by TERRA at a secret facility in the Tormented Valley area near Skagway, Alaska.

PROLOGUE

APRIL 20, 2074

"We're clear of Saturn's gravitational horizon," crackled Mary's voice over the ship's antiquated speakers.

The captain was standing in the washroom drying his rugged face, freshly scrubbed with soap and water, when he heard the update. Some orange hydraulic fluid had dripped on him while working in the engine bay and he'd stopped by his quarters to get cleaned up. He believed it important to lead by example and maintain a clean look for his crew, even if the crew consisted of just two other individuals.

He pounded the speaker button with his fist. "I'll be right up. Set a course straight for Pluto."

He looked at his reflection in the mirror. A few more gray hairs had sprouted in his beard and moustache. Age had made its presence known and even hair coloring wasn't concealing the slow march of silver across his head. Whoever said a freighter captain's job was easy was delusional. The work was lucrative, but the stress could be hell. Maybe if he had an easier job, his head would be a lot less gray. The captain's girlfriend was going to enjoy teasing him about his looks when he returned to Earth.

"Already done, Captain," Mary replied.

The captain flipped the speaker off without a response. He hadn't been in a good mood this entire trip. They'd just finished up a nonstop run from Earth to Mars, delivering plants to the colony nestled on the red planet. With no stopover at Luna, the trip had seemed lengthy and was taking its toll on the captain. He used to be able to handle such runs without missing a beat. Now that his youth had evaporated, these assignments were becoming increasingly cumbersome. He preferred the short jaunts between Earth and Luna.

He'd planned to schedule the ship's next few jobs delivering supplies to the moon from Earth. Screw Mars! They could get their cocoa beans and tomato plants from someone else. But first, he'd been looking forward to a relaxing three-month sabbatical on Earth.

That had been the plan—until the government contacted him with an unexpected job offer.

The captain's initial reaction had been to say no. Actually, *hell no*! But the money was simply too good to pass up. Despite feeling older, greed always got the better of him. He could be on his deathbed and would still try to sucker-punch the Grim Reaper if someone dangled enough money in front of him.

The best part of this deal was being paid in full before completing the job. Talk about a windfall. No company ever paid a full advance in the freighter business. With the amount of credits the government was paying, the captain would be able to enjoy a lengthy vacation.

——— ——— ———

Up on the bridge, first officer Mary reclined in her chair and kicked her feet up on her brightly-lit console station. She gazed out of the panoramic window spanning the small bridge area and saw nothing but empty space. Only the flickering stars dotting the background provided any depth to the view. It would be several weeks before they reached the outer rim of the solar system. This was the longest stretch any of them had spent in space.

Mary looked over at her pilot and navigational support, Juan, who was sleeping peacefully at his station. He was curled up in his seat like a baby in the womb, which didn't bother Mary. It was rare for anything to happen during a flight, and with Juan asleep, she could oversee navigational control from her seat, giving her something to do.

Sleep was elusive for Mary during space travel. It was a problem she worked hard to surmount. Over time, the trips between Earth and Mars had gotten easier. She'd taken baby steps to overcome her insomnia. At first it was two days with no sleep, then a daily nap. She'd eventually worked her way up to four hours of sleep a night.

While awake, Mary found ways to pass the time by stargazing. She had never been this far out of the solar system before and was hoping for some good glimpses of astronomical markers from the Oort Cloud. The captain usually prevented her from partaking in such indulgences. He'd kept her busy almost nonstop this trip, having her check the ship's systems constantly and make minor, unnecessary repairs.

Earlier the computer had detected a small spike in the ship's power core, which was a normal occurrence for an extended flight. Nevertheless, the captain had gone down to the engine bay to ensure there were no problems in either the power core or the engines.

Mary didn't consider him a true spacefarer like herself. Over the years, she'd dealt with all sorts of emergencies on ships. You name it, she'd experienced it. Nothing bothered her anymore. Even something as critical as a hull breach didn't scare her.

As long as the captain was flying the familiar routes between Earth, Mars, or Luna, he was fine. But out here he seemed like a skittish child, lost and unsure of himself. If the government hadn't offered so much money for this reconnaissance mission, Mary was certain the captain wouldn't have agreed to come.

"Ohh, ma," Juan muttered in his sleep. Mary nudged his shoulder with her foot, not wanting to hear him babble in his sleep. "Get up," she ordered.

Juan sputtered as he woke up. "Wha...!" He looked around the bridge as he stretched his stiff body. "We there yet?"

"Hardly." Mary adjusted the angle of her seat.

Juan rubbed his eyes and looked down at the instrument cluster. "Aw, man! Why you wake me up so soon?" the young pilot whined.

It grated on Mary's nerves. "You're not being paid to sleep."

It had been some time since she'd trained a new crewmember. Their last pilot had served for five years, and Mary had had him trained exactly to her liking. When he quit, she hadn't relished the thought of bringing someone new onto the team. She'd even argued with the captain that the two of them could operate the ship.

In the end, it had been his decision and Mary had to abide by it. She was only a hired hand, but she felt her twelve years of service on the RENAULT should have counted for something. At the very least, she should have been consulted on the new hire. But the captain had neglected to include her in the hiring process. He'd chosen Juan and expected Mary to get him up to speed on their operations.

The situation infuriated Mary, and she intended to talk to the captain about firing Juan once they returned to Mars. The pilot was too inexperienced and immature. Since Juan's arrival, she'd felt like a babysitter, and she despised the feeling. Her only consolation was that Juan was being paid a flat rate for this run instead of the usual commission crewmembers earned.

"We've cleared Saturn, so you might as well deploy another sensor package," Mary instructed Juan.

Juan grudgingly complied. He didn't understand why Mary couldn't deploy the satellites herself. It seemed like a waste to be woken up to punch a few measly buttons. He hit the sequence of colored buttons on his console to open the small launch bay. "Where's the loco at?"

"The captain," Mary replied, stressing the word, "is doing a check of the engines."

"Man, I never met anyone more paranoid than him," Juan said as he waited for the computer to signal that the probe package was ready for launch.

Despite his immaturity, Juan's perception was correct. The

captain had been on edge this entire trip and he wasn't masking it from the crew. Mary had confronted him, and he'd admitted that something about this job bothered him, but he couldn't put his finger on exactly what. His instincts were telling him to turn back to Earth, but he had no reasonable explanation why.

"He may be concerned, but I don't blame him," Mary said, trying not to draw too much attention to the captain's nervousness about the mission.

"Are you worried?"

"A little bit, but I'm actually more curious. I'd like to know why the HORIZON stopped transmitting."

The HORIZON was the International Space Agency (ISA)'s pride and joy. It was to be the first ship to depart the solar system and travel through interstellar space, thanks to the sophisticated jumpgate it was carrying.

"What do you think happened?" Juan asked, eager to hear what an experienced space junkie like Mary thought.

Mary wasn't interested in feeding his spacefaring fantasies. "I think it's just a busted transmitter." She couldn't count the number of 'rescue' missions she'd done where a supposedly lost ship had fallen victim to nothing more than failed communications equipment.

"Ahh, bullshit! You're not any fun. You know what I think? The HORIZON encountered something."

"Oh really?" Mary was amused but not surprised by his theory. It was typical for a young man to let his imagination get the better of him. "Some little green aliens we didn't find on Mars are actually living on Pluto?"

"Maybe. I'll bet you the HORIZON is in a thousand pieces, blown away by a ship or weapon hidden on Pluto."

"You've been watching too many movies." No one took the thought of aliens seriously. The ISA had been sending out communications signals for years but never received any replies. Personally, Mary didn't believe in aliens. It was the stuff of fiction, not reality. "The HORIZON is probably already at Alpha Centauri."

A blip from the computer interrupted their chat, drawing

Mary's attention to her console. She immediately sat up straight and looked at the information the sensors provided her. "We've got an object moving at high velocity in our general direction."

Juan checked his monitor, which registered the same blip. "I have it on my scope. Is it the HORIZON?"

That was Mary's initial assumption. The RENAULT and HORIZON were the only ships known to be in the outer solar system, but the sensor data indicated the object was moving faster than the HORIZON's top speed. The HORIZON could only achieve such velocity if it used Pluto's gravity well to slingshot back to the inner solar system.

Mary also noticed the mass of the projectile was smaller than the HORIZON's. She tried to glean more details, but the RENAULT wasn't equipped with sophisticated scanners. It was only a freighter, not a science vessel.

"Alter our course by thirty degrees portside," Mary ordered.

Unnerved that she'd never answered his question, Juan did what she asked.

Mary got on the ship's speakers to inform the captain of their current situation. "Captain, we've got a UFO moving in our direction." There wasn't a hint of nervousness in her voice.

"Unidentified? Damn it! I'll be right up."

Mary clicked off the speaker and stared at the screen. What could it be? The object was smaller than the RENAULT, and Mary couldn't recall any other commercial craft with the ability to move so fast. They'd been told the military didn't have any long-range ships. Even if what they were tracking was a military craft, it would have broadcasted a transponder identification code.

"Shit, man! It's changed direction to match our course correction. It's still heading right toward us."

"Relax, Juan, it's not little green men coming after us." Mary tweaked the scanners to their most sensitive setting, hoping to glean what the object might be. But the sensors wouldn't yield any new information.

Now Mary was becoming worried. She'd thought it might be some interstellar debris or a comet, but that assumption had flown out the window when the object had matched the RENAULT's course correction. She always had logical explanations for any situation, but this defied all logic. The only conclusion here was that the object was a ship.

"Fire up the top cannon and target the object," Mary ordered. Her instruction confirmed Juan's fears that they were in trouble, but she had no interest in coddling him. "If we can't avoid it, we'll have to stop it from colliding with us."

As Juan worked the cannon controls, Mary altered their heading by another twenty degrees and fired up the ship's thrusters to full speed. Again, the object matched the RENAULT's change in course. Mary said nothing, but a lump developed in her throat. Her lack of knowledge about what was approaching them was beginning to scare her. She still hoped it was a military vessel, but the lack of a transponder code made it unlikely. In addition, the captain had received specific information from the military stating they had no long-range ships out this far. If it wasn't the HORIZON, and assuming the military was telling the truth, what could this object be?

"The cannon's charged and ready," Juan announced. He was beginning to sweat.

Mary didn't look at him as he spoke. She focused her attention on the blip on her station screen.

"I said the cannon's ready," Juan repeated.

Mary ignored his panicked tone, speculating on what they were dealing with. The object continued to move toward them at the same rate of speed. Given its rate of velocity, a collision would certainly destroy the RENAULT.

Then it clicked. They hadn't done the obvious.

Mary turned on the communications antenna. "Unidentified object, this is the ETS RENAULT. Repeat, this is the Earth Transport Ship RENAULT, Mars registry M-B412. Please identify yourself." She wanted to hit herself for letting her fears get in the way of her thinking, but now she felt a bit more at ease. Certainly, they would get a response from it.

She held her breath, hoping to hear an answer to the hail. At first only background static filled the speakers. Then, without warning, a loud screeching sound came through. It was deafening and painful.

Juan clamped his hands over his ears in a vain attempt to block out the sound, but Mary ignored the pain, despite feeling like a hundred knives were stabbing her brain. She scrambled in her seat and turned off the speakers to get relief from the sound.

"Chica," Juan said, removing his hands from his ears, "the object is moving faster."

Mary checked her scope. The object had indeed accelerated to twice its previous speed. It was moving too fast now to avoid it. The RENAULT couldn't outrun something so fast. Fear gripped Mary, paralyzing her. It had been years since she'd felt this way.

"Juan, how long will it take to deploy and activate the sensor packet on the probe?"

"Two minutes. Why?"

"Deploy the probe and activate its sensors. Have it send all data to the nearest listening post around Mars."

"What's that going to do to help us?" he sputtered hysterically.

"We don't have much time," Mary said, becoming calm as her fear subsided. It was strange, but somehow, she knew their fates were sealed. "Launch the probe."

"Aw, shit, shit, shit." Juan hit the release button and launched the probe. They both watched on his monitor as the probe glided away from the RENAULT.

Once it had reached a far enough distance from the ship, he activated it. Its silver cylindrical casing blew off, and two large poles extended outward. Within moments, the sensor pallet on the probe powered up and became active. Juan linked the probe to the ship's scanner system. "It's done."

Mary didn't respond. She just looked out through the bridge windows.

"Chica, what is it?"

"It should be in visual range any moment." Mary tried to catch a glimpse of the object. "As soon as it's in range, fire the cannon."

Juan set the cannon to auto-fire on the object once it got close enough. "What should we do?" he asked, looking for additional direction, but she said nothing. He turned around and looked at her, panic visible on his face. "We need to do something."

He was young and inexperienced. Mary didn't have the heart to tell him they were out of options, and she was too preoccupied with trying to spot the object outside.

Juan jumped out of his chair. "We can't just sit here!"

"There's nothing else we can do," she said, never taking her eyes off the bridge window.

For what seemed like an eternity, they searched for signs of the oncoming object. Neither of them noticed the captain entering the bridge behind them.

He'd heard everything they had said over the ship's internal speakers as he made his way up to them. His instincts had been correct. He should have never accepted this job. All they could do now was see what would come.

A bright light blinked in the distance, catching the crew's attention. It grew bigger and bigger, as if a star was being born and shining its light for the entire universe to behold. The hearts of the RENAULT's crew began to pound in unison. The captain and Mary stood their ground, but fear finally overtook Juan. He scurried to the rear of the bridge like a scared animal.

The light grew in size and intensity as it reached the ship and enveloped it. The cannon never had time to fire as the targeting system malfunctioned from an energy overload.

For a moment, in the vacuum and darkness of space, a bright ball of orange light shimmered where the RENAULT held its position. When the light dissipated, all that was left were burnt shards of metal. The only movement was that of the unknown object, a green triangular ship.

The ship slowly passed by the remains of the RENAULT. It paused as if observing the wreckage, then turned and sped away from the scene, racing out on the same path it came in. The only witness was the sensor probe that had survived the incident. It floated unassuming through space as it continued to transmit its data back toward Mars.

CHAPTER ONE

DECEMBER 2142, SIXTY-EIGHT YEARS LATER

LOCATION: GOVERNORS ISLAND - NEW YORK CITY, NEW YORK
PLANET EARTH

The electronic bells sounded off in unison, reverberating through the corridors of the academic buildings at TERRA Academy. Students burst from the lecture rooms in Liberty Hall and spilled into the hallway. Cheers echoed throughout the building as the cadets celebrated the end of the winter semester. A mixture of first, second, third, and fourth year students wasted no time in sharing tales of final exam horrors as they poured out of the building.

One student strolled through the crowd without speaking a word to anyone. He was oblivious to his peers and did not care to participate in their banter. Only a shout from behind stopped him.

"John! Hey John! Wait up!"

John turned to see his best friend racing up to him. "Hey, Billy."

The young men headed out of the building onto the campus grounds, which were flooded with cadets. "How do you think you did on McLeeland's final?" Billy asked, brushing his hand through his short, dusty-blond hair.

"Wasn't a problem," John replied nonchalantly.

"No kidding. I saw you finish it in like twenty minutes."

John smiled. "What can I say? McLeeland's tests are never that hard."

Billy shook his head. "Maybe for you. You're the only person who would say something like that." It was the student body's consensus that LaDonna McLeeland gave the toughest exams on campus. "If only I could get by without studying."

"Hey, I actually read the textbook this semester," John said. Billy just stared at him. "Okay, only portions of it." Billy continued staring at him. "All right! I only skimmed the chapter summaries."

Billy rolled his eyes as they walked through campus. "So, you actually turned on your DAT this semester." Short for Data Acquisition Terminals, these small rectangular computer devices had replaced paper throughout TERRA as the primary form of holding information. "You're probably the first one to pass spatial physics without reading the book."

The cadets stopped when they reached the central campus area, known as The Quad. "We're done with finals, so no reason to hang out on campus," Billy said. "We better head back to Dorm Row to get ready for the parties tonight."

"I've got to see Superintendent Mortino in a couple of hours," John said. "I'm going to hang around here until the meeting."

The request from the superintendent's office had come in on John's DAT just before the start of his last final. It wasn't unexpected. He and the superintendent had a long history.

Billy wasn't surprised either. "You either got a spring assignment in the fleet or pissed Mortino off again."

"I doubt I'm at the top of their list to work in the fleet this spring." John laughed as he rolled his eyes.

Those seniors lucky enough to be chosen for a spring assignment had the opportunity to spend their last semester getting hands-on experience in the field. Competition was fierce, and cadets spent their four years at the Academy proving to the faculty they were worthy of selection. Cadets posted to the fleet their last semester typically climbed faster through TERRA's ranks.

John had never made an attempt to solidify his chance for an assignment. It meant trying to ingratiate himself with the staff, and he didn't operate that way. He went out of his way to challenge his professors and didn't hesitate to mock them in front of the other students. Very few professors cared for John, and he was certain none of them would recommend him for a fleet assignment.

"No, I'm still scheduled to take classes," he said. "So that means I'm seeing our superintendent because I pissed him off again."

"Any idea what it's about?"

"Who knows. I'm sure it'll be a lecture about me *not putting forth my best effort.*"

Billy laughed; John almost sounded like Mortino on one of his tirades. "It sucks if you're stuck here 'til June."

John shrugged. "I don't care. I'll gladly pass up a post this spring as long as I get a position on one of the capital ships after graduation."

"I heard Martin Freeman got picked for an assignment. He's going to be working in orbital control on Luna Station."

"Martin's a brownnoser and an asshole. He probably slept with an admiral to get selected."

"Sheesh, John! Aren't we a little bitter. You may have standards, but I'd sleep with the superintendent's eighty-year-old wife just to get a spring post."

John shuddered at the thought. "That is the sickest, most twisted thing you've ever said! Thanks for the visual. I'm going to have nightmares."

Billy playfully shoved his friend. "Oh, come on! People would do anything for an assignment, and you're no different."

"Yeah, but I'm a realist." John's cavalier attitude about his studies and his view of the faculty as inferior had alienated him from any chance of being sponsored for a spot in the fleet for his last semester. He would have to join the rest of the graduating class in applying for positions after the spring.

The pair approached the fork where the walkway split in two different directions. "Whatever Mortino is going to lay into you about, don't let it go on too long," Billy said. "I'll be with the guys at Sirk's, celebrating. So, hurry up. Otherwise you'll miss the fun."

"I'm not missing out on tonight," John said as the young men shook hands and parted ways. He was ready for a night of party-hopping and drinking. "I'll call you when I'm done with Mortino."

"Sounds good," Billy yelled back as he gave a thumbs-up.

——— ——— ———

Superintendent Paul Mortino stood alone in the conference room on the top floor of the administration building. He watched from the window as the students scurried around the campus grounds like ants. It was a process he watched each semester.

The campus itself was a scientific wonder. Every conceivable plant life on Earth was displayed here. Plants that couldn't thrive on the outside grounds were housed in one of four large crystal domes that sat at each corner of the campus. The domes were fifty stories tall and served as a physical marker to locate the campus from the air. The domes were interconnected by walls that were actually buildings. It gave the feeling that the campus was a fortified installation. The building at the north entrance was split in two at the location of the main entry gate.

The superintendent enjoyed watching his students go about their activities. He felt like a father figure as he observed their interactions with one another as they meandered off the campus grounds. He took his duties as superintendent seriously, and believed their academic performance reflected his ability to run the Academy. He felt pride seeing the students heading home after another semester of hard work.

With finals over and the stress of their studies behind them, the cadets wasted no time heading back to Dorm Row for a weekend of celebration. The campus would soon be nothing more than a ghost town. Everyone would be hurrying home to spend time with their loved ones for winter break. No instructor ever graded final exams on campus. In a matter of hours, only the maintenance bots would be left to tidy up the grounds.

The creak of the conference room door opening interrupted Mortino's thoughts. He turned to see the campus instructors file in.

"Ah, ladies and gentlemen. Please come in and sit," he said in his usual formal tone. He moved to the head of the conference table and waited patiently for the instructors to take their seats. "I know you're all anxious to head home, so I won't take too much of your time."

As the last instructor took his seat, Mortino handed a stack of papers to the instructor sitting closest to him. "What I'm passing to you is a list of some of the seniors graduating this year. As you know, TERRA is overburdened with excess personnel and has been looking to curtail their numbers. Lowering the number of applicants we accept to the Academy has not had an appreciable effect. These past few weeks, you've all heard the rumors about a new program being instituted to solve this problem. I'm here to confirm those rumors are true."

The faculty looked at one another. They *had* heard about a new program circulating through the rumor mill, but hadn't given it too much credence. For years, TERRA had discussed ways to reduce the number of people entering the program without upsetting the population. The problem had been examined for so long that no one ever expected a solution.

Mortino continued once he felt they had digested the news. "The list provided to you is of this year's graduating seniors selected to go into the new program."

"It looks like almost a quarter of the senior class is on here," said tactics instructor George Paez as he reviewed the list.

Mortino nodded. "Correct. As you know, each graduating senior that enters TERRA is guaranteed financial security and benefits for life. The fleet simply does not have the means to support this arrangement any longer. To remedy this, the command council created a reservist program that these seniors will be the first to enter. Rather than work as TERRA officers, they will be placed on reserve status and will only be called upon to serve during times of war."

Everyone in the room knew that would never happen. TERRA hadn't fought a war since its inception. "And what exactly does reserve status mean?" engineering instructor Brandi Marcus asked.

"These reservists will not actively work in TERRA. They'll be applying the skills they've learned here in the private sector. They will receive no pay or support from TERRA whatsoever."

McLeeland interrupted Mortino. "Our cadets work hard and sacrifice a lot to qualify for entry into the Academy. Most spend their entire lives preparing themselves for the entrance exams. What's the point of them going through all that if they won't become officers?"

"The reserve program won't diminish the public's respect for TERRA graduates. Our academic program rivals those of the best civilian universities. Private companies will be begging to have graduates work for them, if for nothing else but the prestige of an Academy graduate on their payrolls. Reservists will enjoy the same respect as officers."

"Except that they won't be officers," McLeeland stressed.

The instructors chattered amongst themselves and offered their opinions about the new program. Mortino gave them a moment to talk before continuing the meeting.

"I understand some of you may have the same concerns as Professor McLeeland, but the decision has been made. The command council has asked for your support in helping these seniors transition into the program."

"I notice John Roberts on the list," Marcus pointed out. "Is there a particular reason why?"

Mortino cleared his throat. He had hoped no one would have noticed that cadet's name, but was ready if someone pointed it out. "It was decided that Cadet Roberts would be a better fit for the reservist program."

"The most intelligent cadet ever to come through the Academy isn't officer material?" McLeeland asked in a sarcastic tone. She never minced words, always going straight to the point. "I know everyone here has had their own experience with him, especially you, Superintendent. But punishing him by denying him a place in the fleet is a bit petty."

"It's no secret that Cadet Roberts has been a difficult student for us. A TERRA officer must respect the chain of command and his peers. Cadet Roberts does neither. He openly mocks TERRA's philosophy and our methods. With placement in the fleet mandated to be cut, we cannot afford to waste space on individuals who may prove to be a disruption. I'm not concerned about Cadet Roberts. With his intelligence, he will undoubtedly have the choice of any job in the private sector."

The usually-quiet field maintenance instructor Alfred Hither spoke up. "Our students aren't here to get rich in the private sector. They come here so that they can serve in the fleet. As Professor McLeeland pointed out, they sacrificed a lot to make it here."

"They will continue to serve TERRA, but in an auxiliary capacity," said Mortino, his patience coming to an end. "The purpose of this meeting was to inform you of the program. The debate of its merits has already been thoroughly discussed by the command council. Our job is to provide a united front and support it when it goes public on Monday. I don't want to keep you any longer, as I'm sure you're all anxious to see your families."

Mortino was always good at politely telling people to get the hell out. He was a natural politician, which is why he was considered by both the faculty and command council to be one of the best superintendents to ever run the Academy. He knew how to get things done and how to deal with people.

The faculty filed out of the conference room, talking with each other as they left. McLeeland approached Mortino as he was gathering his papers. "Who has the fortune of informing the selected cadets about this?"

"The cadets will be informed of their assignment no differently than those entering the fleet." Graduating cadets were given their assignments the first week in May each year.

"Even Cadet Roberts? Seems to me he deserves better than a letter delivered to him by a mail bot."

"I suspect he will not take the news lightly, which is why I will be informing him personally today."

"Don't try to enjoy it too much, Paul," warned McLeeland. "Despite what you told everyone, it will appear that Cadet Roberts was selected out of spite. It's well known you and he don't get along." Without waiting for Mortino to respond, she turned and left the conference room.

She was right. Mortino had personally chosen John because of all the trouble he had caused. He had humiliated and undermined Mortino's authority these past four years. The superintendent had bided his time to get back at Cadet Roberts, and thankfully, that time had finally arrived.

CHAPTER TWO

John looked at the large analog clock on the campus tower, checking the time. It was fifteen minutes past two. He was already late for his meeting with Mortino. He'd lost track of time, letting his mind wander—a frequent habit. For most students, the end of final exams was a huge weight off their shoulders, but not for John. He never worried about tests and never stressed over any of his classes. He studied very little and walked into class knowing he could pass any exam handed to him.

John's mind was preoccupied with the upcoming spring semester, and it wasn't regarding a fleet posting. He'd already resigned himself that he was never going to get one. In May, those seniors not on a spring assignment would be notified of their placement in the fleet, and John was going over the possibilities of where TERRA might put him.

Cadets could submit requests for assignments to the placement board, letting the board know what career track they wanted to pursue. John had made a request to serve on a capital ship, but he didn't specify a position. He didn't care if he was assigned to sweep the decks or unclog toilets, as long as he was on a ship.

For years, John had dreamed of living in space, and the only way he could fulfill that dream was to secure a position on one of TERRA's five capital ships. He wasn't expecting to get a desirable position if he was posted to one. The evaluations on his transcripts were less than stellar, but his grades in ship operations, starship design, and engineering were top notch. He thought that after twenty or so years, when his reputation at the Academy had faded, he would have a chance to command a capital ship. Maybe by then humans would be exploring space outside the solar system.

John believed that an assignment to a capital ship was a realistic goal, but venturing into deep space? That was an entirely different matter. Deep space exploration wasn't a possibility, with the threat of the Screen looming over humanity. Exploring space was what John wanted to do, but he knew that it wouldn't happen in his lifetime.

John finished his lunch and got up from his seat on the bench. He threw his leftovers in the trash bin and brushed the crumbs from his uniform. He was prepared for another encounter with Mr. High-and-Mighty Superintendent.

To say the two of them nursed a mutual dislike was putting it politely. John had wound up in the superintendent's office numerous times over the course of his four years at the Academy. Rumor had it that he held the Academy record.

Mortino had threatened to expel John on more than one occasion, saying he couldn't hide behind the safety of his good grades forever; it was a privilege to attend the Academy and every teenager on Earth, Luna, and Mars competed fiercely to earn a spot on the freshman roster. Usually at that point in the lecture John would roll his eyes, incensing Mortino further, and tune him out. He'd grin while Mortino spouted his holier-than-thou TERRA philosophy and went on about what it meant to be an officer. He was certain that Mortino's evaluation of him was the most scathing in his records.

As he thought about the superintendent, John trekked across campus to the administration building at the eastern wall. It was composed of a polysynthetic glass that acted as a large mirror. The inner wall was red brick that comprised the actual building. A line of windows stretched across it, allowing those inside to watch who was coming in or out. Unfortunately, Superintendent Mortino's office was one of the offices located on the inner side of the building, so he had the advantage of seeing John approach. The first thing Mortino would probably comment on would be John's nonchalant pace despite his tardiness.

A few jumps up some small steps, and John was at the main entrance. He gripped one of the door handles and took a deep breath, trying to expel the nervousness in his body. He would never admit it to anyone, but he always got butterflies in his stomach prior to meeting with Mortino. It wasn't that he was intimidated by the superintendent. He thought Mortino was nothing more than a puppet who couldn't handle a real-world crisis. He couldn't explain his trepidation—but he felt it, nonetheless.

John pushed open the glass door and entered the large, circular lobby. Several snapshots of the campus during its construction adorned the walls. Each picture had a caption, including the year it was taken and a brief description of what it was depicting.

Anyone entering the lobby immediately zeroed in on the central receptionist area. Like the lobby itself, the reception desk was round. It was elevated to the chest level of most students, so the receptionists had to look up at the visitors to speak with them.

Sally Cornich was the head receptionist. She had worked at the Academy for the past seventeen years and had become a permanent fixture. Unlike the other two receptionists she oversaw, she excelled at her job. Sally didn't need to consult the directory when a visitor checked in. She knew the names of every administrator and instructor as well as the campus layout, and possessed comprehensive knowledge of the school's academic programs.

It wasn't unheard of for students to get Sally's advice on their choice of courses when they were unsure of the information given to them by academic advisors. She had a pleasant personality no matter who she dealt with and could turn a person's bad mood into a positive outlook. Students considered her their mother on campus.

Sally was always supportive of the students. She considered them her extended family and would do whatever she could to help them through their years here. John was no exception. Whenever he was summoned to see the superintendent, Sally would always say, "You're such a good boy, why must trouble always find you?"

as if John was innocent of everything he did and merely a victim of circumstance. But she never frowned at him. She gave him a big hug after every reprimand, telling him everything would be fine. Her positive demeanor was an antidote to Mortino's harsh words.

Sally's bubbly personality was no different today. She was by herself, having let the other two receptionists take the day off. The lobby was deserted, not a soul to be seen anywhere. The students had long since vacated the campus, with celebrations already underway throughout the city. John likened the empty campus to a Screen alert, which the campus underwent once a year. When the alarms went off, the students and faculty headed to one of the numerous underground shelters, leaving the topside of the campus deserted.

During his second year, John had decided to go against protocol and hadn't gone to a bunker. As the alert sounded off, he'd snuck away and hid in the bathroom while his starship design class joined the rest of campus underground.

After about fifteen minutes of hiding, he'd headed outside. It was eerily quiet, as the entire top level was devoid of people. Even the campus bots were programmed to head to their stations and shut down during the drill.

John had meandered down toward the center tower and even taken a couple pictures of himself alone on the grounds with his DAT. He'd been sure no one would catch him, and that he would just rejoin the other students as they emerged from the bunkers. Unfortunately, he hadn't known that a TERRA fighter squadron was doing reconnaissance sweeps over the campus during the drill, and they'd locked onto John when their scanners picked up the only sign of human life topside.

John had never seen Mortino so angry. He was surprised the superintendent hadn't blown a blood vessel. Mortino had rambled on about TERRA ethics and standards, his arms waving wildly as he stomped around his office, swearing numerous times that John had ended his career with that stunt. But a day after the drill, Mortino had changed his tune and instead of being expelled, John was disciplined by working a week in the campus kitchen.

John had been surprised by this change of heart, and he wasn't the only one. Everyone had expected him to be booted from the Academy. For weeks rumors had circulated about what John had done to avoid expulsion. His favorite rumor was that his father was an admiral on the command council and had smoothed things over with Mortino. Not a lot of people knew that John's parents had been dead for years.

When John wasn't kicked out for the emergency drill stunt, he knew he would never be expelled. He'd become bolder in his brash comments to Mortino—which hadn't done much to improve their relationship.

"Good afternoon, John," said Sally, interrupting John's thoughts. "Finals go well for you?"

"I did okay." He leaned on the desk. "How bad is it?"

"He's actually in a very good mood," answered Sally as she scratched her curly red hair with her stylus. "He finished a staff meeting not too long ago and seems quite upbeat. I don't think you have to worry."

John smiled. "I never have anything to worry about."

Sally chuckled and patted John on the cheek. "You're such a good boy. Why does trouble always follow you around?"

"Dumb luck, I guess."

"I'm sure he saw you coming. Go on in," said Sally, waving John toward the hall. "And good luck."

John gave Sally a quick smile before heading down the hallway. Mortino's office was the first one on the left side, so it wasn't much of a walk. He reached the door and knocked, not wanting to stall any longer. His mind was already shifting toward getting over to the bar for some fun.

"Come in," came Mortino's voice from behind the door. As usual, John shuddered to hear the snotty tone of the superintendent's voice. He took a deep breath, turned the knob, and opened the door.

The superintendent was an enthusiastic fan of various forms of artwork, and the paintings and sculptures littering his office reflected that appreciation. The wall behind the desk was a bookshelf, filled with books that included philosophy, TERRA tactical manuals, and literature from some of history's famous writers.

John wondered if Mortino kept the books in some sort of order, but never had a chance to carry on a civilized conversation with him long enough to find out. He'd always thought it would be a great prank to break in and rearrange the books on the shelf, maybe throw in a few DATs loaded with pornography. It would be a great farewell senior graduation prank.

The other item that caught John's attention was a table where a lamp and several pictures of Mortino's family were arranged. The pictures were of his wife and two daughters. John had never met them, but he assumed the daughters were probably bitches and the wife some upper-class socialite who flashed a phony smile whenever in public. Any of the superintendent's family members had to be as despicable as he was.

Mortino was standing in front of the window, looking out at the campus. His hands were clasped behind his back. He didn't turn when John walked in, so the cadet announced himself.

"You wanted to see me, Superintendent?"

"You seem to have forgotten that we had an appointment at two, Cadet Roberts."

John decided to start Mortino's vacation off to a good start by getting him mad. "No, I didn't forget," he said, his tone matter-of-fact.

The superintendent didn't react to John's comment, which was disappointing. Instead, he walked over to his desk and sat down. "Have a seat, Cadet," he said as he reclined in his chair.

John sat in one of the two chairs that faced the superintendent's desk. He watched as Mortino picked up a DAT, curious about what the superintendent was looking up. His eyes gravitated toward Mortino's large bald spot. The superintendent's gray hair now covered only the sides of his head. John prided himself on thinking he'd helped accelerate the man's baldness.

"I received your grades for some of your classes already. Not bad, three A's so far. Looks like you might have your best semester ever."

"I chalk it up to an easy semester. But then again, all my semesters here have been pretty easy." John knew that any insult to the Academy was an insult to the superintendent.

"Yet you are ranked in the middle of your class. If the classes have been so easy, I would think you would have earned straight As and be at the top of the class."

John's lack of stellar grades was another source of the faculty's frustration with him. They all recognized he could do the work and consistently demonstrated his understanding of the material in class—but when it came to exams, he frequently did not apply his ability to earn top marks.

"I'd hoped your roommate's academic habits would have rubbed off on you. She's ranked in the top five."

"Yeah, well, grades are nothing more than letters and I wouldn't want to embarrass the Academy by pointing out how substandard the coursework is."

"You always have an answer for everything, don't you, cadet? Well, I guess after four years of sliding by, you've become accustomed to getting away with things. All talk and no action."

John didn't say anything. He just wanted to get this meeting over with so he could go have fun with the other cadets. They did the same song and dance each meeting and John was not interested in a repeat performance now, not when there was drinking to be done.

"All right, Cadet Roberts," said Mortino. "I'm sure you're anxious to celebrate with your fellow classmates and I do believe I have something for you to celebrate."

"Huh?" John was confused. His first thought was that he'd gotten a spring assignment with TERRA. But he knew Mortino would rather sacrifice his kids to the devil before letting that happen. Something was up.

"I'm happy to inform you that you will be the first graduate from the Academy to be inducted into the newly formed TERRA Reserves."

"What the hell is that? I never heard of it."

Mortino leaned further back in his chair, grinning. "It's a new branch of TERRA. Graduates who are placed in the reserves are on inactive status until such time they are called for service, primarily during warfare. It'll provide you an opportunity to work in the civilian community."

"You've got to be kidding."

"No, cadet. I am quite serious."

"What dumbshit came up with such a stupid program? And why the hell does TERRA need a reserve staff? It's too chickenshit to go to war with anyone to need a branch like that. This is ridiculous." John tried to restrain his temper. Maybe this was some sort of practical joke—but he had the sinking feeling that Mortino was being sincere.

"Mind your tongue, cadet."

"No one spends four years busting their asses to get placed on the sidelines."

"Well that's the thing, isn't it? You didn't work hard in your studies. You just got by doing the minimum, wasting your talents and our time."

"Now wait a minute." John was beginning to fume. "I'm in the top half of the class."

"Which is unacceptable for a man of your abilities," shot back Mortino— the closest he had ever come to giving John a compliment. "You've done nothing but taken for granted the opportunity given to you. Other students have sacrificed their personal lives to succeed while you've squandered your time here. There are others who are more deserving of a post in the fleet than you."

"Oh, I see." John stood up and leaned toward Mortino, his hands braced on the desk. "I'm being punished because I don't salute the flag, know the fleet song by heart, or kiss your scrawny little ass. You were just waiting for the chance to sabotage my career."

"It takes more than intelligence to be a successful officer, and you're a perfect example. You mock everything TERRA stands for and what it represents. The only person who has sabotaged your career is you, cadet. You really think your antics these past few years have gone unnoticed?"

"Oh, I'm sure you documented every little misstep in my file," John hissed as his entire body tensed. He knew his dream of serving on a capital ship was all but gone. "You just couldn't wait to tell everyone how insubordinate I am."

"Oh no, Cadet Roberts! You managed to pique the attention of the admiralty all on your own, something rarely accomplished by a student. They have concluded you are too much of a risk to be allowed to serve in the fleet."

John had heard enough. The decision had been made and no amount of pleading or ranting would change Mortino's mind. Not that John would ever conceive of begging. Even a chance to work on a starship wasn't worth swallowing his pride. He bolted for the door.

"Cadet Roberts," called Mortino as John opened the door. "Do not look at this as a setback. A graduate of the Academy will have a choice of any job in the private sector. Perhaps you will have the opportunity to work on a civilian vessel for a shipping company."

After four years of trying, Mortino had finally pushed the right buttons. John snapped. "You can take your fuckin' reserves and shove them up your ass! And you can quote that on my transcripts!" He slammed the door as hard as he could, stomping down the hallway and through the lobby. He didn't notice Sally standing there, her mouth open.

"John," she called, but he ignored her. He tore through the campus grounds, knocking aside several maintenance bots that tried to scurry out of his way. His only thought was to escape and hide himself from the world. The pain welling up inside him was too much to bear. He wanted to numb that feeling.

He'd never expected to get a quality assignment in the fleet, but to be railroaded from ever serving at all? He'd never seen it coming. As long as he could graduate from the Academy, he'd thought there would always be a place for him somewhere in TERRA. How could he have been so wrong? His entire life had been a waste, working toward a dream that would never be.

Through the window of his office, Mortino watched John

storm away. Four years. It had taken four years, but the superintendent had finally prevailed. He could not help but smile at his accomplishment.

CHAPTER THREE

New York was considered one of Earth's premier cities. It was a hallmark of what humans had accomplished over the past 120 years. As a highly-regarded institution, TERRA could have established its operations anywhere on Earth, Luna, or Mars. The organization's headquarters were on Luna, but 95 percent of the human population still lived on Earth, so it made sense to establish the Academy there.

When it came time to choose a locale for the Academy, TERRA had chosen Governors Island. The world's financial center had been relocated to Tokyo, so the area once called Wall Street had been converted to what was now known as Dorm Row. Cadets resided here while attending the Academy, and it was the center of student life.

A cadet's needs were paid for by TERRA—dorm apartments, living expenses, everything. TERRA took care of its own. Every year, thousands of young men and women applied for a shot at one of the Academy's admission slots. The chances of acceptance were slim.

High school applicants spent two years of intense physical and academic training to prove their worth to the admissions board. The lucky few accepted into the Academy made a lifelong commitment to serve in TERRA. No one ever retired.

A TERRA officer was admired by the world and treated like a celebrity. Many would argue that officers were more highly regarded than even the president of the Interstellar Republic Alliance.

Neon and Sirk's were the two most popular hangouts for cadets. Neon was far more popular, as it was in the heart of Dorm Row. Students could be found there day or night; it was the only establishment in Dorm Row open twenty-four hours a day. On weekdays, cadets would congregate in study groups while watching the latest news developments on the monitors. Fridays and Saturdays consisted of drinking to forget about the rigors of the week's academic challenges. Sunday was all about drinking coffee and recovering from hangovers.

On this Friday, Dorm Row was an explosion of festivities. The end of the semester meant the streets would be full of cadets letting loose after surviving a week of final exams. Cadets were either celebrating in the streets or hanging out on the balconies of their dorms. Young people from all over New York flocked to Dorm Row at the end of the semester, as it was well known that TERRA cadets threw the best parties.

Neon was filled to capacity, with most students already intoxicated. Cadets crowded the bar and chatted, regaling each other with tales of heart-wrenching exams and all-night study sessions. In the middle of the bar sat one lone individual who was oblivious to all the chatter around him. He was surrounded by his peers, yet he refused to partake in the celebration. He was in complete solitude with his thoughts of despair.

John had come straight to Neon from his meeting with Superintendent Mortino and had done whatever he could to erase that encounter from his mind. In three hours, he had consumed two screwdrivers, three apple martinis, two Cosmopolitans, four Washington Apples, and was now working on a cranberry vodka drink, which he finished with one gulp. It was a miracle he hadn't thrown up yet.

"Sammie," he mumbled, barely able to formulate coherent words. "Another one." He hit the empty glass on the bar. Any harder and the glass would have shattered.

The petite young bartender walked over and grabbed the

empty glass from his hand before he could break it. "Forget it, John. You're overdoing it. I don't need a case of alcohol poisoning tonight."

"Nonsense. Nonsense. Nonsenseses....non..." He smiled, as if he'd had a remarkable revelation about the word.

"Something's been riding your ass since you walked in. You only drink this much when someone or something has pissed you off. You flunk a class or something?"

John pointed to the empty glass she was holding. "Fill 'er up and I'll tell ya all about how my future went kaput...kaputo..."

"Fine, but you're getting water," she said grabbing a new glass from the rack behind her. "And I swear you're out of here if you puke."

John stuck his tongue out at her as she walked away. During his freshman year, he'd incorrectly gauged how much alcohol he could put away. After getting up on the bar and spinning around, he'd promptly tossed his cookies over everyone and everything around him. Sammie refused to use her bot to clean up the mess and instead made John do it. Still, she swore the stench had lingered for several weeks.

"Whose future went kaput?" boomed a loud voice behind John. Billy clasped his hands on his friend's shoulders. With him was David, a close friend of both Billy's and John's.

David's father was an admiral in the fleet, and a force to be reckoned with. The same could not be said of David. He was quiet, unassuming, and the frequent target of bullies. Despite being, well, a wimp, David was honest and dependable. But his honesty tended to be a little too honest, which got him into trouble.

On one occasion, fellow cadet Greg Jacobs had started hassling David when he caught the meek young man staring at him in the student lounge. When Greg asked what he was looking at, David replied that he wondered how someone with such an ugly and distorted face could have a knockout girlfriend. John was nearby, and on hearing those words, instantly wanted to be friends with David.

That day John rescued David from a brutal beating. To keep

Greg's attention away from David for the rest of their freshman year, John hacked into the grading system and failed Greg in base operations. The instructor never accepted paper submissions. Everything had to be on a DAT, which made it easy for John to doctor phony exam results to support the F. Greg was so mad at having to repeat the class that he forgot all about David. It was one of very few stunts John had gotten away with.

John peered at his friends through his bloodshot eyes as they squeezed up to the bar on either side of him. "Hey," he muttered.

"Jeez, man. You could've waited for me before starting," said Billy, looking at the drunken mess that was his friend. "I told you we were going to be at Sirk's." He called over to Sammie. "How much has he had?"

"Too much," said the blond bartender. "You need to get him out of here. He's cut off."

"Bleh!" David said, getting a whiff of John's breath. "He smells like a drunk. Let's get him outside for some fresh air."

"Phit!" was all John managed to sputter, sticking his tongue out at David. "You get blesh aired..."

"Come on," said Billy, turning his friend around and helping him stand up. David did what he could to keep John propped up.

"I want another drink," John said half-defiantly, but he was in no condition to offer any resistance.

"We'll get one at your place."

Billy and David headed out of the bar as they towed their friend between them. David looked over at Billy. "I guess the meeting with Mortino went well."

Luckily for the two sober cadets, John's apartment was only a block from Neon. They managed to get halfway there before John's legs gave out and they had to carry him the remaining distance. As soon as they got him up the two steps in front of his place, John leaned over the railing and let loose.

Vomit spewed from John's mouth onto the flowerbed in front of his apartment. Billy patted his drunken friend on the back as John leaned over the railing. David, too squeamish to watch his friend throw up, left Billy to handle getting John in the apartment.

David had a legitimate excuse to leave, as his father was flying in from Mars and his mother wanted the entire family home for his arrival.

"I hate this," John managed to blurt in between spewing puke.

"Yeah, yeah. But you're so good at it," said Billy. "And you're giving the plants plenty of protein."

John struggled to lift himself off the railing. Billy helped him up, trying to avoid smelling his friend's now-rancid breath.

They worked their way up the stairs to the door, Billy struggling to keep his friend upright. There were a couple of instances where John almost toppled over, but Billy was quick to balance him and prevent them both from falling over. They finally reached the door and Billy punched in the code on the keypad to unlock it. As soon as he heard the lock click, he turned the knob and kicked open the door.

TERRA apartments were spacious accommodations provided to students. When the old Wall Street area was selected as the location to house cadets, all the buildings were torn down and the new dorms erected. Each apartment was identical in layout, so no one student had a better apartment. A large living area was the first room people entered from outside. The balcony was accessed from the living room through the large sliding glass doors, which provided a scenic view of the streets of Dorm Row. The kitchen was on the other side of the living room, separated by a long breakfast bar. A hallway led to a pair of bedrooms that each had their own bathroom.

Students were housed in pairs and stayed in the same apartment throughout their four-year stint. The Academy had strict rules about students changing dorms, primarily to prevent them from moving in with friends. No one knew how the Academy matched roommates, whether by some selection criteria or simply at random.

Although the apartments were furnished by TERRA, students could redecorate their new homes at their discretion. So over time, each apartment looked radically different from the next. John's apartment was bright and had a homey feel to it. The walls were cream-colored, and potted plants were scattered throughout.

John had a preference for cacti, and had several of them in the living room and his bedroom. He didn't have much of a green thumb, and had a knack for killing any plant he cared for. Cacti were the only ones that seemed immune to his touch of death. It was the sole contribution he'd made to change the apartment's look.

His roommate, Julie Olson, handled the rest of the redecorating responsibilities. She had spruced up the apartment with various paintings done by artists in her home state of Nebraska. Julie had a fondness for art and believed the best works were done by unknown artists struggling their way up in the art world.

Redecorating an apartment was typically a bonding experience for new roommates to get to know each other better, but John and his roommate hadn't been able to tolerate each other from day one.

Julie was sitting in the recliner, reading a TERRA career manual on her DAT. Distributed to the senior cadets in October, the manual detailed all of their possible career choices. Julie, like the rest of the senior class, had already put her request in with the placement board, but she enjoyed passing the time by reading all the career descriptions offered in the fleet. She even read up on the ones she had no interest in pursuing.

TERRA offered a litany of job specialties to cater to the cadets' various interests. Julie's first pick was a career in bridge operations. It was one of the most desirable career tracks cadets vied for, as it typically led to a command position on a capital ship or support vessel. Julie was confident in obtaining a position on a capital ship, as she was ranked fourth in her class and had recommendations from the entire Academy faculty.

Julie had heard some commotion outside but dismissed it as rowdy cadets passing by. As she heard the door open, she put her DAT down on the coffee table and stood to see who was coming in. She wasn't too surprised to see Billy carrying in her roommate.

"It's only nine o'clock. You finished early?" she asked in an amused tone as she watched Billy struggle to haul John inside.

"Maybe for him," Billy replied as he led John over to the couch.

Julie got a whiff of John's putrid breath and moved out of the way to let Billy through the living room. Dropping John face down on the couch, Billy collapsed on the recliner, exhausted. After a few moments of trying to catch his breath, he looked up at Julie and gave her a smile.

"Hi."

"Hi. You want something to drink?" she asked as she went to the kitchen. Julie considered Billy a close friend, even though he was John's best friend and Julie and John didn't get along. It didn't make sense to be friends with someone who was best friends with a person she loathed, but there it was.

Billy considered having a beer, but one glimpse of John's condition squelched that thought. "Water's good. John's barfing killed any desire I had to drink."

Julie cracked a grin. She opened the refrigerator to get some cold water. "How'd you do on finals?"

She didn't want to talk about John. Their relationship had been bad from the start and had only gotten worse as time passed. She'd requested to move to another apartment during freshman year. Unfortunately, the request had been denied. Eventually, the two cadets learned to avoid each other. Any interaction they had always seemed to end in a fight.

"Pretty good," answered Billy. "Even though spatial physics was a bitch, I think I nailed the final."

Julie returned to the living room and handed Billy his glass. She sat down on the futon next to the recliner and took a sip of an iced tea she'd poured for herself.

"Did you get an assignment for next semester?" Given Julie's ranking in the class, he'd assumed she would be working in the fleet this spring.

Julie shook her head. "No, I never received a letter."

"Impossible. You have a higher GPA than Martin, and he got an assignment."

"I know, I heard. I was thinking about talking to Superintendent Mortino about it." Julie put her glass down on the coffee table.

When the mail bot hadn't delivered a letter today, it had devastated her. Very little rattled Julie, but this had caught her completely off guard, and she'd spent the entire afternoon crying. It had never occurred to her that she wouldn't be selected. Even her instructors had asked about her spring assignment.

She had put off calling her dad back in Nebraska to tell him the bad news. What had gone wrong? Had she done something to eliminate herself from consideration? She'd racked her brain trying to find an explanation, but couldn't come up with any viable reason.

"I'd wait a couple of days before talking to the superintendent," said Billy. "John had a meeting with him today and I don't think it went well."

Julie stole a quick glance at her roommate—then looked down at her lap. It didn't surprise her that their meeting had resulted in John infuriating Mortino yet again. But this time was different. John was rarely bothered by anything. When something really upset him, he drowned his sorrows with whatever bottle of liquor was lying around. At first, Julie had thought John was an alcoholic, but he could go six months without touching booze. He just used it as a tool to get away from the world and whatever awful feelings he was experiencing. It was another habit that prevented Julie from respecting him.

Billy noticed Julie had bowed her head after he'd mentioned the meeting with the superintendent. "You know what happened, don't you?"

Julie lifted her head back up, resigned. "A couple of students were at the admin and saw John storm out of Mortino's office screaming and yelling."

"Ah shit! I hope he didn't get expelled."

"No, I called Sally. She told me that John's been assigned to the reserves after graduation."

"The reserves?! I thought that was only a rumor."

"Apparently not. They're going to make an official announcement Monday, but Sally already knew about it from Mortino. John's part of the first group being assigned to the program."

"Aw, hell! Four years of hard work and for what? A job in the civilian sector? John's the smartest student in the Academy. He can do amazing things for TERRA, but they're not even giving him a chance."

Although Julie disliked John, she couldn't help but admire how Billy had come to his friend's defense. Billy and David were John's only friends. John's aloof attitude toward his studies and outward confidence had alienated him from his fellow classmates. She still wondered how she'd managed to stay sane as his roommate. They fought whenever they interacted and each time it left her frustrated and upset.

"It *is* unfair how John is being treated," she admitted. Despite her disdain for him, she had to give credit where it was due. When he chose to, John excelled at anything he did. It wasn't right that someone with his skills would be written off to the reserves.

Billy was surprised to hear Julie utter any words of support, given the discord between the roommates. "I'm sorry for talking about John's problems with you. I know you'd rather not hear about it."

"No, no. It's okay." Julie took another sip of her drink.

Billy clasped his hands. It was his turn to change the subject. "You know what? Finals are over. We should be out there having fun. Why don't we go out and join the celebration?"

Julie shook her head. "No, I'm not much in the mood for celebrating tonight."

"You love to party as much as the rest of us. Don't let the spring assignment thing get you down. Come on, I'll buy you your favorite drink."

"The whole spring assignment thing has really hit me hard, Billy. I'm just not in the mood for anything."

"If you have to forgo a fleet assignment this spring to get the posting you want after graduation, maybe it'll all work out for the best."

He had a point. As long as she got posted on a capital ship, she'd be able to forget about this bump in the road.

"Did you put your request in with the placement board?" she

asked.

Billy nodded. He moved over to one of the stools at the kitchen bar counter. "It's between the monitoring center on Mars or the sensor team in Madrid or Luna. I'm still up in the air if I'm offered both."

"I hope you go for the monitoring post. Then we could see each other regularly."

"You're going for the SOLARA, aren't you?" It was no secret to anyone that Julie wanted to start her career on a capital ship with the goal of becoming a starship commander someday. TERRA's five capital ships were old, and the SOLARA was the youngest in the fleet.

She nodded.

"Well then, I guess I'll have to go for the Mars post," said Billy.

At that moment, the apartment's comm link beeped.

"Hang on," Julie said as she went over to the door to answer it. She hit the screen and it lit up, showing several TERRA students. They were obviously drunk, hanging all over each other with big smiles on their faces.

"Hey Jules!" said one of the students. "Where's Billy? Bunch of us saw him dragging John outta Neon."

"He's right here," she answered as she motioned Billy over.

As soon as they saw Billy pop up on the screen, the students went wild. "Billy! Come on! We're heading to Central Park for the bonfire," they all chanted in a slurry discord.

Billy laughed. "Okay, I'm there. Where you all at?"

"Outside at the booth across the street," one of them shouted. "We're all waiting."

"Be there in a sec." He hit the comm link off and turned to Julie. "You sure you won't come along?"

She shook her head. "No, I'd just sour the mood. Besides, I'd better stay here and make sure John doesn't throw up on the floor."

"Don't let this get you down," Billy said as he patted Julie on the shoulder. "Think of it this way. The seniors who got a spring assignment actually have to work while you get one last semester of cruising through classes."

"Yeah," Julie replied halfheartedly. She appreciated that he was trying to make her feel better.

Billy headed out the door. "Tell John I'll call him tomorrow before I head to David's place."

"I will. Have fun."

Once the door closed, she went to the balcony window. She watched as Billy joined the jovial band of students on the street. Before long, they were marching down the sidewalk toward Central Park. They corralled an innocent city bot on their way to the park. The square bot found itself usurped from its street-cleaning responsibilities as they forced it into the middle of the pack.

After watching the students fade away down the street, Julie returned to her seat on the recliner. She couldn't shake the depression that had gripped her since realizing she hadn't been selected for a post. She began examining what could have happened that eliminated her from consideration again. The top ten cadets always got an assignment. There wasn't any reason why she shouldn't have been chosen.

She looked over at John, who was passed out on the couch. Could he be the reason she wasn't offered an assignment? She didn't want to believe it. They were only roommates, nothing more. They didn't associate with each other, and, except for David and Billy, she had her own circle of friends.

Superintendent Mortino had once warned her about being associated with John in any way. Julie had brushed off the warning, figuring it wouldn't be a factor against her. But could it have been? Had John somehow sabotaged her chance of being chosen?

She got up off the recliner and looked at her roommate. "It's probably all your fault." It was an irrational statement, but she had no other explanation.

She left John alone in the living room and retired to her bedroom. He could drown in his vomit for all she cared. Tomorrow she would head home and forget about TERRA for a month. She was looking forward to spending some downtime with her father in Nebraska.

Julie didn't know John wasn't asleep, and she didn't hear his muffled cries. John laid face down, weeping, as thoughts of losing a career on a capital ship floated through his intoxicated mind.

CHAPTER FOUR

The myriad celebrations in Dorm Row were curtailed by an unexpected snowstorm. It wasn't severe, but enough flurries descended on the city to convince people to head indoors.

Julie woke up early and spent the morning sitting out on the balcony in her winter robe, sipping hot tea as she watched the city bots plow the small amount of snow from the streets. There was hardly a soul outside, as most of the residents were sleeping off the previous night's festivities.

Julie enjoyed the crisp air the cold weather brought, but after a couple of minutes it became too chilly for her. She retreated indoors to make some more tea.

John moaned as he turned over on the couch. One arm was over his head in an attempt to cover his eyes from the morning light. He wanted to crawl into bed, but couldn't force himself up and to his bedroom. His body felt like it had been hit by a shuttle.

"Morning," said Julie in a flat tone. She briefly considered being courteous to John, given the news he'd been dealt yesterday. But this was a man who made it a point to make her life miserable, and she quickly got over any notion of being sympathetic.

"Mm-uh," was all John muttered. He didn't want to talk to anyone, especially his roommate. Slowly, he shifted himself on the couch to get comfortable. He didn't have a headache yet and didn't want to spur one by moving too fast.

"You need some water?" asked Julie as she put some water in

the boiler unit.

When he nodded, she said, "Then get up and get some. I'm not your maid."

John extended his arm and gave her the middle finger salute. Julie expected nothing less.

The door chime rang, which caught Julie by surprise. Who the hell would be at their door this early in the morning? "You expecting someone?" she asked John.

John sat up and tried to adjust his vision. "No," was all he could manage to crack from his dry throat. His head was spinning and he focused on one of Julie's paintings to try and shake the sensation.

Yesterday seemed like a dream, but John knew in his heart that his meeting with Mortino had happened. The events of the previous day replayed in his mind.

He might have not been expelled, but John couldn't help feeling that going back to the Academy was an effort in futility. Even if he did shape up in his last semester, the decision had been made and nothing was going to change it. There was no career on a capital ship in John's future, no opportunity to live in space. Maybe he should cut his losses and leave now. No one would miss him and he couldn't fathom taking his last set of classes with the knowledge that they would do him no good.

Since John didn't get up, Julie was forced to answer the door. As she re-tied her robe, she opened the door and almost stumbled back as she saw who was standing there.

"Good morning, Cadet Olson."

"Admiral Johnson!" Julie stared, disbelieving. The person standing before her was one of the most powerful men in TERRA.

"May I come in?"

Stunned, Julie didn't respond. Admiral Oliver Johnson was the head of TERRA operations. Every division reported directly to him. The only individuals the admiral reported to were those on the command council, of which he was a member. He wielded enormous influence in TERRA and was held in high regard in the fleet.

"Miss Olson," said the admiral, snapping her back to reality. "Are you still trying to wake up?"

"I'm...I'm sorry, sir. Please...come in," said Julie, motioning the admiral inside. She quickly closed the door and walked ahead of the admiral to the living room.

John had managed to get to his feet and was stretching. Julie had hoped he'd retreated to his bedroom rather than wait to see who was at the door. She didn't want the admiral to associate her with him.

"John," said Julie, trying to contain both her excitement and nervousness. "Admiral Johnson is here." She wanted to scream at him to clean up and be on his best behavior, if behaving civilized was even possible for John. She could only hope her roommate knew of the admiral. But how could he not? Admiral Johnson was a celebrity in TERRA.

"Huh?" muttered John as he looked past his roommate. It didn't look as if John recognized the admiral, which made Julie more nervous. She prayed that he wouldn't say anything offensive. It wouldn't surprise her if John used the admiral as a scapegoat and blamed him for what had happened yesterday.

"Cadet Roberts," said the admiral, extending his hand to John as he walked past Julie. Hesitantly, John complied and shook hands with him as he continued staring at the admiral. He did recognize Admiral Johnson, but couldn't reconcile the fact he was standing in their apartment. Had he drunk so much that he was now hallucinating?

He looked over at Julie and assumed the admiral was here for her. That would just cap everything off. Now TERRA was having admirals personally visit their best cadets. John was disgusted at the thought. He wouldn't be surprised if Superintendent Mortino had set this up to twist the knife further.

"I'm sure you two have a lot to talk about," John said, making no effort to be polite. "I'd love to stay and gab, but as you can see, I'm hung over and look like shit. I'll be in the shower."

Julie was speechless. Was it impossible for John to act civilized at all?

"Actually, I'm here to speak with both of you," the admiral said.

Surprised, John halted his retreat to the bedroom and turned around.

"Cadet John Roberts and Cadet Julie Olson," the admiral said in a tone that sounded as though he was in awe of them. "I've waited a long time for the privilege to meet you."

Both cadets were perplexed.

Julie was the first to say something. "You have?"

The admiral nodded. "I've been watching the two of you for a long time."

John wanted to burst out laughing at this statement, but restrained himself. He'd assumed his constant defiance wasn't worth the attention of anyone outside the Academy, unless Mortino was telling tales of his unpleasant encounters with John at TERRA pow-wows.

"You have both demonstrated skills and determination far beyond what I've seen in years. You're exactly what I need for the assignment I have in mind."

A spring assignment? Could it be true? Julie felt relieved. They hadn't forgotten about her. This was unprecedented. She must have impressed the placement board so much that a letter was inadequate.

"We're honored that you would consider us," she said, and the admiral smiled.

None of this made sense to John, and he had no qualms about speaking up. "Wait, wait, wait. I was told yesterday I was being placed in the reserves and now you come waltzing in offering me a post? Excuse me for being suspicious, but TERRA doesn't make a habit of contradicting itself."

"Goddamn it, John! Why do you have to spoil this?" Julie knew her outburst wouldn't impress the admiral, but she wasn't going to sit by and let John run his mouth.

John crossed his arms. "Because yesterday I was being thrown to the wolves, and now the head of operations shows up offering an assignment." He gave the admiral a defiant stare. "So, which is it? Am I out or one of the good old boys? Because I've got shit to do."

"For once would you keep your mouth shut and listen to what the admiral has to say?" Julie was close to yelling at him.

Admiral Johnson chuckled, drawing their attention back to him.

"Admiral, I'm sorry about this." Julie felt humiliated that she'd allowed John's behavior to get to her again. "This is not how officers should act in the presence of a superior officer."

John rolled his eyes. She always had to be the suck-up. He made a couple of kissy noises, but Julie ignored him.

"No, no, Ms. Olson. No apology is necessary."

"Hey Julie, I bet if you ask nicely the admiral will bend over and let you kiss his ass."

Julie took a step toward John, ready to smash his face in. She wasn't about to let him throw insults at her in front of the admiral.

"This is exactly why I've chosen you," said the admiral. "If nothing else, you're honest with each other." He looked to John. "I know about your assignment to the reserves, cadet. I don't agree with the commission's choice."

John felt better hearing that not everyone in TERRA agreed with what had been done to him. But he was still unsure of the admiral's motives for his visit.

"Admiral, I appreciate that you don't agree with my placement. If you don't think I should be in the reserves, couldn't you just overrule the board and put me in the fleet? I don't expect a spring assignment if that's what you're here for. I only expect a career after all my work at the Academy."

It was Julie's turn to roll her eyes.

"What I'm offering is better than any entry-level position in the fleet," said Johnson. "Quite simply, it's a once-in-a-lifetime opportunity."

Both cadets were now intrigued. The admiral had captured their interest.

"What's the assignment?" asked Julie.

"I'm afraid I cannot discuss it here. In order for you to fully grasp what I have to offer, I must show you. My shuttle is right outside and ready to take us. All I need is a yes from both of you."

Julie needed no time to think and immediately agreed. Despite the admiral's words, though, John couldn't help but be suspicious about his intentions. It was in his nature to question people's motives, and this was no exception.

Then again, Admiral Johnson would not have shown up unless he sincerely wanted them. John had read the biographies of all the command council members and high-ranking military officers. From everything he'd read and heard, the admiral was a man of honor.

"Sure, why not," he relented. "But can I least clean up first? I look like hell."

Julie could only clasp her hand to her head in embarrassment.

——— ——— ———

A shuttle rose up over the buildings of Dorm Row and took off. It sped effortlessly along, neither land nor ocean inhibiting its progress.

The cadets sat side by side in the back. John had cleaned up and was wearing a fresh TERRA uniform, but it wasn't one cadets wore. Before they left New York, the admiral had given them gifts: TERRA officer uniforms. These presents reinforced the notion that they were being given positions in the fleet. The only thing missing from the black-and-gold-trimmed uniforms were command bars.

It was a rare privilege to wear a TERRA uniform. It let people know that the wearer had persevered through rigorous mental and physical training and was now part of an elite institution.

Admiral Johnson had John and Julie change into the uniforms before leaving, and they were only too eager to fulfill his request. Both felt a renewed sense of accomplishment as they settled in on the shuttle for the ride to wherever it was they were heading. They didn't speak to each other throughout the trip, preoccupied with trying to figure out their destination.

John was beginning to relax and let his guard down. He

fantasized about stopping at Mortino's house so he could show off his new officer uniform. John relished the thought of driving Mortino into a tirade after seeing him in his new outfit, hanging out with Admiral Johnson. It would make up for the hell the superintendent had put him through yesterday.

Julie was enjoying her unexpected good fortune. She'd known TERRA wouldn't let her sacrifices go unrewarded—and what a reward they had given her. Admiral Johnson had personally chosen her for an assignment and elected to deliver the news firsthand. It didn't matter what the job entailed. Just to be selected by the head of operations was an honor. Julie would gladly do whatever the admiral asked of her.

Admiral Johnson was seated across from the cadets. Twice he went up to speak with the shuttle pilot. The cadets could overhear them talking, but neither could discern what they said.

Neither John nor Julie could bring themselves to ask the admiral about their destination. They were both a bit starstruck. Oliver Johnson was a famous figure, not only in TERRA but also in the public eye. Everyone knew of him and how proud he was to represent TERRA.

"I would've thought the two of you would be more talkative," the admiral quipped. "Don't let my presence prevent you from speaking your mind."

"Uh, sorry sir," Julie stammered. "It's just that we're...well...*I'm* still surprised by your offer."

"And you, Cadet Roberts?"

"Honestly sir, I'm waiting for the other shoe to drop," John said. "Superintendent Mortino was quite blunt about why I was going to the reserves, and I didn't take the news very well. I'm sure he wasted no time telling the whole command about my blowup."

"You are correct, Mr. Roberts," said the admiral. "The superintendent notified several executive officers of your behavior yesterday. I expected your reaction based on your academic file. The superintendent holds little regard for you."

"You did read the right file." John had begun to think the admiral had mixed him up with somebody else. "Not to brag or anything, but I'm considered a black sheep at the Academy."

The admiral laughed, and Julie frowned a bit. She was jealous that John seemed to have garnered the admiral's favor by acting like himself. She was following all the proper protocols expected of a TERRA officer. She was polite and respectful to the admiral, making sure not to utter any offensive or controversial remarks. But John's in-your-face attitude seemed to be having a positive effect on Admiral Johnson and it bothered her.

"Yes, cadet," said the admiral as he regained his composure. "I did indeed read the correct file. Let me see if I can remember...ah yes! *Has little regard for complying with authority figures. Immediately questions any order given to him. Has the unique ability to create discord in any unit or project in which he is a participant.* I believe I've stated the basics of your evaluations."

"Yeah, that'd be about right," said John as he folded his arms.

"You act like you know what's in your file," said Julie. "Cadets aren't permitted to view their records."

"Oh please. I accessed my file a long time ago. Everyone knows the Academy's records aren't that hard to break into."

"I can't believe you just admitted to breaking into confidential Academy files in front of the admiral," said Julie. "That's grounds for immediate expulsion."

"Well if it makes you feel better, I looked at your file too. You're such a suck-up."

Julie glared at him, then looked at the admiral. "You see how he is? He's bragging about breaking rules. This can't be the person you had in mind for what you're offering us."

"Such behavior would be considered unfit for any position in TERRA," admitted the admiral.

"So again, I ask, why I am here?" asked John. "All you have is a file saying I'd make a terrible officer and, as you just witnessed, I have a big mouth."

The admiral became serious. "Let me ask you this. Why did you enter the Academy?"

"Huh?" The question caught John off guard.

"You spent years preparing for the entrance exams. You gave

up your youth to have a chance to become a TERRA officer. To those who have watched you, it seems that you have little respect for TERRA. So why work so hard to be a part of it?"

It was a question Julie had always wanted an answer to. John mocked and belittled TERRA at every turn, and she couldn't understand why he'd ever applied to the Academy.

"Simple," said John. "I want to live in space."

"You could do that with a private company," Julie pointed out.

"It's not the same thing. I don't want to haul freight, captain a pleasure craft that goes to the same place over and over again, or work for a mining company. I want to live on a capital ship and explore what's out there in space."

"There's not much left to explore within the inner solar system," the admiral said.

"Maybe, just maybe, in my lifetime TERRA ships will travel to other star systems. If it happens, I want to be on one of those ships. As much as I don't care for TERRA, it's the only path available toward my goal of living in space."

Julie found that notion idealistic. The Screen had prevented human ships from leaving the solar system for decades. Every time a vessel tried to pass the boundaries beyond Mars's orbit around the sun, a Screen ship would appear and destroy it. No one knew why this alien race wanted to keep humanity contained. But as long as humans stayed within the inner solar system, the Screen left them alone.

Before the admiral could respond to John, the pilot spoke up.

"Admiral, we're at the perimeter."

"Excuse me." The admiral got up and relocated to the co-pilot chair. John and Julie could hear the pilot being hailed over the communications system.

"EXODUS Station to shuttle ARIES ONE," came a female voice over the shuttle speakers. "Please identify yourself and provide clearance code."

"This is Admiral Johnson on board ARIES ONE. Clearance code Alpha-Zeta-9-0-Theta."

"Confirmed, ARIES ONE. Welcome back to EXODUS. You are

clear for approach to the hangar deck."

John whispered to Julie, "What's EXODUS?" He figured it was something mentioned in one of the Academy textbooks he'd never read.

Julie shrugged. "I have no idea."

The admiral turned from his seat to his guests. "Cadets, would you join me up here?"

The two approached the front of the shuttle. As they stood behind the admiral and shuttle pilot, they got a clear view out the front window. What they saw took their breaths away.

Before them was a massive ship, hovering just above the ground. Describing the ship as *massive* seemed inadequate. It was enormous and easily eclipsed any of TERRA's capital ships. The vessel seemed to encapsulate the entire valley it towered over. Its sheer mass captivated John and Julie as it appeared to stretch to the horizon and beyond.

The vessel was unlike anything either had ever seen. It wasn't in any textbook they studied at the Academy, and it didn't conform to any specifications of which they knew. TERRA ships were rectangular. This ship seemed almost organic in nature. It was a large, elongated, dome-like structure, its hull shimmering and glass-like. Light radiated off the hull as if the ship was alive. TERRA ships seemed artificial and inanimate by nature, but the ship before them seemed to exude a pulse of life.

The admiral smiled. "Julie Olson. John Roberts. I'd like to welcome you to the EXODUS Project."

"EXODUS," muttered John, transfixed by the ship. He couldn't get over how unique it looked.

"Yes," the admiral said. "What you're looking at is the result of twenty years of hard work."

"That's a human ship?" Julie's voice was hushed.

"I can assure you this ship is 100 percent human, built from the ground up here by a dedicated team."

"It completely departs from traditional ship design," Julie said.

"Yeah," John agreed. "Human ships seem so..." He fumbled, trying to find the right word.

"Mechanical," said the admiral.

"Exactly." He continued to gaze at the ship as the shuttle flew closer, unable to take his eyes from such a fantastic sight. "It looks like it could be a living creature."

"You're the first one to describe it like that," said the admiral.

Details of the ship began to emerge as they approached it. The vessel was a light tan, unlike the metallic silver of most TERRA ships. The cadets could see small windows and portholes dotting the hull. John tried to see if he could spot people walking past the windows, but no matter how much he strained, he couldn't catch a glimpse of anyone.

"How many people can this ship hold?" he asked.

"Fifty thousand," answered the admiral. "It can hold more if necessary. Currently, there's a little over 5,000 people on board."

The number seemed incomprehensible. The ship was big, but was it really large enough to hold such a complement? The largest TERRA capital ship was the SYRIA, which staffed about 800 people and, in a squeeze, could get over 3,000 on board. Given the enormity of EXODUS, John wasn't surprised it had taken over twenty years to build.

A blip on the shuttle console caught the cadets' attention. "We're passing through the anti-gravity field," the pilot said. "Switching to thrusters and activating internal gravity."

John and Julie both felt the change to artificial gravity as the shuttle passed through the anti-gravity field that surrounded EXODUS. It made sense to John that such a field surrounded the ship. Its sheer mass would cause it to collapse in upon itself in Earth's gravity well unless it was composed of some top-secret alloy. John had kept up on all the technology relating to starship design and felt he would know if such a thing was possible.

"Admiral, why is there an antigravity field here?" asked Julie.

"As you see, EXODUS is a massive ship and is far too large to operate in a gravity environment." *So much for the new alloy theory,* John thought. "We have four towers generating the field surrounding the ship. Without them, EXODUS would implode under its own weight."

"It's a spacefaring vessel," John guessed.

"Correct," replied the admiral. "The ship is of multipurpose design, specifically meant to operate in space. For planetary missions, the ship has a wide range of smaller support craft available to use."

"Admiral, just from the number of people it can hold, I assume the ship is designed to be completely self-sustaining," said Julie. "The Luna and Mars orbiting stations wouldn't have the resources to resupply a ship like this."

"That's one of the primary goals of the EXODUS Project," the admiral said. "The ship can operate without the need of station replenishment. It's fully autonomous and can operate for years in space without any external support."

That statement caught John's attention. Why would TERRA need such a vessel? As Julie pointed out earlier, ships were restricted to the inner solar system. They weren't even permitted to have hyper-drives. Building a ship for interstellar travel would be meaningless, not to mention illegal.

"EXODUS is equipped with all necessary tools to conduct mining and exploration missions," continued the admiral as John considered the possibilities this ship represented.

"Admiral, why have you brought us here? Are we to work aboard EXODUS?" Julie felt compelled to ask. Surely the admiral wouldn't have brought them here unless he intended for them to work on the ship—but she wanted to make sure they weren't simply passing through on the way to another destination, before she became too excited.

"All in good time. First I want to give you a brief tour of the ship before explaining what your roles will be."

Julie only nodded. She rejoined John in looking out the front window as the shuttle passed alongside EXODUS.

John noticed the rear of the ship seemed to expand a bit and assume a more rectangular shape. He couldn't make it out from this distance, but he swore that the curved configuration of the ship's hull stopped at the rear. As he speculated what the area housed, the shuttle began to ascend. It climbed above the ship and made a ninety-degree turn, allowing the cadets to see a subtle half dome sitting atop EXODUS, barely discernable to the eye.

A large opening presented itself on one side of the dome facing the rear of the vessel. Shuttlecraft and auxiliary service ships entered and exited the opening at regular intervals. John correctly concluded that it was the hangar bay.

"This is ARIES ONE, requesting clearance to the hangar deck," said the pilot.

"This is EXODUS hangar control," a woman replied over the speakers. "You are cleared for entry."

"This is Admiral Oliver Johnson. Inform the crew I'll be conducting a tour with some guests."

"Understood, Admiral."

Julie and John looked at one another with anticipation. They were going to get the opportunity to see the inside of EXODUS. John's mind raced, wondering what sort of new things he would see on board. He could only imagine what new technologies the ship would contain.

The shuttle cruised into the hangar deck. The cadets looked on either side to see a variety of small ships lined in rows along the walls. John could make out at least five different vessel types, from reconnaissance Scouts to attack Interceptors.

The shuttle landed not too far from the hangar doors. The rear hatch opened as the pilot powered down the shuttle systems. The admiral got up from his chair and turned to see that, although Julie was still standing where she was, John had already exited the shuttle.

"I'm sorry," Julie started to apologize. "He just bolted..."

The admiral held up his hand to interrupt her. "There's nothing here that you and Cadet Roberts are not supposed to see. He'll undoubtedly ask many questions and I expect you'll not refrain from asking questions either. There's nothing off-limits here for you two."

Julie nodded and moved to let the admiral pass, preferring to follow him out. They stepped out onto the expansive hangar deck and she looked around to get her bearings. The area was enormous.

It was almost the size of three football fields. TERRA capital ships' hangar decks were only one-fifth the size.

John had forgotten about both Julie and the admiral as he explored the hangar, moving between the small ships to see what he could discover. He immediately noticed that the Interceptors were not the same type used in the fleet. Although they looked similar, these fighters had what appeared to be additional weapon ports. John had memorized the specifications of the Interceptors and easily recognized the ones here were packed with much more firepower. He wanted to get a look at the cockpit and was about to open one up when he was interrupted.

"Who the hell are you?" bellowed a growling, deep voice.

John turned to see a man dressed in a blue security uniform, his arms crossed. He was older, his age betrayed by the lines carved into his face. His five o'clock shadow added to his rough-and-tough appearance.

"John Roberts," John replied in a matter-of-fact tone.

"You with the admiral?"

Admiral Johnson and Julie approached the men. "Ah yes, Chief Sandoval," the admiral said. "Mr. Roberts is one of the guests I told you about."

"I see," Sandoval said as he gave John a good look up and down. The cadet didn't appear remarkable. He certainly didn't come across as the dynamic individual the admiral had described.

John was equally unimpressed with the security chief and was not intimidated by his gruff demeanor. He remained focused on the Interceptor. "You know anything about these fighters?"

"You're asking me?" said a confused Sandoval.

John smiled. "I am."

"You'll have to ask one of the engineers. I just handle security here."

"What? Security doesn't know how to fly a fighter?"

"Thomas Sandoval is responsible for maintaining security operations on the ship," interrupted the admiral. He motioned to Julie. "This is our other guest, Julie Olson."

Thomas nodded but did not address her. "I came down when

I heard your shuttle was docking to make sure everything went okay."

"I appreciate your concern, but I don't want to hold things up for our guests here. Is the command deck ready?"

"It is," Sandoval said. "Lieutenant Brandus contacted me twenty minutes ago and said tests on the new life support systems have been completed. The command deck has been cleared for re-entry and the command deck crew was released back to their posts fifteen minutes ago."

"Good, then we'll head up there after our walk around Central."

"Lieutenant Brandus asked me to give these to you." The security chief extended his hand and the cadets saw two tiny black dots. Neither knew what they could be. Sandoval slid the tiny specks toward the admiral.

"I'll see you tomorrow at the staff meeting," said Johnson.

The chief nodded and left the hangar without saying anything more to Julie or John.

"Nice fellow," commented John. He was tempted to give the chief the finger behind his back but resisted the impulse. "Is he always so charismatic?"

"Chief Sandoval is dedicated to his job," the admiral said. "Security heads are not known to be social types. But enough about him. I have something to give you." Johnson reopened his hand. "These are pips. They're communication devices designed exclusively for use on EXODUS."

"They're so tiny," Julie said as she examined the small devices.

"I thought for a second they were just bits of dirt," admitted John. "Where do you stick them?"

"Just on the inside on your ear," the admiral said. John eagerly stuck out his hand. "It'll be easier if I do it."

The admiral placed one pip at the end of his finger and gently squeezed the inside of John's ear. He did the same with Julie.

"I don't feel it at all," said John.

"Good, they're designed to be inconspicuous. They serve as both a communications and tracking device," the admiral said. "The ship's computer continuously monitors all traffic on the ship, accounting for every crewmember. If you need to contact someone, you just say your name, then the individual's name. *Admiral Johnson to John Roberts.*"

Both John and Julie heard a brief beeping sound. Their eyes lit up.

"Anyone nearby you will hear a beep when someone is calling you," said the admiral. "That way no one thinks you're talking to yourself."

"Remarkable," said Julie.

"You also have full access to the ship's computer. Just say 'computer' and make your query." The admiral lifted his finger. "Computer, current location of TFX EXODUS."

"TFX EXODUS is currently moored at the Tormented Valley ground station," the computer replied in a soft tone.

"Again, anyone near you will hear the computer's reply to your query," the admiral clarified, "unless you specifically tell it to reply via your pip only."

"This is way better than wearing a comm bracelet or carrying a DAT," said John.

"And it's more practical," said the admiral. "With these, we avoided having to install a comprehensive speaker system. We only have speakers in the main areas."

Neither cadet could feel the pips in their ears and quickly grew accustomed to the idea of wearing them.

"Before we head up to the command deck I'd like to briefly show you Central," said the admiral.

"Lead on, sir," said John. Julie noticed it was the first time he had shown any sort of respect to a commanding officer. The sight of this ship must have tempered his behavior.

It didn't surprise her. Because of Admiral Johnson, John was apparently back in TERRA and was controlling his demeanor so as not to ruin this opportunity. How typical of John to be thinking only of himself.

Julie's mind soon shifted gears and became littered with questions. Why would TERRA go through all the effort of making this ship? Even though the admiral had said it was a multipurpose vessel, Julie still tried to classify it. A warship? Maybe. It certainly had the capacity to hold a large number of troops. An explorer? Possibly. However, the sheer size of the ship indicated it had massive power requirements, which could severely limit its ability to travel very far from Earth.

The admiral had indicated that EXODUS was equipped to conduct mining operations to procure resources. Julie couldn't imagine that the ship had facilities large enough to convert raw materials into useable goods. The very nature of this ship seemed to go against everything she'd learned at the Academy. TERRA would never build a vessel that could travel beyond the solar system. It would be a waste of resources and would infuriate the Screen. TERRA always made it clear that it wanted to do nothing to infuriate the aliens.

As they left the hangar, the expansive corridor before them proved yet again how contradictory this ship was to traditional ship design. Capital ship interiors were compact to save on costs. Corridors were only wide enough to allow two people to walk side by side. But this was more than three times the size of a capital ship. It couldn't have been built with the thought of flying it just to Mars or Luna. She was unnerved at the thought that this ship's purpose was based on traveling through interstellar space. Its size was impressive, but it certainly couldn't go up against Screen technology.

Julie looked over at John and saw in his eyes how fascinated he was. He was asking the admiral all sorts of questions, from EXODUS's metallurgical composition to the amenities the ship offered, wasting no time trying to obtain as much information as he could gather. Ship design was one of John's favorite subjects and was one of the few areas he'd chosen to excel at during his time at the Academy.

Julie had been elated when she first gazed at EXODUS, but as time passed and questions kept popping into her head, the euphoria wore off. This was surely a classified project. Julie had noticed the shuttle pilot had flown with the transponder off, which meant the shuttle was undetectable by standard monitoring protocols.

The admiral hadn't wanted anyone to know where they were going. But why would he bring two cadets here? TERRA rules strictly prohibited cadets working on classified projects. Even the head of TERRA operations had to adhere to regulations.

She would just have to be patient. The admiral had assured them he would be forthcoming about why they'd been brought here as soon as he had shown them more of the ship.

"What's the main objective of this ship?" asked John as they stepped onto an elevator lift.

His question snapped Julie back to attention. She looked at the admiral, curious as to how he would respond. Despite John being obviously enamored by the ship, it hadn't allayed his concerns as to why they'd been brought here. Julie was glad to see that his cautious nature hadn't completely evaporated.

"Level 23," said the admiral. The cadets could feel a slight motion as the lift descended. "I was hoping your enthusiasm would've delayed that question until after the tour. But it seems your curiosity doesn't want to wait. Let me show you Central first. After that, we'll talk on the command deck."

The lift made a beeping sound and the doors opened. The group stepped out onto a catwalk. Before them was an open area. There were no decks or corridors, just a large expansive space. Protruding from the ground level of this area were buildings, like those typically found in a city.

"What the hell," John said, amazed. He leaned over the catwalk and saw people walking around the floor level, far below. It looked like a downtown marketplace, with shops and businesses lining the streets.

Julie glanced at the various buildings and could see people through some of the windows. As she continued to look around, she could see catwalks circling the perimeter at multiple levels where deck flooring should have been. There was no doubt what the cadets were looking at: It was a city encapsulated within the ship.

"This is Central," the admiral proudly stated. "A self-contained city situated in the heart of EXODUS that encompasses thirty-two decks. It was designed to mimic a typical downtown city. Most of the civilians live in the apartment buildings here."

"Wow," was all John managed to mutter.

The admiral continued his spiel. "Central was designed to alleviate the stress of extended space flight by providing a planetary city environment. It's where crewmembers can go to relax from the rigors of space travel."

John's head was spinning. This was a concept he'd never imagined could exist on a ship. Such an idea had never been discussed in any of the textbooks at the Academy. "You just gave me a zillion more questions to ask. How's this logistically possible? Wouldn't the shops and restaurants drain valuable power resources from the ship?"

The admiral held his hand up to stop John from inundating him. "I wanted to show you what makes EXODUS unique. It's not just the size of the ship that makes it special. Central's an important component of how it operates. It ensures the well-being of the crew."

"Admiral," interjected John. "I'm grateful you brought me here. But I've got this nagging voice in the back of my head demanding to know *why*. As much as I'd love to see the rest of this ship, I need to know what skills you believe I have that could possibly benefit this project. The more I see here, the more confused I am as to what I could do here."

Julie couldn't have said it better herself. An actual starship was far different than a capital ship. TERRA's current ships wouldn't have many of the facilities a deep space explorer would require. Bringing two inexperienced cadets to this project seemed foolhardy.

"You see the entire picture of a situation," the admiral said, sounding impressed. "Let's head up to the command deck and I'll explain why you're here."

CHAPTER FIVE

he lift door opened and the trio stepped out onto EXODUS's command deck. They had had to take two lifts to get here. The admiral had explained that, as a security precaution, only one lift, accessible on deck two, could access the command deck. No unauthorized personnel could enter unless they had security clearance.

Deck two appeared no different than any other deck, but it was littered with unseen and dangerous security systems designed to halt the advance of any unwanted personnel. Force fields, lasers, and poison gases were just some of the hidden devices.

The cadets walked noticeably faster as the admiral explained the deck's layout. Neither wanted to spend any more time than they had to on deck two.

It was a short ride on the lift to the command deck. Before the cadets had a chance to prepare themselves, the door opened. As they stepped out, Julie and John took their first look at the central brain of the ship.

The command deck was a large, rectangular area. They were on a walkway that lined the walls of the deck, and up against the walls were various computer terminals with lights blinking in a chaotic dance. Above the terminals was a large window that, like the catwalk, circled the command deck and allowed an unobstructed view of the outside. John could see the clouds, with a shuttle occasionally passing by.

As John looked out the window, Julie focused her attention downward. She saw steps leading from the walkway to a sublevel. This pit area had various command stations, with officers busily working at each one. A large circular table sat at the center of the pit, glowing with an array of shimmering lights.

Given everything they had seen so far, Julie had assumed the command deck would have been a unique arrangement as well, but it was no different than the setup found on a capital ship. It was just a lot bigger. She supposed there was no need to reinvent the wheel if it already worked fine.

Two officers passing by the group acknowledged the admiral. The cadets took no notice as the officers stepped off the deck onto the lift behind them. They were too preoccupied with their surroundings to worry about greeting anyone. No one made an official announcement, alerting the command deck staff that the admiral was present.

"This way," the admiral motioned, stepping in front of the cadets. They followed him halfway along the catwalk, where he opened a door on the side that was almost unnoticeable. John almost bumped into him, his attention still focused on the command deck's layout.

The cadets found themselves in what appeared to be an office. Directly in front of them was a clear plastic composite desk. The only contents on it were several reports that were neatly stacked in a pile. A small control panel was embedded on the desk, its yellow and blue lights blinking sporadically. To the left, a black leather couch rested against the wall, a large portrait of Earth hanging above it.

On the wall opposite the couch was a detailed, animated floor plan of the EXODUS's interior. John walked over and inspected the image carefully. He saw the engineering section, Central, and the medical bay, to name a few. Every so often, lights flashed on the blueprint.

"That monitor displays power distribution, security alerts, and crew movements on the ship," the admiral said. "You can modify the display parameters through the computer to show specific information."

John nodded as he looked over the display, captivated.

Julie sat down on the couch, exhausted by what she had seen so far. The sheer enormity of this ship overwhelmed her and she needed time to get her bearings and collect her thoughts. She felt that she had been running around all day, even though they had only been here a little over half an hour.

The admiral took a seat behind the desk. "I've been with the EXODUS Project since its inception twenty years ago. I've overseen every component and system developed for her." John could tell by the admiral's tone that he was deeply invested in this ship. It would be hard not to get attached to something you'd spent twenty years building.

"It's hard to imagine this ship has been here for twenty years," Julie said.

"Sixteen years, to be exact," the admiral corrected. "A ship this size doesn't get constructed overnight. It took two years just to build the ground facilities. We had to do it while concealing the project from the people of Earth, Mars, and Luna."

"Why was this ship built?" John said. "What's its purpose?"

The admiral sat back and sighed. "TERRA initiated EXODUS as a solution to the Screen threat. Years ago, TERRA believed that the Screen attacks were a precursor to a system invasion. Repelling the invasion was deemed improbable, as our technology was considered inferior to the Screen's. Only the use of nuclear weapons on our planets would garner any possible success in driving them away."

"You mean by destroying our own worlds?" Julie was shocked by the admiral's casual tone.

The fallout of the Nuclear Holocaust still had great influence on society. The Interstellar Republic Alliance publicly documented generations of people suffering from genetic disorders, with the hope that humanity would never forget such a horrific lesson. Even with the government encouraging healthy people to have babies, the human population had not recovered in numbers since the war. Nuclear weapons had been dismantled long ago, as well as nuclear plants used as power sources in the civilian sector.

The science of nuclear energy had not been lost, merely put aside. It was disturbing to think that TERRA was considering using nuclear weapons again to fight the Screen. Julie shuddered at the thought.

"It may sound distasteful, but it's a legitimate military tactic," the admiral said. "It's assumed the Screen wouldn't want a planet whose resources have been contaminated by nuclear waste. Annihilating our worlds would remove any incentive for them to invade. However, the command council felt that destroying the human race was never a viable option. The only remaining solution was to build a large ship and abandon the solar system. Take a large group of people and seek out a new planet in another star system. That's what EXODUS was designed to do—allow humanity to survive and thrive in space while searching for a new home."

John eyes widened. " TERRA actually commissioned a ship designed to leave the solar system?"

"From your point of view, this ship is an explorer," said the admiral. "TERRA sees this ship as a final option to save humanity. Call it an escape craft, or a generational ship, it doesn't matter."

"Isn't twenty years a little long to build a ship that's supposed to save humanity?" John asked. "What if the Screen attacked before you were ready?"

"We designed the program to allow EXODUS to be a habitable craft after six years of construction. Each additional year allowed us to add more systems and expand the ship's capabilities."

"Modular ship design," Julie said as she processed what the admiral was telling them. It was a concept that TERRA discussed at the Academy but never implemented into practice. A capital ship spent months going through a refit, a downfall of having fully integrated systems.

"TERRA eventually concluded that an invasion was unlikely, and over time the building of EXODUS became less urgent," continued the admiral. "The command council directed the ship be used as a platform to test new technologies. Its intended mission to depart Earth and venture into deep space was abandoned.

TERRA actually believes the ship is incapable of leaving Earth."

"What about saving humanity?" asked Julie.

"TERRA believes so long as we stay in the solar system, the Screen won't bother us," the admiral said.

John rolled his eyes. "You put a lot of resources into building this ship. It's too bad TERRA's too narrow-minded to allow it to fly."

"I never said this ship couldn't fly," the admiral said. "It's space-worthy and I intend for it to launch the day after tomorrow."

Julie was caught off guard. "What!? Why?"

"I believe that hiding in the shadows isn't a viable option for our future. Rather than try to determine why the Screen has bottled us in the inner solar system, TERRA has forced an unconditional surrender on us. I'm unwilling to let this ship sit here because our military is too scared to act. We need to know why the Screen has contained us."

"I gotta be honest and say you're the first TERRA officer who's talked with any sense at all," John said. He'd never thought he'd see the day when a command-level officer disagreed with the status quo.

"I know you hold the belief that we should be out there amongst the stars," said the admiral. "At the very least, we should determine what the Screen has planned for us. At some point, I believe their approach will change and we must learn what their intentions are before they have a chance to act against us."

"Admiral, I'm a little unsure of what you're proposing," said Julie. "TERRA's views may come across as passive, but they have kept us at peace with the Screen."

John was prepared to challenge Julie, eager to point out how naive she was, but the admiral spoke before he could utter a word. "My dear, it's difficult for an established institution to change its ways. TERRA's a military entity, but over time it's transformed into a social, political, and economic institution. People look up to TERRA in reverence. No one seems willing to stand up, say TERRA's wrong, and demand change. You say TERRA has kept the peace with the Screen. How do you know it's the Screen who hasn't chosen to attack us?"

"I don't," Julie said. "But TERRA hasn't done anything to prompt hostility from the Screen."

The admiral flipped through the stack of reports on his desk and pulled out two files. He handed one to each of them. "Those are your assignments after you graduate. As Cadet Roberts already knows, he will not be serving in TERRA."

John read his file and saw nothing new in it. He chuckled as he read some of the opinions given by the Academy faculty. The list of his infractions and insubordination was lengthy and read like a good book.

Julie opened her file and read its contents. Her mouth dropped as she read her assignment. "This can't be."

"What is it?" John asked as he looked over at her file.

She handed it to him to read, humiliated.

"Tourist Information Specialist of the TERRA Museum of History," John read aloud. He looked at the admiral. "Is this a joke?"

"I'm afraid not. Miss Olson has been assigned to be a museum tour guide," the admiral confirmed.

"But I'm fourth in my class. I'm the first person to win the Academy Flight Tournament as a freshman. I've never received a bad evaluation from my instructors. How can they do this?"

"Because you wield no influence in the fleet," replied the admiral. "TERRA can no longer support placing all their graduates in fleet positions. It's simply become bloated with staff. Only those with family or friends in the higher command structure get a position. It doesn't matter how good you are anymore. What matters is who you know. The only reason you weren't placed in the reserves is because you ranked so high in your class."

John felt sympathy for Julie. Although he was upset about what had happened to him, he understood why he'd been targeted. But Julie? She was an ace cadet and a model example of how an officer should act. She hadn't done anything to deserve such a demeaning assignment.

The admiral stood and approached the cadets. "I've watched

the two of you during your time at the Academy. You're both gifted and have the determination to achieve your goals. You do what you believe is right rather than let yourselves be guided by how to best improve your careers. I brought you here because I want the two of you serving on EXODUS as officers when it departs for space."

These were the words John thought he would never hear. The chance to serve on board a ship was being presented to him. And not just any ship, but an actual starship. This was better than serving on a capital ship.

John's suspicions about the admiral melted away. For the first time in years he was willing to put his faith in someone.

"What positions would we serve?" He hoped he would be given a position on the command deck. Maybe in operations or weapons control.

"John, I want you to serve as ship commander of EXODUS and I want Julie to serve as executive officer."

It took a moment for John to process the information. "Come again?" Had he heard the admiral correctly? He couldn't have just heard him say he wanted John to command the EXODUS.

"I said I want you to command this ship."

"You can't be serious. I know I'm good, but I'm not good enough to command a ship as a first assignment. No one is. Julie and I are only cadets. We don't have any real-world experience working on a ship. What we learned at the Academy about ship operations is completely inadequate to run EXODUS."

"You're the only two I've watched who are not career-minded opportunists," the admiral said. "The other cadets are only interested in the perks and status of being an officer. But you, John, have the instincts of a leader. You can anticipate when to take chances and are willing to gamble on your gut. You don't let anyone intimidate you."

The admiral had said nothing that John didn't already know in his heart, but it was refreshing to hear it come from someone else, especially an individual John respected.

"Julie," the admiral continued, "you don't let your emotions cloud your logical thinking. You're levelheaded, even under the most intense pressure, and can readily make difficult decisions. Your motive for a career in TERRA is to serve and protect. Together you two make a formidable team, and I firmly believe that this mission will only succeed with the two of you at the helm."

"A formidable team?" John thought the admiral was spouting nonsense. "If our interaction back in New York didn't give you a clue, then let me clear it up for you. We fight every time we try to have a conversation. She's nothing but a thorn in my side, and I can't stand the sight of her."

"Admiral, I have to agree with John, except for the thorn in his side comment," Julie said. "Put aside the fact that I don't have the qualifications to be an executive officer, I can't even fathom working under him."

"Nonsense," replied the admiral. "Neither of you realize it, but you have the makings of the perfect command relationship."

"Sure," John said as he winked and gave the admiral a sarcastic thumbs-up. "Together I'm sure we'd be great at setting off the ship's self-destruct system."

He stood up and paced to the other side of the room. It was one thing to serve on this ship, but as the commander? With Julie as his executive officer? The only thing that would come out of such a relationship would be the downfall of the EXODUS, with John and Julie strangling each other on the command deck as fire and brimstone erupted around them while the ship crashed on some interstellar rock.

"What about the officers on board?" Julie asked, more receptive to the admiral's analysis. "Are they willing to do what you ask? How can we expect them to follow us?"

"I've spent my life overseeing this project. The people working here share my dream of seeing EXODUS leave the solar system. They believe that we shouldn't be confined here and have spent their own lives preparing for the day to leave Earth. They trust my decisions and trust me when I tell them you are the only ones qualified to lead them."

"You've already told them?" said John.

The admiral fixed John with a stern look. "Would it matter if I had? The decision ultimately lies with you."

"Well, I'd be lying if I said I needed time to think about this," John said. "Exploring space is all I ever wanted to do and this is my only chance to do it. I think it's a little weird that you believe Julie and I can work together, but what the hell. I've done crazier things in the past. I'm in."

The admiral smiled and nodded, as if he'd never doubted John would accept his proposal. "Thank you Cadet Roberts, or should I say Commander Roberts." He turned to Julie for her answer.

"I, I don't know," she stammered. "This is all so sudden. On the one hand I want to do this, especially after reading what TERRA has planned for me. But TERRA has always been good to me. I don't think I could betray them."

The admiral opened his mouth, perhaps to persuade her, but John spoke up first.

"Loyalty is a two-way street, Julie. It's admirable that you're still willing to stand by TERRA, despite what they want to do to you. But when someone gives their heart and soul to an institution they believe in, that person deserves to be given the same level of respect.

"You've worked hard your whole life because you wanted to make your dad and hometown proud of you. And what has TERRA done? They've ignored all your accomplishments with no regard for you. This is your chance to prove they're wrong. Don't let them step all over you. You deserve better."

"But what if the Screen comes here and attacks our worlds because we tried to leave? I don't want to be the one responsible for humanity's destruction."

"TERRA's been feeding us that same crap for years," John said. "They've done such a good job scaring us that no one is willing to take a risk. Who knows what's going to happen. Maybe the Screen will come in and attack as soon as we leave orbit or maybe they'll run scared at the sight of EXODUS. I'd rather go out there and find out once and for all who they are and what they want. This is our chance to change the course of human destiny."

"Now you're just laying it on thick," Julie said. John could be quite persuasive when he was passionate about something. Despite their differences and clashes, she'd always admired his conviction in his beliefs.

She did buy into TERRA's philosophy and was afraid of the Screen. She'd been taught they were a powerful and destructive force that could not be fought. It was difficult to push a lifetime of teachings aside.

But if she stayed on Earth, she was guaranteed a life of mediocrity giving tours to civilians in a museum. She hadn't gone to the Academy to be a tour guide. On this ship, she had the opportunity to put her training into use. This was her only chance to keep her dream alive.

"All right," she said, standing up. "I'm in."

—— —— ——

After they agreed to serve on EXODUS, Admiral Johnson escorted the cadets to separate quarters on deck seven. The plan was for them to be introduced to the senior staff in the morning.

The news sent a surge of nervousness through Julie's body. She expected the staff would be unimpressed with them as their commanding officers, despite the admiral's assurances that the staff supported his decision. Julie would need to display absolute confidence to convince them she could handle the position of executive officer.

John hardly blinked when he was told. He looked forward to the meeting and was curious to see how the staff would treat him on their first encounter. He had become accustomed to being looked upon with disdain at the Academy. If the senior staff didn't accept him, so be it. He was to be their commander. So long as they followed his orders, he could care less about being their friend.

The admiral requested that John and Julie remain in their quarters for the evening. The main computer was being taken offline for final upgrades and therefore would be unavailable as a guide. EXODUS was enormous, and it would not take much for

John or Julie to get lost within it.

The downside was that they couldn't leave the EXODUS Project to return to New York. The admiral assured them their personal belongings had already been retrieved and would be delivered to the ship by morning. Given the critical nature of this mission, no one who worked on the EXODUS Project ever left the Tormented Valley. It minimized the chance of a security leak and of TERRA uncovering what was truly going on.

Julie sat on the couch in the main living area of her quarters, looking at the DAT sitting on the coffee table. A single lamp was providing the only light in the room, barely illuminating the blue walls.

Julie stared at the DAT for a long time. She was hesitant to use it. Each time she began to reach for it, she pulled back.

The admiral had arranged for her to contact her father without the call being traced back to the ship. Julie wanted to call him, but was afraid. What would she tell him? He was expecting her back home tomorrow. Instead, she was going to have to explain she was leaving and might never see him again. How could she say anything without giving away the existence of EXODUS?

She couldn't tell him about the project, if for no other reason than to keep him safe. Once the ship left Earth, all hell would break loose with TERRA. This could be the last time they would ever speak. He deserved more than a vague explanation.

Her dad was her biggest supporter and had sacrificed a lot to help her prepare for the Academy entrance exams. He took her to every prep class available in Nebraska, driving her countless times to Lincoln and Omaha. He never complained about it once and always encouraged her. But he never coddled her. When she failed, he offered a shoulder to cry on but expected for her to get up and try again. They weren't wealthy, but somehow he always found a way to scrape enough money together to pay for her classes.

Enough of this. She was stalling by reminiscing about her childhood. She had to do this. Julie swallowed hard, activated the DAT, and inputted the access code the admiral had given her. There was no turning back now.

She waited what seemed an eternity for the call to go through. But soon the small screen lit up and she saw her father appear.

"Hello?" He blinked, trying to get a better view of the monitor.

"Hi, Daddy," Julie said as she watched her father rub his eyes. She wanted to blurt out everything to him: where she was, the ship, and its mission. After everything he'd done for her, he deserved the truth. But she knew she had to be strong and remain silent about EXODUS. It was in his best interest.

"Julie, sweetie," he said, smiling. "How are you? I'm surprised you're calling so late. You have an early morning flight."

"I'm okay. I just needed to talk to you." She fought the emotions welling up inside of her, determined to maintain an outwardly calm demeanor.

"Finals went okay, didn't they?" She had mentioned back in September that this semester would be the toughest yet.

"Finals went fine, but something's come up." This was even more difficult than Julie had anticipated. She did her best to remain composed, but try as she might, she couldn't keep the thought of never seeing her dad again out of her mind. All she could do was to quickly get through the conversation.

"Honey, you seem upset. What is it? Is your roommate giving you a hard time again?"

Tears started to stream down her face. This was an impossible task. She never missed the holidays with him. He'd raised Julie as a single parent and they shared a close family bond. She wanted to stay strong, but the thought of maybe never seeing him again pierced her heart. It was because of him that she wanted to become a TERRA officer. She wanted her dad to be proud of her and now she felt she was abandoning him.

"No, it's not about John. I...I wish I could tell you everything, but I can't." Although the transmission had been encoded and encrypted to hide its origin, Julie had only been given five minutes before the call self-terminated. "Listen Dad, I have to be quick. I'm not coming home for winter break. I've been presented with a very rare opportunity and it's something I can't pass up."

"It sounds like you got yourself an assignment. That's great.

You shouldn't be upset about not coming home. Graduation is only five months away. We'll see each other then. The experience you'll gain is far more important to getting your career off on the right track."

"Dad, I'm not going to be here for graduation."

His smile disappeared and was replaced with a look of confusion.

"The assignment I've been given is highly classified. I can't go into specifics for your own safety. But if everything works out, I may be gone for a long time."

"Julie, I don't like what I'm hearing."

"I'm sorry. I don't mean to be so cryptic about this, but please believe me when I tell you what I'm doing may change things for the better. I just wanted to say that no matter what you hear, know that I love you and will miss you. I'm going to do my best to make you proud of me."

"You already made me so very proud of you. You've always done the right thing. I understand you may not be able to tell me what you're involved in, but I trust your judgment. Don't you worry about me. I'll be fine and will be here waiting for you to get back."

"Thanks." Julie wiped the tears from her face. "I wish I could stay on longer, but I need to go. I love you."

"I love you too, sweetheart. You go on now. Be strong." He put his hand up on the monitor and Julie did the same. They smiled at one another for a moment before the screen went blank.

Once the call ended, the emotions she'd held back erupted, and she cried uncontrollably until she fell asleep on the couch, exhausted. Saying goodbye to her father, possibly forever, was the hardest thing she'd ever done.

Over in John's quarters, the mood was less than heartwarming. John was wrestling with whether he should even take advantage of his one call.

It wasn't that he didn't know who to contact. There was only one person he even considered. He hadn't seen his older sister Nicole in twelve years, and she was the only individual he wanted to speak to.

Their parents had died when he was four, and she'd raised him until he was twelve. But one day she'd packed up and left without any warning. She left no word as to why she'd taken off or where she was going.

John didn't think it was because she couldn't handle raising him. Their parents were wealthy and had left each of them a sizable trust to support themselves. He'd tried locating her numerous times, but had been unsuccessful. Now that he was about to leave Earth, maybe he should try and find her one last time.

"Locate number or residence for Nicole Roberts, sister of John Roberts of La Habra, California." TERRA had access to all sorts of databases and could locate anyone on Earth, Luna, and Mars.

"Unable to locate address or number of named individual," replied the DAT terminal as it linked to TERRA's database. It was another dead end, something John wasn't too surprised to hear. But this time he had the resources of TERRA at his disposal.

"Search all databases for last recorded information for Nicole Roberts."

"Last recorded information for individual made June 11, 2133 from North American Bureau of Population. Information is regarding statistical census data."

It was useless information. "Well, that's that." John clicked off the DAT. She had just simply disappeared. But why? They had had a great relationship and had gotten along, even up until the time she left.

John had never felt that he'd done anything to drive her away. For years he'd racked his brain, trying to figure out Nicole's motive for leaving, but eventually he'd given up. He'd have to give up again, and accept that he would have no contact with her before departing. Despite what had happened between them, John hoped that Nicole was happy wherever she was living.

CHAPTER SIX

he sun crept over the barren landscape in a vain attempt to provide some warmth to the cold climate. The activity level at the EXODUS Project had accelerated to a rapid pace during the night. An announcement about John and Julie's appointment as commander and executive officer had gone out over both the ship and ground facility communication systems. Final preparations for launch were underway.

John and Julie were scheduled to meet the senior staff in the military boardroom early this morning. In less than twenty-four hours, their entire world had changed. Instead of heading home for winter break, they were preparing to launch a classified vessel without the knowledge of TERRA.

Julie continued worrying about her father. TERRA would certainly send officials to Lexington to question him once this all became public. She hoped that somehow TERRA would not discover she was on board EXODUS.

John had forgotten about his sister and was instead preoccupied with readying himself to meet the senior staff. A variety of scenarios as to how the meeting might go down raced through his mind.

Command of a capital ship was given to only the most seasoned and respected officers, neither of which described John. Anyone hoping for one of only five coveted ship commander spots usually had to wait until they were well into their fifties to get one. Competition to get into the Academy was fierce, but paled in comparison to the competition to become commander of a capital ship.

There were other options—one could captain a TERRA freighter or support vessel, where the competition was less intense—but everyone vied for a capital ship. Yet here was John, given command of the first human-operated starship at the age of twenty-four. Was he expecting little or no resistance from the crew? Absolutely not! If he was a member of this crew, he'd be vociferously questioning the admiral's decision to appoint a cadet as ship commander. John suspected that his path would not be an easy one.

John and Julie's belongings arrived from Dorm Row, but neither checked their packages as they were too busy putting on their TERRA uniforms. The uniforms were both adorned with the appropriate gold command bars on the shoulders. John wasted no time getting dressed, slipping into the black jumpsuit with ease. He spent far too much time adjusting the uniform on his body as he admired himself in the mirror. All he kept thinking about was Mortino having a stroke if he saw John in an officer uniform. It was the superintendent he should have called last night.

Satisfied that he looked ready, John headed out and met Julie at her quarters. Together, they walked down the corridor to the lift that would take them to the boardroom on deck three.

"So, what do you think?" asked John as they walked. They hadn't had an opportunity to compare notes and John was curious to hear Julie's thoughts about their windfall.

"I think it's an absolute crime for you to be wearing that uniform."

"As much as I would like to get into it with you, we should probably show a united front when we meet the command staff."

Julie bit her lip. He was right. Julie hated it when John was right. She was an executive officer now. Any problems they had needed to be tabled. "Sorry, I'm just waiting for reality to kick back in."

"I hear ya."

"There's something that's still bothering me."

"What's that?"

"It's the admiral," she said. "He was able to staff this ship with all the specialists and trained military personnel he needed. I find it hard to believe that he couldn't find experienced officers to command this ship."

She had a point and John wished she hadn't brought it up. "Don't you think you're being a little paranoid?"

But it didn't make sense to him either that an experienced officer hadn't been offered command of EXODUS. Why would the admiral hand command over to cadets with no command experience? He had too much invested in this project to risk it on them.

"I'm not paranoid," said Julie. "It's a legitimate question. I assume he would have tried to recruit TERRA officers to command this ship. The mission's too important to simply pass off to cadets out of favor with TERRA, especially if he put twenty years of hard work into this project."

"Maybe it's just..." John scrambled to find the right words. He didn't want to come off sounding suspicious, but he couldn't ignore Julie's statement. There were plenty of good officers the admiral could have selected, but he'd passed them up for John and Julie.

Then the light bulb came on. Of course! It made perfect sense. John felt stupid for not realizing it sooner.

"What is it?" asked Julie. She could tell that John had had some sort of revelation.

"It's nothing. Let's just get through this staff meeting. We can bring it up to the admiral later."

John had chosen not to say anything to Julie, but he was seething inside with what he thought had been the admiral's motivation for selecting them. How could he have been so stupid? He would play along with the admiral for now, but John had every intention of confronting him later.

"The boardroom is to the right," the computer said as John and Julie reached their destination. Julie slowed her pace so that she could compose herself before going in, but John never gave her the opportunity. He wasted no time in opening the door and going inside. She followed right behind him.

"Ah, good morning," Admiral Johnson greeted them. He was seated at the head of the table, in the company of five other individuals. John and Julie recognized Security Chief Thomas Sandoval, who was located at the far end.

A young woman was seated next to the admiral, and John noticed how youthful she appeared. She seemed to be around the same age as the cadets. She only looked up at them briefly when they entered the boardroom. After a quick glimpse, she refocused her attention on the paperwork in front of her.

Her hairstyle grabbed John's attention. It was tied up in a bun that was more commonly worn by old women. John tried to picture her with her brunette hair down, but couldn't come up with an accurate portrait.

Seated next to her was a young Black man who gave them a respectful nod. He seemed curious about the new commanders of EXODUS, his eyes darting back and forth between them. His hands were folded on the table, as if he was at a dinner party, trying to be polite.

Next to the young man was a dark-haired man who appeared to be in his thirties. He reminded John of an older version of David—a bookworm who wasn't too concerned with personal appearance. He shifted awkwardly in his seat every so often. John figured that he himself must have really pissed off the brass if the fleet had accepted this guy over him.

Seated between the nerd and the security chief was an older Black man. His hair was a shimmering white, in sharp contrast with his wrinkled, dark skin. He was seated comfortably in his chair and displayed a warm smile. Unlike the others, he wore a white overcoat, indicating he was a medical officer.

"Let me go down the row and introduce you to your senior staff," the admiral said. "This is Lieutenant Alex'sis Brandus, your tactical officer. She's also been acting as the senior operations officer, a role Commander Olson will be sharing as executive officer."

The woman again looked up at John and Julie and nodded to

them without so much as a smile before resuming her review of her documents. John resisted the temptation to roll his eyes. He told himself to keep an open mind. Maybe Brandus wasn't really a bitch. Then again, it wouldn't have killed her to at least say hello.

"Next to Alex'sis is Private Bret Michaels, your communications officer. Then we have Kevin Jacobson, the ship's navigation officer, Chief Medical Officer Joseph Myers, and of course you met Chief Sandoval yesterday."

"Hello," Julie said to all of them. She didn't know what else to say or what proper protocol was when meeting your senior staff. It was something she hadn't thought she needed to worry about for at least another three decades. She certainly wasn't going to salute them.

"Where's the chief engineer?" asked John, who'd picked up on the obvious omission.

"EXODUS does not have a chief engineer of military rank," the admiral said. "The engines were designed and developed by civilians and they run the engineering section. This meeting is for the senior military staff. You'll meet the civilian department heads later."

Julie wondered how many department heads were on a ship this size. "How many civilians are on board?"

The admiral motioned for her and John to sit at the table as he relinquished his chair to John. John sat at the head of the table and Julie sat next to him, facing the senior staff. Admiral Johnson remained standing, no doubt observing how his new additions interacted with the staff.

"There are 4,175 civilians and 872 military personnel on board," replied Alex'sis. Her voice lacked emotion.

John's instincts told him there would be a personality conflict between him and Alex'sis. Alex'sis and Julie would probably get along great, which worried him. John could already picture them leading a mutiny against him. He wondered if they would hold off betraying him until after they were out of the solar system. If they really hit it off, they'd probably take over while EXODUS was still in Earth's orbit.

"How are we supposed to run this ship in a military fashion when most of the crew is civilian?" John asked, refocusing his attention back on the meeting.

"The crew has been working here as a blended group for years," the admiral said. "They're accustomed to working within military protocol and have adapted quite well."

"But what about issues such as disciplinary actions?" John couldn't believe he was bringing up the topic. He was the last person to be asking about punishing insubordinates. He'd spent his entire Academy career either breaking or circumventing TERRA rules.

Again, Alex'sis was on the spot with an answer. "Civilian personnel on board are subject to the same court martial proceedings outlined by TERRA's code of conduct. Civilians will be disciplined by their department heads as needed and as they see fit. If a criminal offense is committed, they will be subject to any disciplinary action deemed appropriate by you, the ship commander."

"Him?" Julie didn't like the idea of John playing the role of judge. He'd probably just brush off any violation of the ship's rules and not punish offenders. EXODUS could quickly degenerate into chaos.

"It's standard military practice for the ship commander to assume the role in the absence of an established court system," Alex'sis said. "EXODUS will be far from the solar system and we've elected not to staff the ship with legal personnel."

John got the sense that Alex'sis was being sarcastic with that last sentence. Lawyers weren't popular and John was glad to hear the ship didn't have any, but he still thought it could present problems. "The crew has agreed to this?"

"Both the military and civilian sides had to make accommodations in certain areas," said the admiral. "The civilians understand the final rule of authority on this ship rests with the ship's commander."

"The Academy has trained us in scenarios where we command a ship exclusively staffed by military personnel," John said to Johnson. "This will take some getting used to."

Alex'sis came back with a quick response. "With all due respect, sir, your lax regard toward military discipline makes you the ideal commander to work under such conditions." Now John couldn't tell if she was insulting him or giving him a compliment. She had a good poker face, revealing nothing of her emotions.

"Well, glad to see I've already got a reputation here," said John. "I take it you've read my Academy file?"

"My point, sir, is that your record shows you can adapt to new and unknown situations rather adeptly."

Julie interceded before John could reply. They were going off track and she wanted to keep the discussion focused on the ship. "Discipline is only one of a myriad of issues we have to contend with. This ship has technology the Academy taught as only theoretical. It's going to take some time for John and me to get familiar with it. I think it's unrealistic to launch tomorrow when we aren't even prepared. Shouldn't it be postponed a few weeks until we get a grasp on some of the issues here?"

"Unfortunately, we don't have the luxury of time to put the launch off," the admiral said. "You're both on winter break for just two weeks. The Academy will notify TERRA when you fail to report in January and will start searching for you. Second, the command council is scheduled to conduct a walking tour of EXODUS at the end of the week. The status reports they've been receiving omit a significant number of details regarding the ship."

"Like the fact it can fly," muttered John. Luckily, no one heard him.

The admiral continued. "If they discover what EXODUS is really capable of, it may complicate our efforts to launch it."

"What about the Screen?" asked John. "As soon as we move beyond Mars's orbit, we'll undoubtedly encounter a Screen vessel. EXODUS will be at a disadvantage with two green officers calling the shots."

John couldn't believe the words coming out of his mouth. He wanted to hit himself. Since when did he talk like that? This was his chance to command a ship and here he was, bringing up the negative points of being commander. He was starting to sound logical like Julie, and that sickened him. Even when he was wrong or wasn't good at something, he never admitted it. It was a sign of weakness.

"I'll bring you up to speed on the ship's offensive and defensive systems today," Alex'sis said, interrupting John's thoughts. "You'll find EXODUS will be more than a match for the Screen."

How was she so confident that the ship could stack up against a Screen vessel? "Doesn't that seem presumptuous?" John said. He didn't care how many assurances the crew gave him. The simple fact was, this ship had never been in battle against the Screen and no human-operated ship had ever survived a Screen attack.

"We have detailed scans of each Screen attack since the inception of TERRA," Alex'sis said. "This ship possesses the appropriate countermeasures to combat Screen technology."

"I thought there wasn't any information on the Screen," Julie said, confused.

"It's one of the command council's many secrets," the admiral said. "The solar system sensor net has been used to monitor Screen attacks and detailed scans were taken of Screen ships during each encounter."

Julie's faith in TERRA was shaken by this admission. Growing up, all she'd ever heard was that the Screen was powerful. Human technology had no way of combating it. She'd assumed TERRA had no viable information about the Screen and their vessels were impervious to scans. She'd never imagined TERRA had the capability to monitor the alien attacks.

"Well, I'm glad to hear that you have something on which to base your assumption that EXODUS has a fighting chance against our enemy," said John. "What about the fleet itself? All hell is going to break loose once this ship leaves Earth."

"Our first step is to leave the solar system as quickly as possible," said the navigation officer, whose confident voice didn't match his awkward appearance. "I've plotted the most direct course out of the system. Unfortunately, given Earth's current position at launch tomorrow, we'll be passing by Mars to take the quickest route out."

"How close to Mars?" asked John.

"We'll be in range of the planet's particle cannon for a brief period."

"Whoa! Hold on!" That was a variable John hadn't expected. "If TERRA decided to fire that weapon, and I'm sure they would, they'd obliterate us."

"EXODUS will be able to withstand the blast," Alex'sis replied in a cool tone.

"You know, you're awfully confident in this ship." John was starting to get annoyed by Alex'sis's superiority complex. "I don't care how big this ship is or what amazing technology it possesses. There's no way it can survive an attack from a planetary cannon."

Everyone in the fleet was well aware of the Mars cannon. It had been designed as a defense against a possible Screen incursion. The cannon was the single most powerful weapon TERRA had ever constructed. It was capable of taking out a TERRA capital ship in one blast.

"EXODUS is equipped with an energy shield," replied Alex'sis.

Silence filled the room as John and Julie processed this. It was yet another surprise.

"You have an energy shield?" Julie asked in disbelief. Both the admiral and Alex'sis nodded in unison. "No one has ever been able to successfully design such a system. What about the problem of high energy consumption or maintaining cohesiveness in the grid?"

"Solved ten years ago," the admiral said proudly. "The current shield system is actually a third-generation model."

According to Academy teachings, energy shield technology wasn't expected to be viable for at least another century. There were simply too many variables that scientists had yet to overcome.

John was almost speechless. He was beginning to realize why Alex'sis was so confident about their chances. "The Academy curriculum is going to need some serious revisions." He looked at the senior staff, dumbfounded. "Uh, okay. Well, if that's not an issue, then I guess we should have no problem with TERRA's fleet."

"None. They pose no threat to EXODUS at all," said the admiral.

"TERRA won't be aware there's a problem until you've exited Earth's atmosphere. The council believes we'll be conducting a thruster test tomorrow. They'll black out the area from sensor scans and ship traffic will be diverted for ten minutes while we conduct the 'test.' But once they detect EXODUS in orbit, they'll realize there's a problem and send a detachment from Luna to investigate."

"I'll be monitoring communications from the fleet," said Bret. "As soon as they're alerted, we'll know."

The admiral stepped close to John. "As soon as you're in space, you're on your own. Do what you feel is necessary, but you must get this ship out of the system. That's your top priority above all else."

"Even if it means fighting TERRA?" asked Julie.

"Top priority, Commander," reiterated the admiral. "You cannot be prevented from accomplishing your mission."

The definitive sound of his voice crept over Julie's skin in an uncomfortable wave. John felt similarly ill at ease. Despite his animosity toward TERRA, he cringed at the thought of possibly killing officers. But if TERRA ships posed no threat to EXODUS, then maybe they wouldn't have to worry about getting into a firefight.

The admiral changed the subject. "We have a full day ahead of us. Julie, you'll accompany Kevin down to engineering to meet the engineers and get familiar with the hyper-drive. Kevin has been working closely with the engineering team and has the most knowledge about their operations. John, Alex'sis will take you down to the floor level of Central where the department heads are waiting to meet with you. The rest of you have tasks to complete to prepare for tomorrow's launch. John, Julie, I'll see you one last time tonight."

The staff got up and headed out of the boardroom. Julie waited by the door for Lieutenant Jacobson and they both left at the same time. That left Alex'sis and John alone in the boardroom.

"I'll get my stuff together and we'll head down," said Alex'sis.

"Sure." John watched her gather up her papers and put them in her file folder. He waited for her to start a conversation, but she said nothing, so he took the initiative. "So how long have you been here?"

"Four years." She didn't even look up at him as she continued to organize her papers.

"You know, if we're going to be stuck in space for years, it'd be nice to know a little something about the people serving under me. At least give me a chance, before deciding I'm the asshole most people say I am."

Alex'sis stopped what she was doing and looked at John. "The admiral was right. You aren't exactly the military type."

"Does that bother you?"

"No, I find it quite refreshing. I have to be diplomatic to get all the departments to work together, putting on a facade of cooperation. But sometimes all I want to do is choke them." John laughed, hearing her words. "You think it's funny?"

"Yeah, I do. I'm relieved your serious demeanor isn't who you are. I was starting to get worried that maybe you weren't a human being."

Alex'sis cracked a small smile. "I'm glad to provide you with some amusement. I met the admiral during my senior year at the Academy. I was on assignment at the Luna shipyards when he approached me." She got up from her chair, as did John, and together they headed out the boardroom. "At first I was apprehensive about what he was offering. But when he explained to me what he was trying to do with the EXODUS Project, I couldn't say no."

"So, you disagree with TERRA's stance regarding the Screen?"

"I do. It's never made sense to me that the council made no attempt to try and communicate with them. It's one thing to do nothing against a superior enemy, but at the very least we should confirm what their intentions are. The Screen's attacks on ships going beyond Mars doesn't conclusively imply that they want us to stay in our own system. It's a pretty good indicator, but not proof."

"And you're okay with having a ship commander who hasn't graduated from the Academy?"

"You'll find many people on this ship who came here under

similarly strange circumstances. Private Michaels never went to the Academy, yet he's a ranking member of the military here."

"How does that work?"

"It's a long story, one that's best told over a cold beer," Alex'sis said as they stepped onto the lift.

"I don't do beer. I'm more of a vodka person myself," John said, in an attempt at humor.

Alex'sis cracked a slight grin. "The point is that even though a cadet being given a command position is highly unusual, it's something we've all become accustomed to here. Everyone has their own unique story about how they came to the project. The admiral doesn't make any decisions without carefully considering all options. You'll find that he's quite close to everyone here."

"I pegged the admiral as not your typical run-of-the-mill officer," said John. "He doesn't use official titles and calls everyone by their first names."

"The admiral was right when he said you were insightful."

"It's a blessing and a curse." The lift opened and they stepped onto the bottom level of Central. "When it comes down to it, I just have a big mouth."

"Those traits may have hindered you at the Academy, but they'll serve you well here. None of us knows what to expect from the Screen and any insight you can provide when we encounter them will help."

"Whoa! You better not expect me to come up with some magic solution on how to deal with them. I'm just planning to go along as the situation develops."

"Then it's fortunate that you'll be helming the most powerful human ship ever made."

John rolled his eyes. He would soon see if EXODUS was indeed as powerful as everyone claimed.

CHAPTER SEVEN

It seemed to Julie that she and Kevin had been standing in the lift for an eternity. The boardroom was located at the front of the ship, and the engineering section housing the engine was located at the rear. Although the lift was high-speed, it still took time for it to travel across the ship to reach the other side.

Neither Kevin nor Julie spoke. Julie was unsure how to start a conversation with the lieutenant. She was now his commanding officer, and military protocol dissuaded commanding officers from intermingling with subordinates on a personal level. It was easy to follow on a capital ship as personnel rotated duties on all five TERRA vessels. But Julie was going to spend what could be years on this ship and she couldn't live here and only make friends with the civilians.

To get through the awkward silence, Julie pretended to be reading the hyper-drive specs Kevin had given her. She had only a rudimentary knowledge of the physics involved. TERRA didn't use the technology, and civilian ships were banned from having it. The Academy did teach the theory behind hyper-drive, but instructors only covered it briefly in starship design. None of the techs or engineers in TERRA could maintain such an engine if presented with one.

Julie was surprised that a functioning hyper-drive could even be fitted on this ship. Recalling her history lessons, the HORIZON had had a large jumpgate in lieu of an engine. That had been nearly seventy years ago. Enough time had passed to develop an engine small enough to install on any ship, but as far as Julie knew, the technology hadn't been further developed since the HORIZON's destruction.

The EXODUS Project had clearly made further advances in hyper-drive engine design. It didn't surprise Julie that TERRA had secret development projects going on, but it contradicted trying to appease the Screen. How was the admiral able to conceal what he was doing here from TERRA?

"Here we go," Kevin said as the lift door opened. They stepped off into an expansive corridor, much larger than the corridors throughout the rest of the ship. Unlike those areas, this one was bathed in a bluish hue, and Julie could hear a low-pitched hum reverberating throughout the area.

"This is the main corridor that feeds into the engineering section," Kevin explained as they headed toward engineering. "Anyone wanting to access this area has to come through here."

"Why only one way in?" Julie was expecting it to be a security concern. She looked around to see if she could identify any security systems embedded in the walls, but couldn't detect any. The walls were smooth and lacked any markings to indicate they housed a system.

"The hyper-drive surrounds engineering, so access has to be limited to a single entry."

"Surrounds?"

"The engine is composed of rotating beams embedded in the walls. The beams generate the Dubois particles, which are delivered into the ship's hull. The power core sits within the center of engineering and transmits power to the beams via conduits below the deck floor. The techs monitor and control the system from stations within engineering."

"I've read up on old hyper-drive specifications," said Julie. Although the construction of these engines was forbidden, it wasn't illegal for scientists and engineers to draw up schematics. "What you described doesn't resemble any schematic design I've ever seen."

"It does sound unremarkable," admitted Kevin. "And the setup is not that impressive when you see it. But the engine does what it's supposed to do."

"Has it been tested?"

"We've been able to bring the engine to full power without sending the ship off to faster-than-light. The data clearly showed that faster-than-light travel was possible."

Julie was impressed. It appeared the admiral had waited for the right time to launch EXODUS. All the critical systems had been tested numerous times to verify their integrity. She felt a bit at ease knowing that the key systems had proved reliable.

The two reached the end of the corridor, where a single door stood before them. Kevin punched the nearby panel and the door opened. He entered first with Julie following close behind.

The engineering section was not as brightly lit as the corridor. It took a few moments for Julie's eyes to adjust. Immediately ahead of them was a short set of stairs. Kevin had already climbed to the top of the landing, and Julie followed suit. Once she joined him, she could see the entire engineering area. It was quite sparse, unlike the engineering sections of TERRA capital ships. They were compact and littered with computer terminals.

The first thing that caught Julie's attention was a large dome sitting in the center. It was tall and slim, surrounded by eight computer stations spaced equally from one another and manned by engineers. Julie surmised that the dome housed the main power core. The core itself emitted a soothing hum that she found quite comforting. She swore she could almost make out a melody.

Shifting her eyes from the power core to the walls, she could see the outline of the beams stacked on top of each other recessed in the walls. She imagined being in engineering with the hyperdrive active, picturing the beams traveling in some high-speed race to nowhere. To her, it was a technological feat this engine had even been built.

"Lieutenant Jacobson! Lieutenant Jacobson!" The shrill voice brought Julie's attention back from her thoughts. She saw a short bald man stomping toward her and Kevin, as if ready to start a fight.

"Professor Donavin," Kevin said politely.

"That Lieutenant Brandus is giving my people grief about security down here again," the professor said in an upset tone. He didn't even bother to acknowledge Julie's presence.

The professor pulled out a DAT from his lab coat pocket and shook it in Kevin's face. "I still have numerous engineering issues to resolve without having to worry about insignificant matters. Ship security is a military issue and I shouldn't have to be bothered with doing your jobs."

Kevin remained patient. "Lieutenant Brandus requested a report regarding security from each department last week."

But the professor wouldn't hear of it. "You think this engine is easy to maintain, but you have no idea the problems I contend with daily to ensure it is operating at optimal efficiency. Recalculating drive equations to compensate for variables isn't easy, even for someone with a doctorate. But no, you snap your fingers and expect us to deliver perfection on a whim."

Kevin looked over at Julie with a look that screamed, "Help me!"

"Excuse me, professor," Julie interjected, regretting what she might be getting into. "Perhaps I can help."

The professor looked at Julie intently for a long moment. It didn't bother her that he was staring at her, but when his gaze started moving up and down her body, she couldn't help but think that he was mentally undressing her. She wanted to run and hide behind the core, away from his prying eyes. Maybe he didn't have many conversations with women.

"And who are you?" he asked. It was apparent he was enamored by the commander..

"This is Julie Olson, our new executive officer," replied Kevin.

"Ah, then I don't have to bother with you," the professor said, dismissing Kevin. "I can go right to the top."

"I'd be happy to try and resolve any issues you have," Julie said, suddenly thrust into her first personnel crisis.

"The problem is that you military types are intruding in areas you have no business in. I'm trying to run an efficient operation down here, but I can't achieve that goal when your Lieutenant Brandus insists I provide information in areas that really don't concern me."

"You mean security?"

"Precisely! I have no doubt Chief Sandoval can provide adequate security down here for me and my staff. I shouldn't be expected to provide recommendations on a military matter. I'm a scientist, not a policeman."

"I think Lieutenant Brandus wants to avoid any conflicts when establishing security protocols for engineering," Julie tried to explain. "Since engineering is your responsibility, we want to make sure that any protocols we establish don't interfere with your delicate operation."

"I wasn't aware the military was so concerned with matters of civilian departments," the professor said. "I thought as long as you got your end result, nothing else mattered."

"I want to ensure that all operations on EXODUS are fluid and free of needless distraction. Lieutenant Brandus was simply extending a courtesy by inviting your input on how you think security should be established in engineering."

"Humph! Didn't think of it that way." He looked at Julie, as if trying to gauge her sincerity.

"If it'll make things easier, you can send the security report directly to me," Julie offered, trying to cement his favor.

"That would be an acceptable solution," he replied. "I'll send you the report at the end of the day. Just be sure that Lieutenant Brandus knows that I'm working with you now. You can tell her she's no longer welcome here."

Julie didn't intend for him to assume he could go directly to her all the time, but before she could utter a word, the professor turned and headed back to his colleagues near the core.

"Thank you," Kevin said in a low voice. "Once he gets going, it's almost impossible to get him to stop."

"Is he always this charming?"

"The professor is highly intelligent. Unfortunately, that doesn't include knowing any social graces. He's harmless, just a bit of a klutz when dealing with people. When it comes to his work, he can be passionate."

"I hope he wasn't serious about Lieutenant Brandus. And what was all that talk of the hyper-drive being delicate?"

"The professor tends to have a dramatic flair. Despite what he says, the hyper-drive is one tough engine. It's been tested and reworked so many times over the years. It's one of the most reliable pieces of equipment we have." Kevin's reassurance gave Julie some peace of mind. "You handled the professor just right. Make him feel that he's running the show and he'll be easier to handle."

"Only easier?"

"The professor is a difficult man. It's just a matter of lowering the degree of difficulty."

"Thanks for the tip." Julie looked over at the professor. "By the way, what were those glass things on his face?"

"Oh, those are called bifocals. It's an old tool people used to wear to compensate for diminished vision."

"He's not a mute, is he?" she asked. A 'mute' was short for 'mutant.' It was a nickname for someone who descended from a Nuclear Holocaust victim and suffered from genetic disorders resulting from their ancestors' radiation exposure.

Mutes weren't permitted to serve in TERRA and were not allowed to live on Luna and Mars, as their conditions were deemed a drain on the limited resources of both colonies. The Interstellar Republic Alliance required all citizens to undergo genetic profiling to ensure no mute left Earth, so that they could receive all the necessary medical treatment they required. The government's goal was to eventually eliminate the genetic defects that still plagued a significant portion of the population.

"Oh no, his genes are good," replied Kevin. "The professor just doesn't like doctors and refuses any treatment, no matter how minor. Dr. Myers has tried on numerous occasions to get the professor to have his eyes fixed, but he has a hard enough time getting him through a routine physical."

Julie was not surprised to hear this. She hoped that her

interactions with the professor during their trip would be few and far between. Executive officers were expected to handle the day-to-day issues on a ship, but Julie felt that John would be better off dealing with the professor. Her former roommate was not intimidated by anyone.

The rest of the day's events exhausted the two newly minted commanders. John and Julie each met what seemed to be hundreds of crewmembers and were given comprehensive reviews of many of the ship's systems. The launch was looming tomorrow and both tried to prepare themselves as best they could for it.

Trying to retain all the information thrown at them and becoming familiar with the vessel took its toll. Despite her fatigue, Julie wanted to spend a few more hours in her quarters reading over the technical manuals of the ship. After everything she had seen on board, she was beginning to feel inadequate and wanted to eliminate that disadvantage by digging into as much information as possible before tomorrow.

One of the more unique systems Julie read about was the ECON (short for economics) system. The ECON was a computer system independent of the main computer and the rest of the ship's networked systems. It was the method developed to regulate and distribute the limited resources the ship carried. The ECON monitored resources such as food, water, and clothing and assigned monetary amounts to them based on availability and usage. Based on their position, crewmembers were given credits each week to buy goods or services.

The system was highly secured; only the ship commander had the authority to alter its parameters. The merchants of Central, initially skeptical of ECON, had fully embraced the system after living with its operation the past few years. Julie thought it was an ingenious way to moderate ship resources.

Unlike Julie, John had had his fill of schematics and procedures and just wanted to go to bed. Twenty-four hours was too short a time to absorb all the information thrown at him about EXODUS and he wasn't about to kill himself trying to keep it all straight in his head. A good night's sleep was what he needed to be alert for tomorrow's launch, but Admiral Johnson had invited him and Julie to his quarters for dinner. Even though he was tired, John felt obligated to attend and reluctantly agreed.

This farewell dinner was John's final opportunity to confront the admiral and learn the real reason he'd chosen him and Julie for this command. His whole speech about the cadets' personalities making them a perfect fit for this assignment wasn't sitting well with John. The admiral's explanation reeked of bullshit and John wasn't going to be played as a pawn by anybody—but he chose not to call out the admiral right away. He wanted to give him the opportunity to come clean without any cajoling.

"To the EXODUS," the admiral said, raising his wine glass at the dinner table. John and Julie joined him in the toast.

"To the mission," added Julie.

"The mission," echoed John as they each sipped from their glasses. John didn't have much of a taste for wine; he pretty much limited his alcohol intake to whatever hard liquor was available. The wine had a dry taste that didn't appeal to him. He liked his drinks sweet, and the wine wasn't helping to get him into a celebratory mood.

"So, Admiral," John started, not wanting to wait any longer to address the issue that had plagued his mind all day. "There's something that's been bothering me. You had plenty of opportunities to find an experienced commander for this ship. Hell, you've had years." The tone in his voice did a poor job of hiding his suspicion. "You chose two cadets with no experience to helm this vessel. You've explained your decision by claiming that no TERRA officers would jeopardize their careers in taking on this mission, but I'm having a hard time believing that."

"You personally know the sacrifices and years of hard work required to make it to the Academy and earn a commission in the fleet," replied the admiral. "No officer would be willing to throw away a career for this mission."

"So, you choose two people who have nothing to lose?"

"John," Julie tried to interject, seeing the inevitable confrontation that was about to take place, but he held his hand up to silence her.

"No, Julie, we need to know." John gave the admiral a penetrating glare. "We have no promising careers if we graduate from the Academy. But you just swoop in and offer us a job. Of course we'd take your offer, as we have no other alternative. We worked hard to get into TERRA and we're not about to accept a civilian or dead-end job." John's eyes didn't waver as he kept his gaze on the admiral, waiting for him to dispute his statement.

Julie could only sit there in silence. Everything John said had a sickening ring of truth. She couldn't ignore it.

Admiral Johnson continued to eat his dinner as John spoke, but eventually pushed his plate away and wiped his mouth with his napkin. John took his silence as confirmation. "So, it wasn't our great skills that attracted you to us. You played us."

The admiral cleared his throat. "You have to understand, I couldn't risk approaching a commissioned officer to take this assignment. TERRA officers are fiercely loyal, and I couldn't risk an officer reporting my proposal to the council. We all know what would happen if this mission failed and EXODUS didn't make it out of the system. The commanding officers would be courtmartialed and stripped of their ranks. They'd be barred from ever serving in TERRA. No officer would take that chance."

"But you figured we might," John said. "Because we have no careers and no loyalty to TERRA."

"I anticipated you'd be more receptive to my proposal." The admiral tempered his words, attempting to sound diplomatic. The mission hinged on them staying. "You said you weren't going to let a lifetime of training go to waste."

John threw his napkin on the table. "Don't try to sugarcoat this. You're only using us as a matter of convenience."

He got up and went to the window, looking out at the stars hanging motionless in the sky. He wanted a life in space, but on his own merits. Getting command of a starship as a matter of convenience made him feel cheated. He felt stupid for imagining it was his intelligence and independence that had gotten him here.

"I firmly believe you're the only ones who can make this

mission a success," reiterated the admiral. "I wasn't lying when I said that."

"We're just not your first choice," John replied sarcastically.

"Is your pride so wounded that you would consider leaving?"

Damn him. As upset John was, the admiral had him there.

"No, I guess it wouldn't matter." Despite how they'd been selected, it didn't change John's mind about taking this mission. It was his only chance to serve on a ship.

Julie spoke up. "Isn't there any chance we can have a legitimate career in the fleet? Maybe I could talk to the placement board."

Admiral Johnson shook his head. "I made inquiries before I approached you. I knew there was no recourse for John. His reputation was simply too undesirable. No department or squadron would want him serving in their ranks. As for you, Julie, you'd make an excellent officer. But the fleet is not what it once was. TERRA has gone from being a military institution to an elitist organization. Unless you have a high-ranking officer looking out for you, your career will only go so far."

"No surprise there," John said.

"I don't think you understand the extent to which the corruption extends. Individuals are no longer judged on their merits. What happened to Julie reflects what TERRA has turned into."

He looked at Julie with sincerity. "You come from a middle-class farming community in Nebraska. You're the first member of your family to attend the Academy and thus your family holds no influence in TERRA. You could've been number one in your class and still would've been relegated to the museum assignment. The most desired positions are being given to the Freemans, the Mortinos, the Daleys, the Blocks—families that hold powerful positions in TERRA. The future of the fleet is one where these 'royal' families will control TERRA and they will make choices that benefit themselves, not humanity. It's more important to them to maintain the status quo rather than protect the interests of the human race."

"Is that why you're doing this?" asked John. "To fight corruption in TERRA? Taking down elitist snobs doesn't sound very personal, and I don't think something so vague would motivate a high-ranking admiral to risk his own career. Julie and I have our reasons for going into this. What's yours?"

The admiral did not immediately respond. He stood up and walked over to John by the window, looking at him with a sorrowful expression. John was caught off guard. Something he had said had touched a nerve. Seeing the expression on the admiral's face, John regretted coming across so harshly.

"You remind me so much of my son," the admiral struggled to say.

John didn't know how to respond. His regret changed to a feeling of discomfort as the admiral gazed at him intensely.

"I didn't know you had children," said Julie. She had read the biographies of all the command council members and didn't recall the admiral's biography listing any family members.

"My son was an Interceptor pilot in the fleet. I lost him fifteen years ago." The admiral looked at John once more, his eyes red as they welled up with tears. He went back to the table and sat down, staring at his plate. He did not want to relieve painful memories, but would have to if he was to convince them his intentions were honorable.

Julie looked to John, who only shrugged. He was as perplexed as she was by the admiral's behavior. He stayed by the window, not inclined to pursue an obviously uncomfortable subject.

Julie took the initiative and sat down next to the admiral, putting her hand on his arm. "What happened?"

The admiral looked at Julie and smiled weakly. "The fleet holds many secrets. One of them is tightly guarded. It's a routine mission only the council members are privy to. Not even the president or anyone in the civilian government is aware of it." He cleared his throat before continuing. "Every year the council has the sensor net shut down under the guise of upgrading it. The real reason is to conceal a clandestine mission. A pilot is sent out in an unarmed Interceptor beyond the Mars orbital boundary to gauge the Screen's reaction."

Both Julie and John were equally appalled to hear this. "TERRA has always been so adamant that no one does anything to antagonize the Screen," said Julie. "Why would they do such a thing?"

"It's the only way for the council to monitor the Screen and see if their hostility toward us has changed. This has been done for decades, but no record is kept of the activity. By conducting this reconnaissance, the council can be confident in their long-running stance that no one leaves the solar system."

John was less restrained in his opinion. "The hell with the Screen! What about the pilots they send to their deaths?"

"The pilots volunteer to go out," the admiral replied in a cool tone.

John couldn't comprehend anyone willing to throw away their lives for such a foolhardy task. "What half-brained lunatic would agree to fly a suicide mission?"

"There are officers who are so loyal to TERRA they're willing to do anything the council asks them, including sacrificing their lives."

"For what?" John asked angrily. "To maintain the status quo?"

The admiral nodded. "That's why the council will never approve an interstellar mission. They have thousands of loyal officers who have bought into the council's passive philosophy. It's been passed down for generations. They're so devoted to protecting TERRA that they're willing to give up their lives to see that nothing changes."

"Sounds like a cult," John said. "TERRA's nothing but a goddamn cult." He looked at Julie. "I hope you see now what kind of underhanded operation TERRA is."

Julie ignored John's comments. "The council just picks the officer to fly this mission?"

The admiral nodded. "It's not difficult for the council to identify the most willing candidate. They've never had an officer say no."

"And your son was one of the pilots?"

The admiral looked at Julie with an expression of pain, as if a knife had been plunged and twisted inside of him. "My Kory was so devoted to TERRA. There wasn't anything he wouldn't do. I was proud that he chose to serve in the same institution I spent my life in. But I didn't realize how deep his commitment to TERRA was. I told him privately about the secret operation. The next day he volunteered to test the Screen. He knew I would never permit him to go out, so he convinced the council to keep me in the dark. It was the only reconnaissance mission I never observed. It took three days for the council to inform me..."

Recounting the tale was too much for the admiral. He got up and walked to the other end of the room.

John felt horrible for making him recount that part of his life. His own personal problems with TERRA seemed insignificant in comparison to the loss the admiral had suffered.

The admiral regained enough control of his emotions to resume his tale. "I knew things couldn't go on like this. I promised myself that no one else's son or daughter would die needlessly. When I returned to the EXODUS Project, I began bringing in people who shared my vision that we needed to change TERRA. EXODUS was transformed from a test bed of technology to a ship of exploration."

There was a long period of silence in the room. There were no more secrets between them now. Everything was out in the open.

Julie felt a great deal of sympathy for the admiral. She imagined her father must have felt the same when Julie's mother died.

"Thank you for telling us," said John. "I understand why you weren't upfront about it."

"I suppose if I'm asking you to risk your lives, you should know my motives," the admiral said. "I'm sorry I wasn't upfront with you. I was too afraid that you would say no to me."

Despite the painful nature of the admiral's story, Julie decided it was time to bring up an issue she'd discovered inadvertently during the day. "Admiral, if you believe in what the EXODUS stands for, why aren't you staying on board when it launches?"

John gave the admiral a surprised look. He'd naturally assumed the man would be part of the crew.

"My only role has been to prepare the ship to launch. If I remain on board, I'd be expected to command the ship. I just don't have it in me anymore. I lost my faith in the military when my son died. Once EXODUS is launched, it doesn't matter what happens to me."

"It matters to me," said John. "If you remain on Earth, TERRA will capture you. I hate to think what they would do to you."

"It doesn't matter."

"Admiral, you're the first person who's stuck their neck out for me," John said in a passionate tone. "Please stay on board. The crew knows and respects you. I don't even have to command this ship. Just having the chance to explore space is enough for me."

Julie was surprise to hear such selfless words coming from John. The only other time she'd witnessed such behavior was when John had stayed up all night, helping Julie prepare for her battle tactics final their junior year. To this day, she didn't understand why he'd helped her.

The admiral put his hand on John's shoulder. "My boy, you don't need this old relic helping you out there. It's young minds that are going to help EXODUS succeed. I made my decision long ago. This is the best arrangement. The council can imprison me or execute me. The two of you, and this ship, are all that matters."

There was a prolonged silence in the room. Neither Julie nor John knew what to say. Despite feeling guilty for forcing the admiral to explain himself, John felt more at ease taking command of EXODUS. For better or worse, he was going to be in charge out there and wouldn't have the admiral to fall back on for support.

"It's late and tomorrow's a big day," the admiral said, breaking the silence.

"We better get some sleep, John." Julie got up from the table. "Thank you for dinner. We'll see you in the morning."

"Yeah," John said as he followed Julie out the door. He stopped before heading out. "You didn't have to tell us about your son. You could've lied."

The admiral nodded to John. "You deserve no less than the truth, Commander."

John smiled at being addressed by that title. "Good night," he said and left the admiral's quarters.

The admiral turned and looked out the window. He was pleased that he had been able to maintain his composure during dinner. It had taken an enormous effort.

"I told you the angel wouldn't allow the kingdom to fall," he said aloud. "He knows his destiny."

He went to the bathroom, opened the medicine cabinet, and took out several bottles of medication used to treat psychiatric disorders. After gulping down fifteen pills, the admiral looked at himself in the mirror.

"Just one more day, then you can have me. I just need to see this ship off."

——— ——— ———

While John and Julie retired for the evening, the rest of the senior staff were still enjoying their downtime.

"I'm in," Alex'sis said as she tossed two blue chips to the center of the table.

Poker night happened to fall on the day before the launch. It would have made sense for tonight's game to be cancelled, to ensure the officers got a good night's rest. But poker night was serious business and only a disaster of major proportions could stop it from being held. The gathering allowed the participants to vent their stress.

The single rule for poker night was that rank was checked at the door. Everyone was an equal at the table and therefore they went by first names only.

Tonight's gathering was being held in Alex'sis's quarters, and Kevin, Bret, and Thomas were present for the game. They were seated at a circular table littered with cards and poker chips. So far, Bret was leading the group with the most chips.

"So, what do you think of our new commander?" Kevin asked Alex'sis as he mulled over his hand of cards.

"It's only been a day," she replied with no apparent hint of emotion.

"In, and raise you five," Bret said as he threw a chip in the pile. "You spent a good portion of the day with him. What's your opinion of him?"

"He's just as the admiral said, open and direct. But he's undisciplined and has no field experience."

"He's only a cadet," Kevin reminded her. "Of course he's going to be at a disadvantage."

"You don't think he'll cut it as ship commander?" asked Thomas.

"I'm not going to speculate on his chances," Alex'sis said in a stern tone. "He's our commanding officer and our job is to support him. We have other hurdles to overcome besides an inexperienced commander."

"Such as?" asked Kevin.

Alex'sis rattled off a list. "The ship not falling apart at launch, systems blowing up, TERRA shooting us down, the Screen shooting us down..."

"Geez! Relax, Alex'sis," said Bret. "Nothing's going to happen with the ship, otherwise none of us would have signed up."

"Out." Thomas tossed his cards down and redirected the subject back to John. "It seems to me that you already think favorably of him."

"That's your opinion," Alex'sis replied as she gave the security chief a defiant look.

Kevin could feel the tension between the two. Both had strong personalities and often clashed openly when they disagreed. He decided to speak up to break the mood. "I had the chance to spend time with Commander Olson. She's very professional and by the book. She's quite knowledgeable about TERRA procedures."

"Good to hear," replied Bret. "You in or out?"

"Oh, out!" Kevin tossed down his cards. "She seems to be a nice individual."

"She must be a great officer if she's nice," Thomas said sarcastically.

"I was just making a general observation," said Kevin. "She did meet Professor Donavin today."

"Poor girl." Alex'sis chuckled as she tossed in a couple more chips. "I hope he wasn't too hard on her." The professor's reputation was well known throughout the ship. No one wanted to deal with him if they could avoid it. Even Alex'sis tried to minimize her interactions with him.

"No, no! She actually handled herself quite well and managed to put the professor in his place," Kevin said.

"Sounds like good officer material to me," Bret said as he looked over at the chief.

Thomas was surprised to hear that Julie had handled the professor with apparent ease. "If that girl can take on the professor, then maybe she's the right person for the xo job," he admitted.

"Sounds to me that you have a positive opinion about Commander Olson," mocked Alex'sis. Thomas ignored her.

"Call," said Bret. "What do you got?"

"Two pair," Alex'sis said as she showed her cards.

Bret threw his cards down triumphantly for all to see. "Full house."

"Take it." Alex'sis took a sip of her drink. She had a fondness for mixed cranberry and vodka, which she always had during poker games. However, with the launch tomorrow, she'd omitted the vodka and was just drinking the cranberry juice. The others assumed she had liquor in her drink, but she felt no obligation to tell them otherwise. "Have you all made your final contact with your families?"

"I managed to get a hold of my father," said Kevin. "The conversation was just as brief and unimportant as always."

They all knew Kevin's relationship with his parents was shaky at best. Kevin's father had wanted a career in TERRA, but had never qualified to enter the Academy. He lived vicariously through Kevin, who was never given a choice about pursuing a life in TERRA. His dad pushed him hard through all the preparatory courses when he was young. He routinely bragged to anyone within earshot how it was he who encouraged Kevin and got him into TERRA. All his father ever wanted to talk about was TERRA, and it infuriated his son.

The anger and frustration that had built up in Kevin over the years had finally exploded in one spectacular argument. Since the blowup, his father had been distant and cold to his son. If Kevin didn't take the initiative to call, they would have stopped speaking years ago. His mother had never been attentive and loving toward Kevin, and they hadn't spoken in fifteen years.

Alex'sis turned to Bret. "And you?"

"Yup," was all the young man said. "Said all my goodbyes."

Alex'sis looked over to the security chief. "Thomas?"

"My business is done." She hated that he seemed to never answer a question directly. He always threw out some vague statement to pacify people.

Out of everyone at the table, Thomas was the individual they knew least about, despite his many years with the EXODUS Project. Alex'sis wanted to chalk it up to him being a private person, but wasn't entirely convinced that was the case. She hated secrets.

Alex'sis dismissed Thomas's comment and held up her glass. "Here's to a successful launch tomorrow."

"And that we get out of the system in one piece," Bret added as he held up his glass.

"I'll drink to that," said Thomas.

CHAPTER EIGHT

E XODUS's liftoff was scheduled to commence at 2305 local time. Although it gave the crew the entire day to prepare for the launch, the staff on the ship and ground were instructed to finish all preparations by noon. All morning, people scurried in and around the ship like ants finishing up their final tasks.

It had been another sleepless night for Julie, as she mentally reviewed all the technical specifications she had read. The amount of information was overwhelming, and she tried to retain as much of it as best she could. But she was finding it difficult to concentrate. She kept dwelling on the admiral's son. It must have been awful for Johnson to lose his only child. Julie thought about her own father and how much he must have suffered when her mother died.

Unlike Julie, John slept soundly. Any notion that this whole proposition was some elaborate trick had faded after last night's dinner. There was nothing left for him here and he was ready to leave Earth behind and explore the galaxy, assuming they got out of the solar system.

Despite his deep sleep, John woke up early and was anxious to get his day started. After donning his TERRA uniform, he took a walk through the ship to get more familiar with its layout and burn off some of his excess energy. He didn't consult the ship's computer as to where he was or where he was heading. He chose to randomly walk down the corridors and catwalks.

Eventually, he wound up in Central. He meandered around the floor level, looking up at the buildings in awe. He was amazed how walking around Central reminded him of being in a city on Earth. The streets, sidewalks, and city lights all contributed to the illusion. The only indication he wasn't outside was the ceiling far up in the distance instead of blue skies.

As he made his way along the main street, he spotted a café called Stardust that was open. Large square flowerpots lined the white gate along the café's outdoor seating area. The pots were filled with colorful plants and small trees, none of which John could identify. He wasn't the gardening type. The café's exterior had a French design to it, as if it had been plucked from the streets of Paris.

John could smell the aroma of eggs and bacon drifting from the restaurant and decided to take the opportunity to have a nice breakfast and enjoy the atmosphere of Central. Once he got to the command deck, he doubted he would have another chance to eat a meal today.

As he took a seat at a table outside and ordered, John watched some of the morning crew walking down the street, heading toward their work areas. Many of them acknowledged the new commander with a nod or a hello. One even called John 'Captain,' which made him chuckle. It was already unusual to go from a cadet to a commander. John had no doubt the crew needed time to adjust to him being in charge now, despite the admiral's assurances. Admiral Johnson would have been pushing his luck if he had made John a captain.

An orange bot passed John's table and emptied the garbage bin near him. John watched as the bot's dome head opened and it dumped the garbage inside itself, where its internal compactor squeezed the collective trash into a compact cube. The process took only seconds, and before John knew it, the bot's dome closed and it continued on its way, sweeping up the area as it went.

"Here you go, Commander," the café's owner, Mario, said as he placed a plate of eggs, bacon, sausage, and toast in front of John. It looked and smelled divine. John could hardly resist diving in and swallowing the meal in one gulp, but etiquette told him otherwise. He forced himself to take his time with his meal.

"Thanks," he said as he savored the food's aroma. "And you can call me John. Only the military calls me Commander."

Mario shook his head. "Lieutenant Brandus made it clear the senior officers should be called by their rank by both military and civilians."

Sheesh! That girl needed to relax a bit. John couldn't help but roll his eyes. "I understand where she's coming from, but that's not how I operate." He realized as ship commander, he could now call the shots on which protocols he would choose to follow, and TERRA had a lot of protocols he didn't like. In John's opinion, civilians were under no obligation to address ranking officers by title, and he wasn't going to force that protocol on them.

John looked around and saw Mario had no other customers, so he decided to try and learn about the café owner. He wasn't about to spend the entire trip socializing with just military personnel. The sheer thought made John want to slice his wrists.

"What brought you to EXODUS?" asked John.

"Well, if you're up for a story..." started Mario. John smiled and motioned for the owner to join him at the table.

Mario was more than happy to chat. "I'm here because I needed something to do. I ran a successful chain of restaurants in Chicago for twenty-four years. I opened my first one when I was twenty-two. Married, raised three kids, got divorced."

"It sounds like the ideal life, except for the divorce part," said John.

"Oh, it was," Mario said as he wiped his greasy, grey-streaked hair. "When my kids got older, I decided to turn the business over to them. I had plenty of credits put away for a good retirement, even after that bitch tried to clean me out."

John almost choked on his food at Mario's comment about his ex-wife, but managed to maintain his composure.

"What a mistake that was. Those kids managed to run the business right into the ground. I tried to give them advice, but they thought they knew everything. When the restaurants failed and I wouldn't give them any more money, they stopped talking to me."

"Sorry to hear that."

"Are you kidding me? Those kids were good-for-nothing brats. I still can't believe I'm related to them." John was amused at how unapologetic Mario sounded. "I guess it's my fault for not teaching them the value of a credit."

John had been fortunate to have a trust fund growing up. But neither he nor his older sister took advantage of it. Nicole never spent extravagantly and neither had John after she left.

Mario continued talking. "What irked me more was retirement. I wasn't happy sitting around playing golf or some other crap like that. I was restless and felt I needed to go back to work. But I wasn't about to reopen another restaurant. That bitch would've tried to get a piece of it. But owning a restaurant is the only thing I've ever been good at. Oliver...Admiral Johnson offered me the opportunity to open a restaurant on this ship. It was a challenge too good to pass up."

"Even if it meant never seeing your family again?"

Mario gave John a stern look. "Didn't I just finish telling you how much I hate my ex and kids?"

"You really don't have a problem with the ship leaving the system?"

Mario leaned back in his seat. "Please! We should've been flying out to space years ago. Oliver used to come by my first restaurant every weekend. We'd sit there talking about the merits of interstellar space travel. I have no problem defying those scrawny Screen aliens. Far as I'm concerned, they're nothing but a bunch of pussies."

John had to gulp down his orange juice—otherwise he would have spewed it everywhere. "Interesting point," was all he could say between coughs. He'd never heard of anyone describing the Screen as scrawny, let alone *pussies*.

"As soon as we pass the boundary line I'll bet you they'll turn and run like rabbits." Mario waved his hands around as he spoke.

"You sound confident about our chances," said John.

"I'm fifty-six years old, Commander. My kids are ingrates, the ex-wife's a bitch, I probably eat too much fatty food, and I'm too old to be having affairs. I ain't got much to look forward to in this world. If we don't make it, oh well. I lived a full life. If we do make it, great! I'll be the first aging Italian running a restaurant out in deep space. I look at it as a crapshoot. It doesn't matter to me which way it goes."

John took a bite of the eggs on his plate. "Well, with food like this, I'll make sure we make it."

Mario knocked on the table. "Glad to hear it. I'll stop gabbing so you can enjoy your food. It's the only freebie you get." He got up and walked past John, patting him on the shoulder. "Next one will cost you fourteen credits."

——— ——— ———

Although watching the crowds of people walking through Central fascinated John, he didn't take too long to finish breakfast. Once he was done eating, he headed out of Central up to the command deck. He purposely took the long route, as it gave him an excuse to see more of the ship. As he walked through the corridors, John noticed that there weren't any bots. He had only seen the one while he was at Stardust.

TERRA capital ships were stocked with bots that handled many routine tasks, such as cleaning and minor maintenance repairs. Alex'sis had told John that it would have taken up too much room to store all the necessary spare parts to maintain a dedicated bot group on EXODUS.

Unlike the bots on Earth, Luna, and Mars that ran on solar power, ship bots ran on batteries that needed recharging from the ship. Such power consumption was deemed too high for the benefits of having a large bot staff for EXODUS. So only five maintenance bots were actively used for the entire ship, and they all operated in Central. This allowed the merchants working here not to worry about cleanup or trash disposal.

There were 600 bots stored all over the ship within hidden bays in the corridors. In the event of a catastrophic incident, these bots would be activated to assist the crew in making emergency repairs. However, once they became damaged or broken, there were no maintenance parts available to fix them. It was odd to think a ship this large and sophisticated had to forgo such a basic convenience of everyday life.

John found himself on the same deck where the medical bay was located. He strolled past it and took a quick glance inside as he passed by the entryway. When he spotted Dr. Myers, John decided to speak with him for a few minutes. It was another chance to learn more about a senior staff member.

"Hey, doc."

As soon as Myers looked up and saw the new commander, he smiled. "Commander Roberts," he said in a gracious tone.

John was really enjoying the sound of that title. Hearing the words coming in the doctor's slight accent gave them a hint of royalty. He couldn't tell what the accent was; he'd never been good at discerning them.

"I hope your morning's going well," Dr. Myers said.

"So far, so good. But ask me again after the launch."

The doctor laughed. "Keep that sense of humor and you'll always weather the bad days. A good ship commander needs an outlet to release the stresses of command."

"What do you think about our chances of getting out of the system?" John had asked every crewmember he'd spoken with that question. They all seemed to have complete confidence in the EXODUS's abilities. Maybe they knew something he didn't.

He had read about many of the ship's capabilities to see if he could find that one element that could explain their confidence, but he couldn't identify anything. There was the shield system, but it was unproven and untested against the Screen. The crew seemed to have a devotion to the ship that both intrigued and troubled John.

"I believe we'll have no problem eluding the fleet, but I do have some reservations about the Screen. As you know, no ship has ever survived an encounter."

"Then why are you here? Everyone else seems pretty sure we'll get through."

"Alex'sis told me you don't like to dance around the issue," the doctor said.

Great. John was already getting a reputation amongst the crew.

"I'm just the ship's chief medical officer," he continued. "I don't have the technical knowledge of the ship to say with certainty it will withstand a Screen attack. But the admiral and I have been friends for many years. If he says we have a chance, then I trust his judgment."

"That's an awful lot of trust if you're willing to put your life on the line."

"You haven't known the admiral long enough. If you did, then you would know why he has such loyalty amongst the crew."

John smiled. "I'll take your word on it, doc."

He looked around at the medical bay. There were a lot of computer stations and monitors lined up along the walls. In the center was a surgical are surrounded by observation glass, which provided immediate quarantine protection.

"The ship's weapons and shields were designed based off data collected on the Screen ships that have attacked our ships in the past. Do we have anything on their physiology?"

"Unfortunately, neither the sensor net or any TERRA or civilian ship has ever been able to penetrate the hull of a Screen vessel. We have no information on their organic makeup. The EXODUS's sensors are designed to scan the interior of a Screen ship. However, we won't know if they'll work until our first encounter."

"Have you been able to establish any guidelines regarding the capture of a Screen?"

"I've only been able to come up with a set of general protocols. Putting the Screen aside, we've never encountered any alien life form. I have no point of reference to draw from in establishing guidelines." The doctor walked over to the surgical area. "Any Screen or alien would be brought here for immediate isolation. This area, as well as the entire medical bay, has its own life support system separate from the ship. From here we'd run a battery of tests to learn more about an alien's anatomy. Other than that, there is not much more that can be done until we actually have one on board."

"That will be one of our goals," said John. "We need to learn everything we can about the Screen: their bodies, technology, what their home world might be like. If we ever have the opportunity to capture a Screen, you'll need to devote all your resources to examining one."

"I understand the need to learn all we can about them and I will do what I can," Myers said. "However, there's something I'd like to bring up."

"What's that?"

"I'll do everything I can to help the mission succeed. The Screen is an enemy and our survival is paramount. However, I won't engage in any research to develop a biological weapon of genocide against them. I'm a doctor and won't use my skills to exterminate a species."

"What if genocide winds up being our only option?" John appreciated the doctor's honesty, but things could change once they learned more about the Screen.

"Then, Commander, it will be your job to have options available other than genocide," replied the doctor.

"Fair enough." He hoped that it wouldn't come to such a decision. He wouldn't want to give the order to wipe out an alien race. But if it came down to it, John wouldn't hesitate to make the call.

He decided not to share his position with the doctor. "I better get up to the command deck. Got a ship to launch. I'll see you later, doc."

"If you ever need anything, please don't hesitate to see me," the doctor said.

Despite their differences about how far they were willing to go to stop the Screen, John took an instant liking to Myers. The doctor seemed genuine.

Over the next couple of hours, both John and Julie were thrust into a frenzy of activity as the ship's launch crept closer. Both tried to familiarize themselves with as many systems they could to be best prepared for liftoff. To shorten their learning curve, the admiral had all of the department heads brief them. They wouldn't have a comprehensive understanding of all systems by launch, but at least they'd have a rudimentary knowledge. Both would have to rely heavily on the crew.

John spent most of the remaining morning going over the weapons systems. One advantage of the EXODUS Project's classified status was that it didn't have the prying eyes of the command council watching over it. As the project director, Admiral Johnson had complete control over the flow of information. The command council was apprised of project activities via progress reports submitted by the admiral. Of course, the reports were fabricated to hide what was truly going on.

The project's scientists had analyzed years of data on Screen encounters and developed defensive systems to counter the alien technology. The systems allowing EXODUS to be a habitable deep space explorer had been completed long ago, so the staff had spent the last few years developing the ship's offensive and defensive capabilities. John was shocked to find the energy defense shield had been refined and tested for years. This critical defense system would go a long way toward improving the ship's chance of surviving a Screen attack.

Julie was busy learning about the ship's propulsion systems. Despite its bulk, EXODUS's sub-light propulsion system was so far advanced compared to those on TERRA frigates and capital ships that it could easily outrun any ship in the fleet. The true gem was the hyper-drive. Abandoned long ago by TERRA and commercial shipmakers, as development and manufacturing of hyper-drives were illegal, the EXODUS Project had continued the work started by Francis DuBois nearly eighty years ago.

It was nearly 1800 hours before Julie and John met up again at what was now John's office on the command deck. The new commander was lying on the couch, trying to get some rest before the launch. The boundless amount of energy he'd had this morning had evaporated. He could have easily nodded off to sleep if Julie hadn't startled him by walking in unexpectedly.

John made a mental note to change the entry parameters on

the door to require people to ring the bell first. He hoisted himself into a sitting position as Julie spoke.

"Every theory I learned in my last four years at the Academy has been rendered obsolete with everything I've seen on this ship."

"Yeah, it's remarkable what they've been able to accomplish," John said. "I think we have a good chance of pulling this off."

"You're not worried?"

"No. I know I should be, but the more I see of this ship, the more convinced I am that we can succeed. The crew's confident we'll make it and they've been working here for years. They know these systems better than we do."

Julie could see in John's eyes that he didn't have any hesitation. He was prepared to get this ship lifted off into space and show TERRA was it could do.

"Just remember, this isn't about you," she said.

"What's that supposed to mean?" As was often the case, she came off sounding like a parent correcting a child. It was a characteristic John disliked about her.

"A lot of people have spent their lives working on this ship to make it a reality. You have to think about what's right for them and not do what you want for yourself."

"I don't believe this," John said as he rolled his eyes. "I haven't issued my first command and you're already criticizing me. You could at least wait until we actually get off the ground."

"I'm just saying that you're so excited about getting into space that it might cloud your judgment," Julie said, defensive.

"Isn't it on the books somewhere that insubordination is a punishable offense?"

"Hey, if you bothered to read anything at the Academy you'd know that a good executive officer questions the ship commander. I'm just trying to be a good second in command for you." Julie felt she could never make a critique because she wasn't good enough in John's eyes.

"No, what you're doing is being a bitch. So why don't you do me a favor and keep your opinions to yourself until they're actually needed...or wanted."

That last comment got Julie's blood boiling. Leave it to John to throw out the insults. Mad as his comment made her, she decided to be the bigger person.

"If you don't want to listen to me, fine. But the crew will only put up with an incompetent commander for so long before they take action and replace you. You better take this seriously."

"How nice. Now we're talking about mutiny. Well, I guess as long as they replace me with you, all will be fine and dandy."

Julie knew they weren't going to get anywhere but into a fight if this kept up, so she decided to change the subject. John was too stubborn to acknowledge anything she said might have some truth to it. He would rather spend hours arguing with her before admitting she might be right about something.

"What time are we meeting the admiral?" she asked.

John was only too happy to oblige her by changing topics. It was ridiculous for them to fight before the ship had even launched. He had no doubt they would butt heads many more times, but he was hoping they could put their disdain for one another aside until they left the solar system.

It was hard, though. Julie could really piss him off.

"Eight o'clock in the hangar," he answered as he got up and moved behind the desk.

"Have you had a chance to review the departure plan?"

"No, I figure I'd just wing the launch," he replied with a sarcastic tone. "Of course I've reviewed it."

As Julie sat in the chair on the other side of the desk, John brought up a holographic image of the solar system showing the ship's flight path.

"The ship's central computer will be linked to ground control, allowing them to control the ship's propulsion during lift-off," John said. "The ground station will control the thrusters on all the towers and EXODUS. At 2305 hours, the four towers will detach from their base moorings. Once free, ground control will fire all the thrusters simultaneously. The towers and EXODUS will head up into low orbit around Earth. Once we leave Earth's gravity, the antigrav field will deactivate and the towers will head back down to Earth."

"One of the advantages of being a classified project is there's a communication blackout for the entire area around our liftoff path," said Julie. "But once the ship is detected in orbit, the command council will be notified. They'll realize something's wrong and send a garrison after us."

"You thinking the patrol from Luna Station?"

Julie nodded.

"Can we get the ship moving fast enough before they can intercept us?"

"Surprisingly enough, we can. The hyper-drive keeps the entire ship enveloped in a low level hyper-active field."

"Really?" John was surprised. The main engine was one of the systems he hadn't had time to get familiar with.

"They discovered that they could keep the engine core active and use minimal power to keep the ship surrounded in a field. It reduces the effect the mass of the ship has on its ability to move. EXODUS can take off and stop relatively quickly. Once the patrol sees us, they'll assume it can't move too fast to escape their smaller ships until it's too late."

John nodded. "Good. I don't want to directly encounter the fleet if we can avoid it."

"I'm surprised to hear that. I thought you'd be itching for a brawl with the fleet."

"Our enemy's the Screen. As much as I hate what TERRA did to me, I have no interest in hurting anyone in the fleet. When we take off, we make sure no one who comes after us gets hurt."

"This ship is technologically superior to anything TERRA has in the fleet. We should be able to keep our defenses up and race out of the system."

"Good, because I won't fire on our own kind." John got up from his desk. He could handle being called a lot of things, but he refused to be called a murderer. Whatever it took, he would not harm another human being.

"I'll inform Lieutenant Brandus and Jacobson," said Julie. "I'd suggest we both get a couple hours sleep before the launch."

John agreed with her suggestion. They were going to be up for a while once the ship launched.

He didn't say anything until Julie left the office and was out of earshot.

"Stupid know-it-all bitch."

———   ———   ———

Time passed by swiftly as 2000 hours—the time of the Admiral's departure—crept closer. John spent the remaining time in his office going over the ship's schematics before heading to the hangar bay. Once there, he took a seat in one of the parked Interceptors. For once, he was early.

He took the opportunity to look over one of the new fighters that had caught his eye when he first came on board. But checking out an Interceptor was just an excuse to get some time alone, to think about the recent events that had completely changed his life.

Admiral Johnson had thousands of officers to choose from, but he'd selected John. This was a man who'd zeroed in on John's good qualities while everyone else seemed eager to point out his faults and weaknesses. TERRA saw John as a nuisance, but the admiral only saw his potential. He now had a chance to realize his goals.

In their brief time together, John had grown attached to Admiral Johnson. He wanted to succeed—not just for himself, but also to prove to the admiral that the man had made the right choice. For the first time in his life, John wanted to make someone proud of him.

While John was musing over his impending loss, Julie entered the hangar bay, escorting the admiral to his shuttle. Julie had met up with Johnson at his quarters and they'd spent their walk discussing last-minute details of the launch. Julie wanted to send the admiral off in an official military ceremony, but he wouldn't hear of it. He had already said his goodbyes to the crew and didn't want the publicity of a ceremony.

"There's one more detail I don't want you to forget," said the admiral as they entered the bay.

"What's that?"

The admiral stopped and faced the young woman. "John's a good officer. He may not be the ideal TERRA officer, but he has a lot of positive attributes. Keep that in the back of your mind when you're having an argument with him. You know him better than anyone else. He's going to need you just as much as you and the crew will need him. This will work."

Julie smiled. "I'll keep that in mind." She wasn't convinced, but she respected the admiral enough to give his opinion the benefit of the doubt.

The admiral looked over at his shuttle and spotted John in the cockpit of a nearby Interceptor. "Julie Olson, this is where we part ways."

She was about to salute the admiral, but he grabbed her hands and gently squeezed them. "You'll never know how grateful I am that you agreed to do this."

"Admiral, it's me who's grateful. You rescued me from a mediocre future. I can only hope to repay you someday."

"You already have." The admiral smiled and gave her an unexpected hug.

Caught off guard, Julie didn't know how to respond, so she just stood there with her arms hanging limp. Before she knew it, the admiral released her and headed toward John. He never looked back at her.

A bit bewildered, Julie composed herself and headed out of the hangar bay. If she stayed any longer, she felt she might break down and cry. Her emotions had been a bit frayed since she spoke to her father, and she wasn't up to another crying session.

"You look quite comfortable in there," said the admiral to John.

John's thoughts were far away, and the admiral's muffled voice through the Interceptor's window caught him by surprise. "I didn't see you come in," he said as he opened the cockpit hatch and hopped out of the fighter. He looked around for his executive officer. "Where's Julie?"

"We've already said our goodbyes. Commander Olson was

kind enough to give us some time alone."

"Oh," was all John could muster.

"You seem speechless, my boy. That's not like you."

"It's just that there's so much I want to say but I'm not sure where to start," John said.

"How about at the beginning," the admiral advised.

John looked at him with sincerity He had confidence in himself, but with the admiral leaving John would be responsible for the crew. A moment of doubt hit him realizing he was now in charge. "Come with us. We need you here. If we're going to have half a chance of making it, we're going to need someone with your experience."

The admiral shook his head. "We've already gone over this, my boy. My place is here. I was never meant to go with the EXODUS."

"But what if I'm not ready..."

The admiral cut him off. "Don't. You're not one to question your abilities and now's not the time to start."

John could only nod. The admiral was right. John had never questioned his potential. "What will you do, then? In a couple of hours, your career will be over. TERRA will be crawling all over the planet looking for you. They'll search every ship heading to Luna or Mars."

"Don't you worry about me. You just focus on getting EXODUS out of the system. I have every expectation that you'll accomplish your goals."

John could see the admiral had made up his mind and John's pleading wasn't going to change that decision. But there was one thing left he could do. John pulled a piece of paper out of his pocket and shoved it into the admiral's hand.

"I want you to have this."

The admiral opened the paper and saw an address written on it.

"It's my house in California," John said. "It's in La Habra and sits on a large piece of land in the hills, very secluded. I'm sure you could hide out there for a little while before TERRA discovers I'm commanding this ship. I don't feel right leaving without giving you something."

"Thank you, Commander," the admiral said, looking touched as he tucked the paper in his pocket. "I'm sure it'll come in handy."

John smiled weakly. "Well, I guess this is it." He paused for a moment, trying to find the right words to say. "I'm sorry, I'm not used to saying thank you."

"No thanks needed." The admiral extended his hand to John to shake, which the former cadet did with a bittersweet feeling.

John wished they'd had more time to get to know each other. In some weird way, the admiral had become a father figure to John in their short time together. It was a nice feeling.

"Take care, Admiral."

"And you as well."

The admiral boarded his shuttle and John watched as it lifted off and out of the hangar bay. John was really going to miss him.

——— ——— ———

Admiral Johnson arrived in the ground station monitoring room fifteen minutes later. He went over last-minute details with the ground crew, who assured him preparations for launch were in order. After consulting with them, he took his place at the back wall, watching.

His eyes drifted over to the large digital clock on the wall. The time had finally arrived. Years of planning and construction had brought them to this single moment: the launch of the TXS EXODUS.

The admiral looked through the large panoramic window at the massive ship filling the Tormented Valley. He admired the vessel he'd worked so hard to build. To him, it was a thing of beauty. He looked at the men and women working at their stations. He had asked so much of them and each had committed their lives to this project. He was proud of the effort everyone had put forth to make this day a reality.

He smiled, thinking how easy it had been to hide the project's activities from the command council. They'd never suspected one of their own had been working his own agenda right under their noses.

The hardest part of this launch was staying behind. In truth, he wanted to be on EXODUS when it launched and, for a moment, he had considered John's offer to stay on the ship. But life had a way of interfering with one's plans.

He fiddled with the prescription bottles in his pocket. They only had a couple pills left in them.

He had become too close to the crew. A good military commander kept their distance from those who served under them. The admiral had allowed his feelings to get the better of him. With his son gone, the people of the EXODUS Project had become his family. But he had to let them go if they were going to succeed.

Besides, he didn't want any of them to see what would become of him. In just a few hours, when the effects of the medications wore off, he would become a different person.

"Admiral, we're ready to begin," the ground commander announced. "Preflight check is green across the board."

"Well then, let's send her off."

Over on the EXODUS, activity had reached a fever pitch. The crew scrambled, making last-minute checks and adjustments to key systems.

This would be the first time the ship would move from its position. Although the crew was confident in how she would perform, there was still a sense of trepidation. What if something went wrong because a process or system was overlooked? What if TERRA discovered what they were up to and grounded the ship before it could even leave the planet? Years of planning and preparations had all come down to this moment. They would either succeed or fail.

——— ——— ———

John stepped onto the command deck to find the staff at their stations, in preparation for the launch.

He looked over to see Julie speaking with Bret. John was still mad at her for the way she'd behaved earlier and wasn't inclined to speak to her at all. He'd rather have Alex'sis as executive officer.

She was a typical military officer, but at least John got along with her.

Julie thought that *he* had to worry about being replaced? Hah! It was Julie who should worry about being replaced. A ship commander could replace his xo at any time and John had no problem taking such action if Julie became problematic for him. He would see how she performed while they were in the solar system. If he concluded things were not going to work out, he would demote her en route to the next star system.

Alex'sis was standing at the operations table, checking the ship's tactical systems. "What's our status?" John asked her as he descended into the pit.

"We've done a complete check of all systems," Alex'sis said. "All departments have reported in as ready."

Kevin joined Alex'sis and John at the table. "I've transferred navigation control to ground station. They're set to do a simultaneous launch of the ship and tower units. We'll be able to monitor ground station's control of the launch from here." Kevin punched a few buttons and brought up several data reports on the table.

"How long to get us up in space?" asked John.

"About ten minutes," Kevin said. "We've done everything we can to reduce the ascent time into orbit."

"That's still a significant amount of time," Alex'sis said. "The shields can't be activated with the antigravity field on. We'll be vulnerable during that period."

"What about arming some of the ship's weapons?" Kevin said.

John dismissed that suggestion. He didn't want EXODUS emerging from Earth with active weapons. It increased the risk that someone would panic and fire on them.

"The increased power level would be detected by TERRA. Even with the sensor blackout mandated, I'm sure the council will be watching us and I don't want to send the wrong message. The admiral said he made all the arrangements for the launch to go uninterrupted and I don't want to jeopardize that. We have to assume that he's taken care of all possibilities."

"Commander," Bret called from his station. "We're being

contacted by ground station. They're ready to go."

John nodded. "Everyone to their stations."

The staff moved into their positions except for Alex'sis, who remained at the operations table. Although she agreed with John about keeping the weapons offline during the launch, she wanted to have her finger on the button in case they needed to defend themselves at a moment's notice.

Even with the shields offline, the hull was extremely resilient to weapons fire, but she wasn't eager to have it tested so soon. She was just as determined as the rest of the crew to get the ship off Earth in one piece and didn't want to take any unnecessary chances.

John headed up to his command seat, elevated above the pit. He climbed the steps and sat in the seat looking directly at a large screen. The monitor allowed John to view any of the ship's systems and tap into anyone's station. After a final check of the critical areas, he opened the communications channel. "Ground station, this is EXODUS."

"Copy, EXODUS. Confirm launch status."

"Launch status confirmed. We're ready to go."

"Confirm, EXODUS. All systems show go for departure. Launch will commence in one minute."

"Acknowledged," replied John. He took a deep breath, then switched over to the inter-ship communications. "Attention, all hands. Stand by for launch." He thought about making some speech to the crew, but decided against it. He wasn't about to turn this into some corny cliché.

This was it. In less than a minute, they would find out if this ship was worth the time and effort put into it.

As the countdown began, John thought about the life he was leaving behind on Earth. He'd always wanted to explore space and had never once considered spending his entire life on Earth, Luna, or even Mars. He wanted to be out in space, uncovering what the galaxy had to offer. But here he was, thinking about what his life could have been on Earth. Would it have really been so bad?

Despite being railroaded from serving in TERRA, his

graduation from the Academy would have guaranteed him a well-paying job in the private sector. It wouldn't have been such a terrible life.

Then again, he would have faded into the populace as a nobody—exactly what Mortino wanted.

An ordinary life was not for John. At least on EXODUS, he would be remembered for something. Superintendent Mortino had once said that John would become infamous, and it looked like Mortino's prediction was going to be right. John had no doubt that, to protect their image, TERRA would paint him as quite the villain to the public. For better or worse, he was going to be in the history books.

"Launch in t-minus fifteen seconds..." reported ground station.

John shifted his thoughts to Billy and David. When John had been unable to locate his sister, he'd arranged for a personal message to be delivered to his friends. He wasn't about to let TERRA drum up a cover story without a fight. Although he would be out in deep space, he could still make life difficult for TERRA.

John looked through the panoramic window at the stars sparkling in the clear night sky. In a few moments, his dream would begin.

——— ——— ———

At ground station, the admiral watched as his beloved starship began its ascent to the heavens. EXODUS lifted off in unison with the four antigravity towers, enveloping the ship in a dark blue field. The energy expenditure was maximized to ensure the ship's protection from Earth's gravity during ascent. The ground trembled as the massive craft lifted off, the shaking subsiding as the ship rose higher.

The admiral stopped listening to the ground staff's shouted status reports, his attention squarely focused on EXODUS. All his hopes now lay with that ship.

Soon, EXODUS rose far enough that he could no longer see it through the window. The admiral headed outside despite the frigid cold, so he could continue to watch it until it disappeared into the night sky.

As he watched EXODUS ascend, the immense vessel became a small dot. The lights that emanated from the ship's hull melded into a single beacon.

The admiral felt a sense of completion as the ship departed, but he also felt a sense of loss. It was almost the same feeling he'd had when he lost his son. He thought of Kory and hoped that if he was watching from somewhere, he understood why his father had chosen this course of action.

"Admiral, it's time to go," his shuttle pilot said, waiting patiently behind him.

EXODUS was barely discernable now, only a blip in the sky. The admiral had to blink to even catch an outline of it. Once he was satisfied he could no longer see it, he turned to his pilot.

"Take one of the spare shuttles," he said. "I'll be leaving alone."

"But sir..." the pilot started to protest, but the admiral interrupted him.

"It's far too dangerous for anyone to accompany me. Security's top priority will be to locate me, and it's best that I'm alone. Go on, now. There's no time to argue."

The pilot nodded and took off toward the parked shuttles. The ground staff was beginning to leave the area, streaming out of the buildings as quickly as they could move.

The admiral looked up into the sky one more time, but could no longer see EXODUS at all. As the ground crew rushed to their transports, the admiral strolled to his shuttle. There was no need to hurry now, no need at all.

CHAPTER NINE

Tonight was a lazy night for the boys. Billy and David were lounging in David's living room, watching entertainment shows on the holovision. It was a stark contrast from the celebrations they'd participated in after finals.

Every winter break for the past four years, they'd alternated spending time at each other's houses. This year it was Billy's turn to stay at the Block family home.

They'd started the tradition for John's benefit, as he had no family to go home to for the holidays. Billy's parents loved John; however, the same couldn't be said for David's father.

Sophomore winter break at the Blocks' home had been particularly unforgettable. John had gotten into an argument with Admiral Block about TERRA philosophy. David had begged him not to, but John hadn't been able to resist egging Admiral Block on.

John's inflammatory comments—the harshest of which had been a question about the size of the bribe necessary to become captain of a capital ship—had made the admiral so upset that he'd thrown John out of the house, barred him from ever coming back, and strictly forbade his son from ever associating with John. Thinking that John was out of his son's life, the admiral never mentioned his name again.

Of course, David didn't listen to his father. He secretly enjoyed seeing his overbearing parent get worked up by a young, opinionated cadet. Even to this day, David, Billy, and John glee-fully recounted that event.

The Block residence was a restored twentieth-century man-sion that Judith Block had redecorated over the fifteen years the family had lived there. David's father, Admiral Edgar Block, over-saw Mars's defense operations. He traveled between Earth and Mars regularly.

Admiral Block had tried more than once to relocate the fam-ily to Crimson City, Mars's capital, but Judith wouldn't hear of it. Earth was her home and she refused to allow TERRA to move them around from place to place. She also didn't like the idea of living within an enclosed dome and was convinced the artificial atmosphere wasn't good for the children's health.

Even the promotion to admiral and a coveted seat on the com-mand council for her husband didn't sway Judith's mind. Edgar had no choice but to make the weekly commute back and forth from Mars.

Edgar always took a week off during winter break to spend time with David. However, that morning, he'd been unexpectedly called back to Mars. There had been times where he had to depart on a moment's notice to resolve some crisis on the red planet, but it had never happened during winter break.

David was glad every time his father was called away. He rou-tinely lectured David on what it took to be a good TERRA offi-cer and often cited Billy as a good example, saying the latter was confident and charismatic, traits that would take him far in his career. Billy was always polite and diplomatic to the admiral, but privately, he thought he was too strict and suffocated David with his rules.

David was taught to respect his elders and he never had the courage to speak up for himself. But he resented his father for his constant lecturing, dictating, and comparisons to others.

With the admiral gone and David's mom in Richmond visit-ing her sister, the boys had decided to spend the afternoon loung-ing on the couch, watching mindless entertainment. They'd spent the day before being quizzed by Admiral Block on TERRA protocols. His departure to Mars was a welcome break for them.

Their night of leisure was interrupted when the front door opened and a mail bot entered.

"Messages for Billy Pedia," the bot announced as it closed the door behind it.

"Huh." Billy looked over the couch at the black mail bot. "Over here." The oval-shaped mail bot entered the living room and approached him. "A little late delivering mail, aren't we?"

"Hey, it's a TERRA mail bot," David said, seeing the orange *T* marked on top of the bot. TERRA used its own mail system, separate from the one used by the civilian population.

"Please imprint hand for identification," requested the bot. TERRA required ID verification for all mailings, even propaganda.

Billy stuck his hand out and the bot passed a red beam over it.

"Identity confirmed."

Two video cards emerged from a slot on the bot's midsection. It grabbed the cards and handed them to Billy. One was marked *One* and the other *Two*. Its task complete, the bot left the house without saying another word.

"You think it's a spring post?" asked David excitedly.

Billy shook his head. "I don't think so. As far as I know, everyone's already been notified. Maybe it's from the placement committee. I've heard of cadets getting their fleet assignment this early."

"Oooohh...open it up then. Let's see."

Billy flipped open the video card marked *One*. It took a few moments for the message to play. Instead of the TERRA logo appearing first, John's face appeared on the screen.

"Billy, it's John. I've sent you two encrypted messages. This is the first one. I need you to watch the second message in private away from everyone. Don't tell anyone about this, except for David. But make sure he keeps his mouth shut. You should be getting this about the same time a large ship is being spotted in Earth's orbit. All I can tell you is that I'm on that ship. The second message will explain everything. You're the only ones I trust. Don't say anything to anyone. Your lives could be in danger if you do. And this isn't a joke."

The message ended and the screen went blank. It left both cadets bewildered. "What the hell?" Billy said in confusion.

"Could be a prank." Billy and John had played little tricks on one another for the past four years. Maybe John had gone home for winter break and had nothing better to do.

"Pretty elaborate setup for a prank," said Billy. "And he'd get into some real trouble for screwing around with TERRA's mail system. He did make it a point to say this wasn't a joke."

"Priority news alert," the house computer announced in a loud tone. Admiral Block had programmed the home AI to switch the holovision over to the news channel when a breaking news story was broadcasted. The admiral didn't want to be caught unaware of any events that might involve TERRA while he was home.

The view switched to the ELM news channel, where an anchorwoman was giving her report. "This is Heidi Flicker of ELM News. Moments ago, we began receiving reports of a large spacefaring vessel of unknown origin in Earth's orbit."

"Oh shit," muttered Billy. This was no hoax.

"Right now we have very little information on the vessel's purpose or destination. However, to avoid the public assuming this is a Screen vessel, we have confirmed several eyewitness accounts from Luna residents conducting telescope observations who saw the ship flying up from Earth. Witness accounts state that the ship does not appear to be a TERRA military vessel; however, we've been unable to verify its origin. According to estimates, the vessel appears to have risen from the vicinity of the North American region."

Offscreen, someone handed the anchor a piece of paper, and she paused to scan it.

"Has your dad ever mentioned anything about a ship in that area?" Billy asked David as he kept his eyes glued to the television.

David shook his head. "He's never mentioned anything. If John's on board, then this must be a TERRA ship. But it doesn't make sense. He was assigned to the reserves."

The anchorwoman continued her report. "We just received confirmation that the private cruise spaceship STAR PRINCESS has made visual contact with the vessel. What we are about to show you are pictures taken by some of the passengers."

Images of the mysterious vessel began to appear on the screen. The cadets were in awe. Neither had seen anything quite like it.

"It looks enormous," David said.

"And weird. Its hull design looks alien. It looks like a round bug."

"The captain of the STAR PRINCESS has informed ELM News that he has been directed by TERRA to move away from the unknown vessel. We are currently working to get more information from TERRA and the president's office and will bring you more information as we receive updates."

"Maybe we should play the other message," said David, but Billy hushed him. Now that he knew this wasn't some sort of prank, he wanted to be extra careful what he said and where he said it.

"Come on. We need to get out of here." Billy stood, motioning for David to follow, and headed out the front door. He didn't think it would be a good idea to play the second message in a council member's home. Who knew what type of listening devices could be hidden?

"David, are you departing the premises for the evening?" The house bot emerged from the kitchen, where it had been busy cleaning up.

David froze, not knowing what to say. Seeing his friend's apprehension, Billy spoke up. "We're just going to walk around the neighborhood. We won't be gone long."

The shiny bot's diamond-shaped ocular sensors swiveled from David to Billy and back to David. "I shall inform your parents if they call."

"Fine, great, whatever," David blurted.

"Bye," Billy said as he pushed his friend out the door.

——— ——— ———

As the cadets left the house, EXODUS floated high in the night sky, orbiting Earth. It was as if the ship was enjoying its newfound freedom, basking in the vacuum of space, no longer constrained by the gravity it had endured for years.

"I can't believe it," John said in astonishment, staring through the command deck's windows at the stars.

The launch had been a success. The ship had made it through the atmosphere and, moments ago, the four towers had deactivated the anti-gravity field and returned to the planet's surface. EXODUS was left alone in space. After twenty years on Earth, she now floated effortlessly in orbit above the planet.

"Commander," Julie said as she stood at the foot of John's command chair. It took him a few moments to break his attention from the scenery outside to look at his executive officer. "All systems check out. Engineering's reporting no breeches to the hull. Lieutenant Jacobson has plotted our course and is ready to execute it."

"Any TERRA ships heading our way?"

"We've detected a capital ship docked with Luna station, the TCS SOLARA. But our scans indicate it's undergoing a refit, which matches the schedule Admiral Johnson provided us. Engines are off and power levels are minimal. We also picked up a civilian cruise ship not too far from our location. The ship's since changed course and is moving away from us."

"We better get moving then," said John. "The cruise ship may have been ordered by TERRA to leave the area."

The admiral had told them that arrangements had been made to keep all vessels clear of the area above the launch site during liftoff. So how had a civilian ship wound up in their vicinity? That was something John would have to figure out later.

As for the SOLARA, it was common practice for TERRA to have one capital ship near Earth. The other four did routine patrols around Mars. The SOLARA was fifteen years old and had recently been sent to the Luna station shipyard for a much-needed refit of its systems. In its current state, it posed no threat to the EXODUS.

Julie headed over to Jacobson's station. "Lieutenant, plot our course out of the system. Set speed at one half."

"Aye, Commander," replied Kevin. With the coordinates

already set, Kevin just had to activate the sub light engines. Seconds later the engines roared to life and EXODUS pulled away from Earth.

John watched on his monitor as the distance between Earth and EXODUS grew. This could be the last time he would ever set eyes on the planet. He wasn't sad about the notion. Leaving Earth, maybe forever, was a worthy sacrifice if it meant traveling through space.

"Commander, we're getting a priority communication from Luna Station," Bret said.

John could only imagine the chaos at the station, with TERRA trying to figure out what the hell was going on.

"I'm detecting a squadron of fifteen Interceptors being dispatched from the station," reported Alex'sis. "They're heading straight for us."

"Put the communication up on speakers," John ordered.

Bret patched the signal through for the command crew to hear.

"TERRA Luna Station I to TXS EXODUS. Cut engine power and come to a complete stop. Repeat, halt your advance from Earth and prepare your hangar bay to receive Luna Alpha Squadron."

"No response to transmission," John ordered. The command council must have revealed EXODUS's existence to the fleet. They hadn't addressed him by name, so they must not know he was commanding EXODUS.

"Should I activate the shield grid?" asked Alex'sis.

"No, keep it on standby for now. Lieutenant, will we be able to outrun the Interceptors?"

"Yes sir," Kevin said. "But when they see we're not stopping, they'll probably alter course and try to catch us further ahead. I can increase speed to full for thirty seconds to keep them behind us. After that, they'll be unable to intercept us."

"Do it and keep me updated on any changes they make on their heading," said John.

Julie approached and motioned John to lean down toward her so they could speak privately. "Shouldn't we have the shields up? I know Interceptors wouldn't be able to penetrate the ship, but we should still have them up as a precaution."

"I don't want to let TERRA know what technology this ship has, at least not yet. It'll give us a slight advantage. As soon as any TERRA capital ship approaches weapons range, we'll raise the shields."

Julie nodded, but she didn't look happy. Although she agreed with John's thinking, she wasn't entirely comfortable with it. They had superior defensive systems and she believed they should take full advantage of them. TERRA would have no way of countering EXODUS's defenses.

"Commander, Luna Station has repeated their orders," Bret said. "If we do not halt our advance, they will order Alpha Squadron to take any means necessary in commandeering the ship."

John read between the lines. They would open fire on the EXODUS and kill the crew if necessary. Luckily, their Interceptors were nothing more than toothpicks against the EXODUS. John sarcastically wished them luck in penetrating the hull.

"Continue to ignore their transmissions." John speculated what measures TERRA would take to try and stop them. Would they send the other capital ships after them or just try to overwhelm them with Interceptors?

He wondered how the admiral was doing. Undoubtedly, TERRA would be looking for the man who'd overseen the EXODUS Project, to get some answers. Was he going to hide?

John couldn't think of many alternatives available to the admiral. He still wished Johnson would have stayed on the ship, but it was too late now. John could only hope he took whatever steps necessary to avoid TERRA.

CHAPTER TEN

"Here we are, President Butu," the doorman said as he opened the limo door and assisted her from the car.

"Thank you, Reginald." It was a little past six o'clock in Sydney, Australia. The president had just arrived at home when her chief of staff had called to inform her of an unknown ship in Earth's orbit. She watched ELM News and, like everyone else on Earth, Luna, and Mars, was fascinated by the reports coming in.

It had taken some willpower to pull herself away from the television and head back to the presidential office, located on the outskirts of Sydney. Her staff had been working feverishly to acquire more information about the ship, but at this point all they knew was that the ship was not Screen. That bit of knowledge brought her some relief, but it was still disconcerting having an unknown ship in Earth's orbit, especially one that was so large.

Her chief of staff was waiting at the front door of the manor, a sizeable stack of papers in his hands. Her staff used DATs rather than paper, but Butu was old school. She preferred reading information on paper rather than on a computer.

"What do we have, Charles?" she asked as they entered the building, flanked by her security detail.

He began handing her documents to read over as he spoke in his mild British accent. "The ship originated from Earth. We've been able to verify telemetry and place its origin near Skagway, Alaska. The ship's called EXODUS and has a TXS registry."

Butu was unfamiliar with that designation. "TXS?"

"It means the vessel is experimental," clarified Charles. "But most importantly, that designation means it's a product of TERRA.

The president looked at some photos of the EXODUS. She was not very familiar with TERRA's ships. There was no need to be as she assumed the military wasn't enough of a threat to the Screen to bother destroying the five capital ships in service. Her focus was on domestic matters, not military issues. Except for its concave shape, the ship did not seem remarkable to her.

"Has TERRA provided an explanation as to why it was launched?" she asked as they entered her office. Several other staff members were already inside, working to get more information about the developing situation.

Charles checked his notes. "The ship was slated to undergo stationary testing of its launch thrusters. It was never intended to launch into orbit. Luna Station's been attempting to contact the ship without success and has dispatched a group of fighter craft to intercept it."

"Isn't the SOLARA at Luna Station?"

"Yes, but it's undergoing equipment upgrades. Currently, the ship cannot leave the station under its own power."

A staff member interjected. "Madam president, we have the TERRA command council on the line for you."

"Put them through." She looked at Charles. "What else do you have?"

"Two days ago, the head of TERRA's fleet operations, Admiral Oliver Johnson, went to New York City, specifically Dorm Row. His shuttle then made a trip directly from New York to an area near Skagway, Alaska. Two senior cadets are missing and are believed to have accompanied the admiral."

The communications terminal on the president's desk beeped. "Find out everything you can about the ship," she said. President Butu had great respect for TERRA, but she always preferred getting information from her own trusted sources. The TERRA command council seemed too far away in their headquarters on Luna, and she'd only had a handful of interactions with them in her three years in office.

She activated her communication line as Charles ushered the other staff members out of the office. A monitor popped up from the desk and flickered on. Seven of the nine TERRA council members appeared on the screen. They were seated around a half-circle black table.

"President Butu," said Fleet Admiral Jeremy Donalds in a respectful tone. He was the head of the command council and as such, the leader of TERRA. The Donalds were one of the founding members of TERRA, and every generation had served the institution faithfully. The family wielded considerable clout in the fleet.

"Admiral Donalds. I hope you can provide some details as to what's going on up there. I need to reassure the public that this is nothing more than an errant ship gone astray."

"We understand, Madam President. The ship's a prototype used to experiment with various new technologies. It has allowed us to thoroughly test new systems before integrating them into the main fleet. The crew was testing new thruster technology when an overload in the main engine occurred. It could have led to a breach in the primary energy grid and caused a ship-wide explosion. Emergency protocols dictated that the ship launch into space in case a catastrophic overload was inevitable."

The answer he provided was a little too well rehearsed for the president's liking. Her years of political experience told her that the admiral had prepared this statement in advance to appease her curiosity.

"Have you been able to contact the ship?"

"Luna Station has made numerous attempts to raise the ship, all without success. It appears the ship's communication system has been impacted by the engine overload. We've been able to communicate with the vessel using visual Morse code and have directed them to head to the orbital facility at Mars to assist with repairs."

"Why not Luna Station?"

"The SOLARA's currently moored at Luna Station undergoing upgrades and cannot be moved in time. We've been able to clear all ships from the Mars facility."

"If the ship makes it there," Butu said. "If they can't control the overload, we should consider mounting a rescue of the crew."

"We're currently preparing a plan and hope to initiate a rescue soon." Again, he seemed to be giving answers to placate her.

"It would be a shame to lose any crewmembers, especially those cadets."

Admiral Donalds gave her a startled look, as if she had caught him off guard. Several council members looked at one another.

"Cadets?" he stammered, looking shocked. He had received no information about cadets being on EXODUS. They were strictly forbidden from being involved in any classified project.

"Yes, the two cadets Admiral Johnson took to the ship a couple of days ago." Butu glanced at Charles's notes for their names. "John Roberts and Julie Olson. I'd hate to see the loss of these two young individuals at the start of their careers."

It wasn't her intention to make the council look like fools, but she wanted them to know that she had her own means of acquiring information. She wasn't going to simply sit back and accept everything they were feeding her.

"Of course. Their safety is of the utmost concern," replied the admiral. He'd maintained his composure, but President Butu was sure he wasn't happy that she possessed information he lacked.

"Then I can issue a statement to the public informing them of the situation. It will be brief, of course."

"We would appreciate it, Madam President. We'll contact you as the situation develops."

Butu nodded, and the monitor went blank. She looked up at her chief of staff.

"We need to discover what we can about this experimental ship, Admiral Johnson, and the crewmembers, especially those cadets."

"You don't believe Admiral Donalds was forthright with you?"

"I've been in politics for twenty-seven years. I know when someone's giving me fragments of a story. The admiral was holding things back. We need to gather as much information as we can before I speak to the council again. They seem to be trying to keep involvement by outside agencies to a minimum. We need to know why. I don't want to depend on them for information; otherwise, we may never learn what's truly going on."

——— ——— ———

The president was not the only one plotting a strategy. As soon as the President disconnected, the council chambers broke out in a multitude of conversations. Admiral Donalds allowed this for a minute before tapping his ceremonial hammer on the table to get their attention.

"Do you think it's wise to make her believe we have the situation under control?" asked Admiral Block.

"The situation will be under control by the time EXODUS reaches Mars," Donalds said confidently. "Our fleet will be waiting for them, and we can use the planetary cannon if necessary."

"You would destroy the ship?" Admiral Vespia said.

"If we cannot gain control of it, then it must be destroyed before it can cross the boundary," said Donalds. "We cannot gamble on a status quo Screen reaction to a ship that size trying to leave the system. Destroying it can easily be covered up under the guise of an engine breach."

"What about Admiral Johnson? Has he been located?" asked Admiral Dennin.

"No," Vespia said. "Fifty-six shuttles left the Tormented Valley in different directions. The ones we've located have all been empty, with the autopilot preprogrammed and broadcasting false signs of life. He hasn't turned up at any of his residences or on any ship."

"Maybe he isn't on Earth," Admiral Block speculated.

"We'll assume he's on Earth until we learn otherwise," said Donalds. "We also need to know why a civilian craft was in the vicinity of a restricted area during the supposed thruster test."

"And what about these cadets?" asked Admiral Rodriguez. "We didn't even know they were brought to the project until the President mentioned them."

"Yes, we can't allow the civilian government to have information beyond our own. Contact the Academy and have

Superintendent Mortino give us all the files he has on these two cadets," Donalds ordered.

"I've met this Cadet Roberts before," Block said. "He was an acquaintance of my son. He's a brash, undisciplined, disrespectful individual. I don't know how he managed to get accepted to the Academy. If the EXODUS has been hijacked, I wouldn't be surprised if he was involved."

"We're assuming the ship has been commandeered by rebels?" asked Vespia.

"Until we get some solid information, we'll proceed under the assumption that a hostile force is controlling the ship," said Donalds. "I've authorized the release of the EXODUS's schematics to the fleet to determine its weaknesses and the most efficient way to halt or destroy it."

CHAPTER ELEVEN

It was just another day for X, and the evening was turning out to be more of the usual routine. The house bot had been in the service of the Roberts family for years. John's father, who carried the same name as his son, had purchased the bot as a Christmas gift for his wife when they moved to their house in La Habra.

Graciella hadn't wanted to buy such a large house on a huge piece of land. Where John Sr. saw privacy, all she could see was work, work, and more work. To convince her that they should buy the home, John Sr. purchased a house bot to handle all the house and yard work. The ploy had worked, and they moved into their new home. A year later, John was born.

Nicole saw X as nothing more than another appliance; however, John saw X as a playmate and delighted in crawling all over the bot. Graciella thought it was nice that baby John had adopted X as a surrogate sibling, and it seemed X's artificial intelligence had adapted to the baby's needs. X played with the baby, helped feed and change him, even sang lullabies to get him to sleep.

John Sr. found the whole affair odd, but since his wife seemed content with the arrangement, he wasn't going to say anything. The baby's love of X eventually changed the family's perception of the bot from a mere machine to a family member. X was even included in the family portrait when John turned four. It was the only picture of all of them together. John Sr. and Graciella died a few months later.

X was in remarkable condition for an old bot. Nicole took X in for a thorough maintenance check once a year, and John continued to do so when his sister disappeared. Even after John left New York, he made arrangements for a technician to service X annually.

With John at the Academy, X's daily activities were limited to maintaining the house and grounds. The days of being a part of a family were relegated to some files in X's memory core.

The house was dark and silent, except for the kitchen light. X spent most of its days sitting in the corner of John's room. Ever since John was little, X sat in that corner when on standby mode. His presence was a comfort to John. Even after John's departure to the Academy, X continued to spend his time powered down in the bedroom.

With John gone, X's programming should have dictated it power down by the front door. Yet, for whatever reason, the bot chose to continue to 'sleep' in John's room.

The round, black robot had only been down for a couple of hours when its proximity sensor alerted it to a large incoming object. X immediately brought all its systems online and extended its four metallic legs from its lower body. The bot walked out of the room and headed downstairs. By this time, its sensors had clarified that the object coming in was a shuttle. The shuttle had just landed in the field by the time the bot reached the porch.

X scanned the perimeter, waiting for the person it detected inside the shuttle to emerge. The bot had already confirmed the individual was not John. This individual was older, taller, and heavier than his owner. The person was also a man, and the bot discounted the possibility the individual was Nicole (unless Nicole had had an operation to change her sex. X gave that scenario a 0.00000000013% probability).

X watched as the shuttle's side door opened and the man emerged. The individual took a few steps before tripping and falling down in the field. X immediately responded by retracting its legs and switching to wheel mode. The bot raced down the steps and across the field over to the fallen man to assist him. It scanned his body for any injuries he might have incurred in the fall.

"Let me assist you," X said in its low, calm, mechanical voice. The bot took one of the man's hands in its claw and helped him to his feet. "This unit detects no damage to your body; however, you must not attempt to rise too quickly."

The man looked at X as he got up. The bot finally had a clear look at his face and accessed its memory files to determine who he might be. The face matched a photo John had transmitted to X only hours ago.

"Admiral Oliver Johnson. Welcome to the Roberts residence."

The man grabbed X by both arm extenders and gripped tightly. X made no attempt to wrestle free, as the pressure was in no danger of causing any damage. He stared at X's two white optical interfaces with a wild look on his face.

"Are you one of them?" he asked.

The question made no sense to X, and the bot spent a few moments processing the query. The man looked to the sky, as if he was checking to see if he'd been followed. "The kingdom will protect me. They won't send a devil."

"This unit is unable to properly reference your statements to compose an appropriate response," said X.

Admiral Johnson looked back at the bot and blinked several times, as if trying to break free of a trance. "No...no. Of course not," he muttered. "He said I'd be safe here."

"I conclude you are referring to John. He has instructed this unit to obey all requests from you. The residence is at your disposal."

"Residence? Right, right. I need to clean up, get organized."

"My scans indicate you are able to move under your own motion. Please follow this unit." X's spherical body turned and it rolled back to the house.

The admiral grabbed a duffle bag that he'd dropped when he fell and followed X, looking back at the shuttle and the sky above.

X had interfaced with the house computer and turned on all the lights downstairs. As it approached the porch steps, its legs emerged once more from its lower body and it walked up the steps into the house. X could hear the admiral muttering to himself, but the words were jumbled. He made several references to a devil, kingdom, and something called Kory. X cross-referenced the words with encyclopedic resources, but nothing matched the probability parameters of this situation.

X went to the kitchen and retrieved a drinking glass. It filled the glass with cold water from the refrigerator door. By the time the glass was full, the admiral was inside the house and had just joined the bot in the kitchen.

"Your body's liquid composition is down 23.53%," stated X as it approached the admiral and offered him the glass. "This will increase your hydration by 8.601%."

The admiral looked at the glass suspiciously. He felt that the bot meant him no harm, but there were too many voices in his head telling him too many different things. It was difficult to sort them out. He hit his head with the palm of his hand repeatedly to try to hush them. When the noises had diminished, he took the glass and drank it greedily. He had very little time left.

"John instructed this unit to interface with your shuttle and use its sensor system to monitor the area. With your permission, I will establish a link."

The admiral nodded. That made sense. There were a lot of bad things out there. Maybe this bot could protect him from lurking evils.

X bleeped as it established a link to the shuttle computer. In no time, the bot activated the shuttle's sensors and began monitoring as wide of an area as the sensors could capture.

"Interface established. This unit will notify you of any incoming visitors," reported X.

The admiral had already forgotten about the bot. He'd just realized he was in John Roberts's family home. He walked into the adjacent dining room, leaving X behind in the kitchen. A large wooden table stood in the center of the room, six chairs pushed in around it.

This room had not been used in years. If it wasn't for X's meticulous cleaning, all the rooms would have accumulated dust. At the end of the far wall was a large glass china cabinet. It was filled with beautiful chinaware adorned with pink roses. The top shelf contained a variety of liquor bottles. Some were empty and others had never been opened.

The admiral crossed out of the dining room and into the large living room. Immediately in front of him was a pool table. But it was the fireplace that caught his attention. There, on the mantel, were numerous pictures. He moved past the pool table to get a closer look.

Many of the pictures were of John's parents. They looked so happy in the photos. The admiral remembered having such feelings when Kory was alive. Where was Kory? He hadn't seen him in so long. Why was that? There was a reason his son hadn't called, but the admiral couldn't think what it could be. He closed his eyes tightly and tried to remember. When he reopened his eyes, he zoomed in on a single photo of a young woman.

"Devil!" hissed the admiral. He grabbed the photo and shook it violently. "How did you get here!?" He'd seen her before. Somehow, he knew she was with the devil. No, she *was* the devil, a devil. He couldn't keep it straight, but his instincts told him she was evil.

X had entered the room moments before and approached the admiral. "Do you have a question about the picture you are shaking?"

The admiral looked at X with wild eyes. Was the bot in league with her? He thought it could be trusted. He thrust the photo at the bot's optical scanners. "Who is she? Why'd you bring her here?"

"The young woman in the photo is Nicole Roberts, John's sister," replied the bot in a flat tone. "She is currently not residing here."

The admiral was confused. He looked at the picture again. "She's not here?"

"Nicole departed this household in 2130," replied the black bot. "There is no record of her contacting the residence at any time since she left. John has made no statements indicating he has had any visual or verbal contact with her."

She wasn't here. That made sense. The admiral was relieved he had nothing to worry about. She was an infection on the road to the kingdom, but he'd taken care of her. The road had been cleared.

"Two shuttlecrafts are on approach to the house," announced X. It jolted the admiral, clearing his head for a moment.

"Where?"

"They crossed the northern border of Whittier. Estimated time of arrival at current speed is eleven minutes. They are conducting detailed scans of the area."

There wasn't much time. He'd known they would come here looking for him. He'd been hoping for more time, but the evil was relentless.

"My metal angel, you must help me avoid the damnation approaching."

"John instructed this unit to follow all of your instructions," replied X. "I am at your disposal."

"Then we must hurry. We must prepare for their arrival."

——— ——— ———

Up in space, EXODUS began its course out of the solar system.

"What is the status of the Interceptors?" asked John as he reviewed the ship's power distribution network.

"Luna Squadron Alpha is fifteen minutes behind us," Alex'sis said. "By the time we reach the Mars defense perimeter, we should have about a twenty-minute lead on them."

The plan had worked. As Lieutenant Jacobson had predicted, the pursuing Interceptors altered their course to try to catch up to EXODUS further along on its projected course. A quick burst at full speed had ensured the squadron would not catch them. John was relieved that one potential encounter with TERRA had been avoided.

"Any activity from the Mars defense perimeter?"

"I'm monitoring high-level communications between Luna and Mars," Bret said. "They've encrypted the transmissions so I can't decipher what they're saying. It looks like Mars is preparing for our arrival."

"Commander, I've acquired telemetry on the Mars fleet," Alex'sis said.

John jumped down from his command chair and joined her and Julie at the tactical table as Alex'sis punched up a visual grid of the ships.

"They've mobilized a group of eighty fighters and two capital ships, the AURORA and the SYRIA. They're in synchronous orbit above the communications center and will intercept us as soon as we pass by the planet."

"If they're above the communications center, that would put them near the planetary gun," Julie said.

"You really think they would use the gun against us?" John expected TERRA would use the cannon to try and disable them, but he was hoping that one of his officers had a different opinion. He didn't want to be right about them using that destructive weapon.

"Tactically, it makes perfect sense," Alex'sis said. "They can slow our advance with their fighters and capital ships. That'll give them a window of opportunity to have the cannon's targeting system lock onto us."

"We could alter course and avoid Mars altogether," said Julie.

"If we alter course, that will allow Alpha Squadron to hook up with the Mars group and stage a line against us when we move the ship back toward Pluto," said John. "According to the specs, the shields should be able to absorb a blast from the planetary gun. They'll only get one shot off before we move out of range."

"Commander, the shields haven't been tested in a live scenario, let alone here in space," Julie reminded him. "There's no guarantee they'll even work."

"I have to agree with her," said Alex'sis. "We're better off against a fleet of ships than that gun."

John hadn't expected this from her. Alex'sis had made it well known that she was fully confident in the ship's capabilities. For her to voice any sort of doubt unnerved him.

"That gun is the most powerful weapon in TERRA," said John.

"If this ship can't survive a blast from it, then we'll have no chance against the Screen."

Julie and Alex'sis looked at each other, as if they were considering the merits of his statement. Then Alex'sis offered a compromise.

"I recommend that engineering conduct continuous tests on the shield system until we reach Mars."

"Okay," John said, "But let them know I want the system online the moment we intercept the Mars group or come in range of the gun."

Alex'sis nodded and headed over to another station.

John looked at Julie, seeing the concerned look on her face. "You don't agree with my call."

Julie shrugged. "I'd rather go up against the ships than the cannon. I understand where you're coming from, but the power output of the cannon is enormous. The shields may overload."

"The specs show the shields are designed to dissipate and absorb the energy from a weapon. The system's designed to minimize any possibility of an overload."

"Commander," Bret interrupted. "We're getting a message from the Mars Communication Center. They're trying to raise us."

John wondered if they were going to demand that EXODUS halt its advance, just like Luna Station had. "Put it up on the speakers."

"TXS EXODUS," the intimidating voice boomed.

"Vice Admiral Rollins," Julie whispered to John, recognizing his distinctive voice.

John winced. Admiral Rollins ran the day-to-day TERRA operations on Mars and reported directly to Admiral Block. He was a tough, no-nonsense officer who wouldn't hesitate to put his soldiers' lives on the line.

"You are illegally making transit through the inner solar system and have defied repeated orders to cease your advance," continued Rollins.

John rolled his eyes. *No shit, genius.*

"You are ordered to stand down, disengage all defensive systems, and allow a troop detachment to board. Failure to comply will be interpreted as a hostile action and will be dealt with accordingly. You have one minute to respond."

Julie looked at John with apprehension.

"Shall we respond to the admiral?" asked Bret.

"Negative," John said. "Do not respond to any of their incoming transmissions." He headed back up to his command chair while Julie stayed at the tactical table. "All hands to battle stations."

The emergency klaxons blared as the crew readied themselves for Mars's greeting.

CHAPTER TWELVE

A cool breeze blew, swaying branches and rustling leaves on the trees, as two shuttles landed in the field in front of the Roberts's residence, near the admiral's shuttle. As their systems went on standby, the main doors at the rear of both crafts opened and several armed TERRA officers exited in rapid succession. The group closest to the admiral's shuttle headed to secure the craft, while the second group set up position in the tall grass to conduct reconnaissance on the house. Two officers used their visual scanners to identify any activity occurring within the residence. The interior was dark. Even with the scanners, they saw no movement inside.

"Commander Pavlenko," one of the officers said over the open communications channel.

The commander joined the team embedded in the grass, and the officer tapped his eyepiece. The commander trained his scanner on the house. "I can't get any readings from the house at all."

The commander looked at the house through his eyepiece. "Looks like a scuzzy's been activated. We should at least be picking up some low-level energy signatures from the house computer."

The team that had secured the admiral's shuttle joined their comrades in the grass. "The shuttle's empty, sir."

"It's possible it could be another decoy," said Pavlenko. "I want one guard by the shuttle. The rest are with me. We'll spread out and encompass the house as we close in. Remember, fire only TPs.

We need to bring in people alive for interrogation."

Via hand signals, the officers relayed his orders. They switched their rifles to fire only taser pulses. As one officer stayed behind with the shuttles, the others advanced toward the house. Within a minute, the house was surrounded by the task force.

"On my mark, we go in," Pavlenko said over the comm channel.

"Please, I don't want to hurt any of you," came a voice from the house, a voice Commander Pavlenko recognized belonging to Admiral Johnson. The commander was caught off guard by the admiral's pleading voice that seemed to be projecting from a speaker somewhere in the house. He signaled the officers near him to stand by, an order which was relayed to the others stationed around the house.

"Admiral Johnson," Pavlenko called out. "My name is Commander Pavlenko."

"You need to go. You can't be here."

"Admiral, I've been ordered to bring you in. Come on out so we can talk. No one wants to hurt you."

"I don't want to talk. I just want it to end. Please understand that I can't continue to live."

Pavlenko instantly concluded what the admiral meant. Suicide. He'd been told that under no circumstances should the admiral die.

"Now!" Commander Pavlenko yelled to his officers. The team raided the house via the doors and windows accessible to them. The sound of breaking glass and splintered wood echoed throughout the house. Each officer tried to locate their target, but couldn't find Admiral Johnson anywhere. A few headed upstairs, but none of the rooms yielded any signs of the admiral.

"Clear," the team reported.

Pavlenko took off his eyepiece scanner and hit the entry hall light switch. As soon as he did, he spotted a black bot sitting underneath the stairway. Before any of them could act, the bot raced out of the house through the front door.

Pavlenko managed to reach the door and take one last look outside before the entire house exploded. The local wildlife scurried away from the explosion as it rocked the ground and debris flew everywhere. The fireball that erupted from the explosion could be seen for miles.

X headed straight to the shuttles, as it had been instructed. Waiting there was Admiral Johnson, standing over the dead body of the security officer who had remained behind. Distracted by the explosion, he'd never heard the admiral approach from behind. Despite the voices in his head, the admiral had managed to remain focused, plunging the knife into the officer's back, directly into his heart.

X's upper body rotated so his optical scanners could view the house. "Scans indicate there are no survivors."

The admiral patted the bot on its top. "Good work, my metallic friend. We've cleansed the planet of those demons. The kingdom is much safer now."

"Your statements do not coincide with the current situation. This unit is unable to reference the meaning of your phrases." Its upper body rotated again as it looked to the west. "Shuttle sensors indicate the city has dispatched emergency response units."

"We need to move then," said the admiral. "They won't stop hunting us down."

X watched the admiral as he opened the shuttle door and climbed in. The house bot rotated its body once more to view where the house had stood. It didn't know why it felt the need to look at the destroyed residence. It was nothing but shattered pieces now. Only fire and debris dotted the landscape, elements that served no purpose for X to watch.

The admiral stuck his head out of the shuttle. "We must leave, now!"

With a snapshot of the house debris now saved as a file in its memory bank, X turned and entered the shuttle. The bot concluded that John would want to see visual evidence of the house's demise.

—— —— ——

His house was the last thing on John's mind right now. EXODUS was within the reach of Mars and its mighty space fleet.

"Commander, Mars's defense fleet is moving at high velocity toward us," Alex'sis reported as she reviewed the sensor data on the tactical table.

John punched up the same data on his command screen to see what they were up against. "It looks like it's the AURORA. It's deployed half their fighters."

The AURORA was moving right toward them. It was the most technologically advanced of all the capital ships, having recently emerged from its refit only two months ago.

"The SYRIA's holding back, but they've also deployed half their fighter group," Julie said. "They're going to try to maximize their chances of slowing us down."

"Where are the other two capital ships?" asked John.

"The JORDAN and GENESIS are on the other side of Mars. They show no sign of rendezvousing with the attack fleet."

John checked EXODUS's speed again, then focused his attention on the Interceptors.

"What would happen if an Interceptor impacted our shields?"

"With no shields on the Interceptors, and at our current speed, any impact would result in the fighter being destroyed," replied Alex'sis.

"How slow would we have to go to prevent a fighter from being ripped apart by a collision?"

Alex'sis ran the calculations on her console. "EXODUS would have to cut engines to one-tenth. Any impact at that speed would cause hull fractures on a fighter but probably wouldn't destroy it."

Julie found John's question perplexing. What did that have to do with them trying to outrun the fleet? She monitored the fleet's telemetry as she listened to John and Alex'sis conversation. "One minute to engagement," she announced.

"Drop EXODUS to one-tenth speed," ordered John.

Julie turned around, looking shocked. "Commander, dropping to that speed will give them every opportunity to lock onto us and fire the cannon."

"I'm aware of the risk. Lieutenant, drop to one-tenth."

"Yes sir," said Kevin.

Julie hurried over to John. "What are you doing?" she started, but John interrupted her.

"Those fighters out there are not the enemy. I have no intention of harming them."

"I realize that, but that's not an excuse to let them take free shots at us. That's not how one defends a ship. What if the shields fail? It'll give them the opportunity to attach to our hull. Do you plan to defend the ship then if they board us?"

John was unconcerned. "We'll cross that bridge if need be. Lieutenant Brandus, target the AURORA's engines. We'll disable them. Under no circumstances are you to lock on or fire on any Interceptor. Just the AURORA."

"Yes sir," replied Alex'sis, impressed with how John had come up with a strategy on the fly. She'd expected that, with his lack of command experience, he'd be out of his element and would cling to some routine strategy taught at the Academy.

"John, this act of compassion is not going to put you in a better light with TERRA," Julie said. "If you're concerned about what people will think of you..."

"I don't care what they think," John said impatiently. He didn't appreciate that Julie was trying to interpret the motives for his actions and wasn't inclined to explain it to her. "Back to your post, officer."

Julie didn't appreciate John's dismissive attitude; she was doing exactly what an executive officer was expected to do, question the captain to ensure he or she was making the best decision for the crew. But at least they agreed on one thing: Now was not the time to get into an argument. Reluctantly, she returned to the operations table.

"Sir, we've got fighters inbound," Alex'sis said.

"Raise shields," John ordered.

Alex'sis activated the shield system and a humming noise reverberated throughout the command deck.

"Shields active," reported Alex'sis. "Power is stable and the grid's intact."

"AURORA's fighters have armed themselves," Julie said. "Commander, do you want us to deploy our fighters?"

"Negative," replied John. The EXODUS would not be able to make a quick run for it if they deployed their fighters. And with the energy shield active, the EXODUS didn't need to deploy fighters to act as a defensive barrier. "Open a communication line to the AURORA Interceptors."

Bret opened a channel as Julie again looked perplexed. She looked over at Alex'sis, who was smiling. "What?"

"He's got some balls, I'll give him that," Alex'sis said in a low tone, so no one else could hear her.

"He's going to get us killed." John had never cared about what people thought of him, yet here he was, going out of his way to be a kind and gentle opponent. Such strategy was never taught at the Academy.

"With all due respect, sir, you don't know what this ship can do," Alex'sis reminded her. "TERRA doesn't have the firepower to stop us."

That may be true, but Julie felt that was no reason to ignore military engagement protocols. "What about the shields?"

"They'll hold."

Julie couldn't tell if Alex'sis was trying to reassure her or convince herself.

"Communication opened to the fighters," announced Bret.

"AURORA fighters," John said. "This is the TFX EXODUS. I know your orders are to engage us in combat. This ship is highly advanced and your weapons will be ineffective. You will exhaust your weapons in an attempt to penetrate our ship's hull. Be advised this ship is surrounded by an energy defense screen. We have slowed our speed to ensure no unintentional impact with any of you. Please maintain a safe distance during combat. We will not fire upon you under any circumstance."

Julie couldn't believe this. John had just told the enemy his entire combat strategy. At that moment, she was convinced Admiral Johnson had made the wrong decision in appointing John as ship commander. He had broken every combat rule in the book. This was worse than waving a white flag from one of the portholes.

"Enemy weapons are hot," reported Alex'sis. Outside the AURORA, Interceptors broke off into five formations and began their run on EXODUS.

—— —— ——

Down on Mars, Admiral Rollins watched the fighting begin on the sensor screen in the command hub. He had heard John's announcement about not firing on the fighter group. After verifying through the computer that the voice belonged to Cadet Roberts, he'd brushed it off as a feeble attempt at strategy from someone who didn't know what they were doing.

"Admiral, the AURORA Interceptors have engaged the enemy," reported the sensor officer.

"Has EXODUS activated her weapons?" asked the admiral.

"Negative, sir. Her armaments remain offline."

The admiral found it odd that EXODUS appeared to be following through on what John Roberts had said they were going to do: not fire on any Interceptor. Only moments ago, Rollins had been alerted by the command council that two cadets were on board the ship. He was still trying to figure out why a cadet had been the one to communicate with them. Usually the ship commander made such transmissions.

"Tactical, have the fighters make two passing runs on the EXODUS, then regroup by the AURORA." Rollins was certain that the enemy ship's decision to not engage would be their downfall.

—— —— ——

Flashes of light flickered from the upper windows of the command deck as the squadrons fired their particle beams. Most of the crew couldn't help but be distracted by the light display, including John. His eyes trailed from watching the sensor data on his command screen to looking up at the random flashes of light outside. He imagined the frustration of the Interceptors' pilots as their weapons failed to inflict damage on the EXODUS, made more evident as the larger ship didn't so much as shudder from the attack.

After a few long moments, the lights ceased. "Commander," Alex'sis's voice boomed, bringing John and the command deck crew back to attention. "Enemy fighters have completed one pass. They're turning about for another run at us."

"Damage report." John expected EXODUS to have incurred at least some minor damage, despite the energy shield.

Julie checked her console. She couldn't believe her eyes. "None, sir."

"What?"

"The ship's completely intact. The shields absorbed all the particle beams. The system successfully absorbed the blasts. I'm reading a 1.5% increase in our energy reserves."

John couldn't hide his amazement. "Holy shit! It actually worked." He looked at Julie and grinned. "This ship actually works."

"I could have told you that, sir," Alex'sis said, grinning back. "By the way, fighter craft are coming around again."

Any hesitation John had had about the ship going into combat vanished. EXODUS had just proven itself combat-worthy.

The lights from the fighters' particle beams lit up the area again in a performance of energized dancing lights.

—— —— ——

"AURORA, Interceptors have made their run against the target," reported the tactical officer at Mars Command. "Groups one and two are regrouping near the AURORA. Group three is maintaining a position ahead of the EXODUS."

"Damage to enemy?" The admiral expected a quick answer, but instead got only silence. He looked down at the tactical officer. "Lieutenant, I asked you a question!"

The tactical officer stammered, "No damage to enemy target, sir."

"What? That's impossible."

"Rechecking the sensors, sir," said the officer. But the results were the same. "Admiral, the attacks had no discernable effect on the EXODUS."

The admiral wiped away the beads of sweat dotting his forehead. How could that be? The Interceptors couldn't have all missed their target. "The Interceptors did hit the target, did they not?"

"Yes, sir. Sensors confirm multiple impacts. But the blasts were repelled by some sort of energy field."

"Are you saying the ship has an active shield system?"

"Yes, sir. Once the impacts registered, the sensors detected the energy field around the vessel."

Admiral Block had discussed the EXODUS Project with Rollins in the past, but had never said anything about the ship having an energy shield system. Such a system was only theoretical and had never been successfully developed.

"Are they still moving?"

"Yes, sir. Vessel is maintaining course and speed to the outer solar system."

"Contact the AURORA. Order her to open all her batteries. I want that ship stopped now!"

The tactical officer nodded and relayed the orders to the AURORA. In took no time for the capital ship to begin her assault on EXODUS.

"The AURORA's opening fire on us," Alex'sis reported as she gripped the sides of the operations table.

"All hands, brace for impact," John announced through the ship's internal communication system. Pop shots from fighters were one thing; pulse cannons from a capital ship were something else entirely.

John waited to feel the impact of the AURORA's weapons hitting the shields, but the EXODUS continued to maintain a smooth and steady course.

"Weapons from the AURORA are being absorbed by the shields," reported Julie. She looked up at John. "It's the same effect as the Interceptors' attacks. No damage to EXODUS."

"Wow," John said in disbelief. This ship continued to amaze him. It was simply unstoppable against TERRA. He had a brief fantasy of flying the ship to Luna and demanding TERRA surrender unconditionally. That would certainly teach them not to screw with him.

"Should we return fire and disable their engines?" asked Alex'sis.

"No." John had originally planned to disable their engines and move out of their weapons range. But there was no need to do that now. They knew EXODUS was fully protected. "They're no threat to us. Let them keep firing if they want. Maintain course."

John almost felt bad for the AURORA's crew. They were only following orders. He had an itching impulse to flaunt his victory by going up to a window and giving the AURORA's commander the one-finger salute.

——— ——— ———

The mood at Mars Command was less joyful. Rollins had witnessed the utter ineffectiveness of a capital ship's armaments against an experimental vessel. It didn't matter that EXODUS was five times bigger. The AURORA should have been able to take down that ship, or at least cause some significant damage.

To say that Rollins was upset was an understatement. He was fuming. A stolen experimental ship was waltzing through Mars's defenses. It appeared the schematic data of EXODUS provided to him by the command council was woefully inadequate.

"Shall the AURORA pursue and maintain fire?" asked the Mars tactical officer.

Without an accurate summary of the ship's capabilities, Rollins could only guess at a strategy. He had no choice but to swallow his pride.

"Order the AURORA to cease fire. Have the fighter group ahead of the EXODUS engage her. I want to make sure that ship doesn't speed up before we fire the planetary gun."

——— ——— ———

"Increase speed by half," ordered John as he watched the AURORA withdrawing from its attack and retreating to Mars. He knew the AURORA was withdrawing for only one reason.

"Lieutenant, do the sensors show if the planetary gun on Mars has been activated?"

Alex'sis checked the sensors. "Yes, sir. I'm reading a power transfer to the gun's batteries. I'm also picking up a targeting lock on us."

"We could increase engines to maximum. Maybe get a chance to prevent their computer from locking on to us," Julie suggested.

"I doubt it," said John as he jumped down from his command chair. "Take a look." He punched up sensor readings on the operations table and brought up a holographic image up for them to see. "The Interceptors ahead of us are moving back toward us. I bet they're going to attack to try and keep us from increasing our speed."

"Then maybe we should increase speed to full," Alex'sis said. "When they see us barreling down on them, they'll scatter to avoid a collision."

"And run the risk of a fighter crashing into us? I don't think so." John wasn't about to abandon his principles. They had already come this far without firing on anyone and were almost to the border.

Bret offered another idea. "Couldn't we jump to the outer solar system?"

That got John's attention, and he raised his eyebrows at the thought. It was an easy solution. But out of the corner of his eyes, he saw Julie shaking her head.

"I've gone over the hyper-jump process," she said. "There are too many variables when trying to jump a ship this size within a star system. We could easily hit a planet, moon, or asteroid. We can't jump until we pass beyond Pluto."

John rolled his eyes. So much for the quick way out.

Alex'sis piped up. "Commander, the shields will easily hold against the planetary cannon."

"And how do you know that?" Julie asked skeptically.

"Because Admiral Johnson provided the ship's engineers with the cannon specs. The shield system was designed with that in mind."

Julie's eyes grew wide. "That's classified. How did...?" She threw up her hands. "Never mind." It was another example of Admiral Johnson using his position to cover all the bases.

But John wasn't so confident. Yes, the AURORA had used its most powerful guns on them to no effect, but the planetary cannon was ten times the size of the AURORA's largest weapon.

"You sure the shields will hold?" John asked.

"Absolutely," Alex'sis replied, unwavering in her response.

John looked at her closely. Though she'd had some reservations a few minutes ago, apparently EXODUS' performance in their brief battle against the AURORA and her Interceptors had changed her mind.

John smiled. "Good enough for me." He looked at the shield readouts. "But just in case, let's activate the ship's planetary bombardment guns. If we need to disable the cannon, I want to do it without delay."

"Yes sir," Alex'sis replied as she moved away from the operations table.

"The planetary gun houses thirty personnel," Julie said. "If we wind up firing on it, we'll cause casualties."

"I know. I hope it doesn't come to that," John said as he headed back to his command chair. It was easy to avoid hurting the Interceptor pilots. They were nothing more than a minor inconvenience. But if the planetary gun proved to be a serious threat to EXODUS, John felt he would have no choice but to destroy the control facility. He crossed his fingers, hoping he wouldn't have to make that decision.

——— ——— ———

Mars's citizens had enjoyed over a century of peaceful existence. Even after TERRA had fortified the planet as a front-line defense against a potential Screen invasion, Martians, as they proudly called themselves, experienced very little disruption to their day-to-day lives. Slowly, the Mars economy transformed itself to cater to the large contingent of TERRA officers stationed there. Ask any Martian where TERRA headquarters was and they'd tell you it was on Mars, not Luna.

Each time a human-operated ship crossed the Mars orbital boundary, a planet-wide alarm sounded, alerting citizens to the impending Screen attack on the brazen ship trying to reach the outer solar system. To prepare for the possibility that a Screen ship would attack Mars, the planetary gun was powered up each time the alarm went off. The public never had to wait long for ELM News to broadcast the identity of the latest victim to fall to the Screen.

The attacks were always swift. However, today would be the first time the planetary gun would fire on a target.

The planetary alarm went off throughout the colony. The civilian population, having been trained by TERRA on emergency procedures, headed straight for their homes and designated shelters. They were accustomed to the scenario, as TERRA conducted drills monthly. But this time was different: a verbal warning accompanied the alarms and echoed throughout the planet over the public speakers.

"Warning, planetary defense cannon powering up," the ominous female computer voice announced. "All nonessential personnel keep clear of red zone," the voice continued, referring to a four-mile radius around the gun. "Warning. Planetary defense cannon powering up. All citizens are advised to head to designated shelter areas."

As the Martian citizens raced to safety, the blast shield formed over the clear, poly-metallic dome housing Crimson City, the planet's capital. Businesses shuttered, and within minutes the city streets were deserted, only the city bots remaining as they continued their duties of keeping the streets cleaned and in working order.

The Mars Command Center became a flurry of activity. Admiral Rollins wasted no time authorizing the cannon to fire. Both the technicians and officers monitoring the gun's systems were double-checking the diagnostic test results.

"Admiral, power has been successfully transferred to the gun's power cells," the tactical officer reported.

"Inform firing control to begin lock-on procedures for the enemy ship," the admiral ordered. "Once they obtain a lock, they are to fire immediately. I don't want to give that ship a chance to escape."

"Yes, Admiral."

——— ——— ———

The command deck crew of the EXODUS was monitoring the activity on Mars. All they could do was wait for the attack as EXODUS passed near the red planet. The crew's tension heightened—the first real test of the ship's might was about to take place.

Despite their fears, the crew remained focused on their tasks. "We're passing by Mars," Kevin reported.

"Second wing of fighters is approaching," Alex'sis said. "Their weapons are active."

"Drop speed to one tenth and bring structural reinforcement to maximum," ordered John. "As soon as the fighters have made a pass, boost the ship's speed back to half."

"Shouldn't we go to full speed across the boundary?" Alex'sis said.

"I don't want us to get too far from the border," John said as Julie and Alex looked up at him. "You know...just in case."

He knew they understood what he was alluding to. If the EXODUS failed to repel the Screen attack, there was a chance they could retreat across the border. Then again, once EXODUS crossed the boundary, the Screen would probably keep attacking until they destroyed the experimental starship.

"Don't worry, sir. This ship will hold up against the Screen," Alex'sis promised. John was glad she was sure about the ship, because he was starting to have second thoughts again.

"Incoming fighters," Alex'sis said as she turned her attention back to the operations table. Flashes of lights from their particle beams lit up the command deck windows. On his monitor, John could see the shields easily absorbing the energy impacts.

"Sir, the fighters are not doing a pass of the ship," Julie reported.

John adjusted the tactical readout on his screen. He saw that the fighters were hanging with the EXODUS. They were conducting quick, darting attacks back and forth. Many of the fighters were getting dangerously close. He hadn't anticipated they would ride with the ship and was worried one might impact the shields.

"Sir," Alex'sis said. "I'm reading full power to the planetary cannon. They're preparing to fire."

John punched up the ship's internal speakers. "All hands, prepare for impact. I repeat, prepare for impact."

In the final moments, the Interceptors pulled away. At least they'd been given a warning to clear out.

From space, an eerie white glow began to glimmer from the surface of Mars. It grew in size and intensity as the cannon's power came closer to being unleashed.

On the surface, Admiral Rollins waited impatiently for the gun to fire. He was convinced that the EXODUS would not be able to withstand the blast and was anxious to report to the council that the target had been destroyed. He would be the hero that eliminated TERRA's problem.

The batteries reached full power and channeled the energy through the cannon's large barrel. A stream of white energy streamed toward the heavens, directly at EXODUS. The blast hit the front of the experimental vessel head-on.

The ship rocked from the intensity of the blast. For the longest eight seconds of John's life, the ship was subjected to the cannon's unrelenting attack. He gripped his chair, hoping the ship would hold up. Images of the hull fracturing and EXODUS breaking up into pieces danced in his mind as the vibrations of the attack reverberated throughout the ship. Down in the pit, Julie had her eyes closed. She looked like she was praying.

The attack finally ended. The intensity of the cannon's discharge had shorted out the sensors at Mars Command. As they came back online, Admiral Rollins balled his hands into tight fists as he waited for the results to be reported.

"Status of the enemy ship," Rollins demanded.

Dumbfounded, the tactical officer rechecked the readings. "Admiral, readings indicate no damage to the rogue vessel."

"Impossible!" In disbelief, the admiral checked the monitor himself. Sure enough, the sensors showed EXODUS completely intact and continuing its course. Its shields were holding, and there was no evidence of any hull damage. Somehow this vessel had been able to repel the blast from the planetary cannon without so much as a scratch.

"What the hell did you do, Oliver?" Rollins muttered as he glanced over the sensor data confirming the vessel's shields had not breached. Admiral Johnson was a loyal officer. What had he been thinking when he'd had this ship built? Why had he launched it? Had the project members mutinied against him and launched the ship themselves?

"What shall we do?" the tactical officer asked.

The admiral was at a loss. He hadn't expected to be planning additional interference measures after the cannon had fired. He'd assumed he would be dispatching a cleanup crew to collect the ship's debris.

"Bring up a visual of EXODUS's proximity to the border."

The tactical officer pulled the information up on his monitor, and Admiral Rollins saw how close the ship was to the border. The attack fleet wouldn't reach it for another attack before it crossed.

"Recall the fighters. Have all capital ships take a defensive position by the planet relative to where EXODUS will be crossing the border. Have them redeploy their fighters as support."

"What about the enemy ship?" the tactical officer asked.

"We've done all we could to retake it," the admiral said in a resigned tone. "The Screen will take care of them now." The ship might have survived TERRA's most powerful weapon, but the admiral was certain it would not survive a Screen attack.

"Yes sir. I understand."

"Contact the command council. I need to update them on the situation." It was a report the admiral was not looking forward to giving.

―― ―― ――

The EXODUS crew was taking a quick assessment of their situation. It didn't take long for them to discover that the ship had weathered the attack completely intact. No one celebrated this second victory, though, as they all knew what was coming next.

Alex'sis was monitoring the fleet's movements near Mars to ensure they weren't going to attempt any more runs when she caught something on the sensors. "Commander," she said in an urgent tone. "Take a look at this."

John stepped down from his command chair and joined Alex'sis back at the operations table. "What is it?"

"One of the fighters grazed our shields during the battle. Sensors show its engines were damaged and it sustained multiple hull fractures."

"Did the pilot eject?"

Alex'sis checked her readings. "Negative. It looks like the ejection system was damaged. The fighter's floating alongside us toward the border."

"That fighter has no chance against the Screen," Julie said, stating the obvious. John raised his hand to stop her from saying anything more.

"Is the fleet sending a rescue out to retrieve the fighter?"

"No," Alex'sis replied. "The fleet has taken a defensive position around Mars. There's no indication they're deploying a Repo."

John wasn't surprised the fleet wasn't sending anyone out to retrieve their fighter. They were too busy worrying about their own hides to concern themselves with one pilot.

"We can't leave him out there," Julie insisted.

John nodded in agreement. TERRA might have abandoned their pilot, but he wasn't about to leave him out there. "I want him in EXODUS before we cross."

Julie wasted no time in contacting the hangar. "This is the command deck. We've got a damaged fighter in need of assistance. Deploy Repo for retrieval ASAP."

"Acknowledged, command deck," the senior hangar deck officer replied.

"Slow the ship to allow for retrieval," John ordered Kevin.

"Have a medical team standing by at the hangar. Better have a security team there as well. If the pilot isn't badly injured, he or she might not take being a prisoner too well."

Julie looked surprised by John's comment. "You're going to treat him as a prisoner?"

"No, but what would you think if the people whose ship you just attacked brought you on board?"

"Hmmm, good point."

EXODUS's huge hangar bay door opened and a single ship flew out, circling underneath toward the damaged fighter. The Interceptor was slowly spinning alongside the EXODUS.

"REPO ONE to EXODUS. I have visual confirmation of the damaged fighter."

"Stand by, REPO ONE." John looked over to Bret. "Send a communication to the fighter. Tell the pilot not to open fire. We're doing a rescue and bringing him on board. He won't be harmed."

"Yes, Commander," Bret said as he sent the message.

"EXODUS to REPO ONE. Proceed," John instructed.

"REPO ONE to EXODUS. Deploying grapplers."

Two metallic wire arms shot from the rescue craft. The arms hit the Interceptor and fastened onto the ship.

"REPO ONE to EXODUS. I have positive lock on fighter."

"Acknowledged, REPO ONE," John replied as he eyed the ship's distance from the boundary on the monitor. "Proceed back to the hangar at highest possible speed. Medical team is standing by."

"Acknowledged, EXODUS." The Repo vessel, with the damaged fighter in tow, made its way back up to the top of the ship and into the hangar.

"Hangar deck reporting Repo and fighter craft secured on deck," reported Julie moments later. "Hangar doors are closed and secured."

"Bring the shields back online," John said.

"Shields up," confirmed Alex'sis.

The comforting hum of the shields brought relief to John. He was glad that he was in a position to help. Even though he had done nothing to damage the fighter, he would have felt guilty if the pilot had perished. As least on EXODUS, the pilot had a chance to survive.

"Commander," Julie said in an ominous tone. "We're about to cross the border."

John made his way back up to his command chair and sat down. It took all his effort to maintain a cool demeanor. The real test of the ship was upon them. It was too late to back out now. The Screen were undoubtedly aware of their presence and were waiting for EXODUS to cross the border.

"Commander Olson," John said in a calm tone. "Bring the weapons systems online."

"Yes, sir." Julie inputted her commands to activate the weapons. A loud hum arose as power was routed to the guns and cannons.

"Maximize sensor resolution," John ordered. "I want to know the second the Screen appear."

John hoped that the same Screen fighter that had appeared in every recorded encounter would show up. Regardless of the type of Earth vessel that crossed the border, the same type of Screen fighter craft always appeared. People speculated whether it was the same ship or merely the same class of vessel. Either way, John was banking that this wouldn't change with the EXODUS.

"Weapons are loaded and at the ready," Julie said.

"Commander, EXODUS is crossing the border," Kevin reported. "Crossing in ten, nine, eight..."

The countdown was broadcasted throughout the ship, so everyone was aware the moment the ship passed beyond the safety of the inner solar system. John did his best to stay calm; as commander, they were counting on him.

"As soon as we're across, bring the ship to half speed," John instructed Kevin.

The navigation officer nodded as he continued the countdown. "Four, three, two, one..."

In the void of space, EXODUS crossed the border into what TERRA considered forbidden territory. No ship had ever gone beyond the border and survived. They had all been obliterated by the Screen. Everyone on the command deck—including

John—seemed to hold their breath as they waited for the inevitable confrontation to play out.

"We're across the threshold," Alex'sis reported in a low tone, but no one heard her. Everyone waited in silence for any sign of the Screen. The only sounds were the blips the computer systems made.

Then the familiar screeching that they'd grown up listening to on ELM News broke the uneasy quiet. The noise seemed to be coming from everywhere. John couldn't pinpoint its origin, but it permeated the entire command deck. The fear it created gripped him—and from the looks of it, the crew—in a cold grasp, but the military personnel managed to hang onto their resolve. John hoped that the civilians in Central were faring as well. He wondered if they were thinking of what Admiral Johnson had told him during one of their conversations about the Screen: "Don't try to block out the fear. Just co-exist with it."

"Sensors," was all John managed to say. A huge lump in his throat prevented him from formulating any phrases beyond one-word statements. His mind was telling him they would succeed, but his instincts screamed for him to run. It took every ounce of willpower to ignore the thoughts tearing through his mind. He wondered if experienced officers would struggle with this sort of terror.

Fighting her own fears, Alex'sis fumbled on the controls as she checked the sensor readings. "We've got a target inbound."

"Is it...?" Julie asked hesitantly.

Alex'sis looked up at her with a confirming glance.

"What type...?" was all John could force out of his mouth.

"Readings indicate it's the same raider-type vessel used in previous recorded attacks," Alex'sis clarified, her fear momentarily replaced with confusion. "Strange that they would send the same small ship to attack EXODUS."

Julie had a theory. "Either their sensors can't specifically discern ships trying to leave the solar system, or they believe their fighter can easily destroy any human-operated vessel."

John had managed to get a handle on his fear. "Activate

targeting scanners and lock on the vessel with our plasmatic beams."

"Shall we fire once it's in range?" Julie asked.

"No. I want it to fire on us first."

"Commander, if our weapons will be in range of the ship first, it would give us a tactical edge that we should take advantage of," Alex'sis said.

"We need to know if this ship can withstand a Screen attack," John said. "A good offense won't do us any good if we have no defense against Screen weaponry."

Julie wasn't buying his explanation. This was the first time a human ship had the technology to perform an initial strike against the Screen and they should jump on the opportunity. "Destroying a Screen ship will have a huge impact on the public," she protested. "People would rally around the idea of fighting back. Destroying that ship is more important than testing EXODUS's shields."

John just shook his head in response. "Hold weapons fire until I give the order."

"The time for debate is over," Alex'sis said, interrupting their argument. "Enemy ship has entered firing range."

"Shields to maximum. All hands prepare for weapons impact," John said.

Julie looked at him disapprovingly. It was one thing to gamble against TERRA, but John was now putting all their lives on the line. Julie would have never chosen this course of action. She wanted to destroy the fighter and collect the debris for analysis. But she knew there was no time to change his mind. If EXODUS had the fighter in weapons range, then they probably had only seconds before the Screen ship had EXODUS in range to fire.

The screeching sound reached a high pitch, a clear indication the ship was getting closer. The piercing sound was almost too painful to bear.

"Shields are at maximum," Julie yelled. Even though the shields had held up to the Mars planetary cannon, it did little to ease her worries. She had read about the shield specifications constructed around the sensor data TERRA collected on the Screen. EXODUS was far bigger and more powerful than the scout-sized alien vessel flying toward them, but the fact remained that no ship had ever withstood an attack. Would the shields hold?

"Enemy vessel is firing," Alex'sis announced, sounding confident the ship would prevail.

The Screen fighter opened fire, and the familiar white beam struck EXODUS's starboard hull. They didn't feel so much as a shudder from the blast. The shields had easily absorbed the energy beam. They'd done exactly what they were designed to do.

"Shields held," Alex'sis reported as she tried to contain her excitement. "Power has been absorbed into the ship's power distribution system."

Julie checked Alex'sis's readings. She couldn't believe it. It had worked. The shields had held. Yet another so-called fact the Academy taught cadets had been shattered. TERRA had developed effective countermeasures against the Screen.

John's heart slowed as he realized they would not be obliterated by the enemy craft. This was their biggest gamble, and it had paid off. They'd proved that EXODUS could go toe to toe against the Screen. There was nothing that could stop them from escaping into deep space now.

The Screen vessel outside fired on EXODUS several more times as it passed by the ship. None of its attacks could breach their shields. After passing by the ship one final time, it turned and started to head back out of the solar system, on the same path by which it had arrived.

"The Screen vessel's trying to retreat," Alex'sis said.

Oh no. John wasn't about to let the ship get away from them. For years, the Screen had showed no sympathy for the human ships they'd destroyed. Now, John was going to show them what it felt like to be the victim. He was going to exact revenge on behalf of those killed by the Screen.

"Lieutenant, activate forward cannons. Destroy the target."

"With pleasure, sir," Alex'sis replied. She had already locked on to the fleeing ship. With a press of a few buttons, the EXODUS fired on its target. The cannons hit their mark perfectly. The Screen ship was destroyed in less than three shots. John looked at the monitor as debris from the ship flew in all directions.

"Screen vessel has been destroyed," Alex'sis reported.

Everyone on the command deck looked at one another in disbelief. EXODUS had been the first human-operated ship to survive a Screen attack and was now the first human ship to destroy a Screen vessel. John glanced around—his crew members looked as if they weren't sure whether to celebrate or keep quiet. They chose to remain silent, but from the looks on their faces, he could tell that they all felt jubilant.

John thought his relief and confidence wouldn't waver now that they had destroyed a Screen ship. Instead, he was deeply concerned. In fact, he felt near panic. He'd never thought much about what to do after this point. Getting this far had been almost inconceivable.

They might be flying out of the solar system, but John remained focused on the tactical situation. What he came up with disturbed him.

"Commander," Julie said. "We should proceed at full speed out of the system."

"No," John said with unexpected vehemence. "Lieutenant Jacobson, increase speed to one-half until we reach Neptune, then drop down to one-quarter speed. Lieutenant Brandus, I want our scientists to analyze all sensor data from our Screen encounter. Make sure our defenses were foolproof. Private Michaels, go over the communications data. See if that ship sent out any sort of transmission. We're to maintain tactical alert until we leave the system."

John headed out of the pit. Julie followed on his heels, stopping him on the catwalk. "Why are you so worried? We won. We should increase to full speed and jump out of here as quickly as possible."

"We've finally destroyed one of their ships. Don't you think they're going to send reinforcements to find out what happened?"

"All the more reason for us to leave. We only need to worry if the fighter sent out a distress call before we destroyed it. Otherwise, they'll probably wait a few days, until it fails to return to wherever it came from."

"That's what humans would do. We don't know how the Screen operates." John stopped at the door to the lift and paused for a moment. "A lot can happen between here and Pluto and I don't want to rush to the finish line without the time to prepare ourseleves."

"You sound like that's going to be a challenge."

"It may be. That's where the HORIZON was destroyed by the Screen back in 2073. The first encounter humans had with them was near that planet."

CHAPTER THIRTEEN

"Impossible." Admiral Donalds couldn't believe what he was hearing.

"I'm afraid it's true," Vice Admiral Rollins replied meekly over the DAT. "That experimental ship withstood a Screen attack and destroyed the alien fighter. It's continuing on a course out of the solar system."

Donalds reclined in his chair. The reports Admiral Johnson submitted over the years on the EXODUS Project had not indicated it had any of the capabilities it had displayed against both TERRA and the Screen. It appeared that Johnson had been planning the EXODUS's departure for quite some time. He must have doctored the project's progress reports to hide what they were really doing.

Donalds was incensed that this had happened under his watch. But he couldn't do anything about that now. He had to focus on controlling the fallout he was certain was going to come from all of this.

"Who knows about the ship's status?" Donalds asked.

"I restricted monitoring of the EXODUS to my senior staff and command deck officers of the capital ships. A planetary sensor blackout has been instituted. None of the civilians should be aware of what's going on."

The door chime to the admiral's office rang. He checked the camera: it was Admiral Vespia and Superintendent Mortino.

"Continue monitoring the ship. Don't talk to the media. I'll be issuing a cover statement to them shortly."

"What about the government? I've been receiving requests for updates from President Butu's office."

"Ignore them. I'll deal with Butu."

Rollins nodded and the DAT turned off.

Donalds wasn't happy about losing control of the EXODUS, but he couldn't do anything about that now. He needed to focus on maintaining TERRA's public image, showing that they were still in control.

Donalds wasted no time in hitting the button to open his office door. Vespia and Mortino walked in together.

"Karla, Paul. I hope you have some information I can use." He buried the frustration he had about Rollins and his failure to stop EXODUS. He didn't want his visitors to see how upset he was that the situation had developed contrary to his expectations. A good leader had to maintain a competent, assertive demeanor to instill confidence in his subordinates.

"We've apprehended several members of the EXODUS Project on Earth," Vespia reported. "Most are not cooperating with us, but we were able to encourage a few of them to disclose some pertinent information." She hadn't used the word *torture*, but Donalds knew exactly what she meant. Admiral Vespia was quite skilled in the art of interrogation.

She handed him a folder. "You're not going to believe this, but Oliver gave command of that ship to those missing cadets."

Donalds was shocked at the news. "That can't be. No one with any common sense would give command of a capital ship to cadets."

When Rollins mentioned that they had identified John Roberts issuing communications from EXODUS, Donalds assumed he'd been assigned communications duty. He'd never considered that a cadet would be commanding the ship—and why would he? Such a thing was unheard of.

He flipped through the folder and glanced at the dossiers of John Roberts and Julie Olson. What the hell had Johnson been thinking? He was held in high esteem in TERRA and had built his career in service to the military. For him to take such an inconceivable action was out of character, to say the least.

"I verified the information about the cadets with several project members we've apprehended," Vespia said.

"Johnson must have been desperate if he resorted to cadets commanding the ship." The thought irked Donalds even further. It made it more embarrassing that a ship had broken through the fleet under the command of inexperienced cadets. "Do we have any idea why these cadets chose to throw away their careers like this?"

Mortino spoke up. "Cadet Roberts has always been a problematic individual. He's the worst cadet to go through the Academy in my experience. His combative behavior made it impossible for him to serve in the fleet. He was selected to enter the reserve program as a means of barring him from service."

"And the girl?"

"Cadet Olson has an excellent record. I can only believe that Cadet Roberts somehow coerced her, perhaps forcibly, into boarding that ship. They were roommates."

Vespia countered Mortino's assessment. "According to what I was able to glean from our captives, she was a willing participant in this plot."

The superintendent shook his head. "Cadet Roberts can be quite persuasive, and Cadet Olson's file indicates she has a high regard for following the rules."

Donalds held up her dossier. "According to her file, she was assigned to be a tour guide at the museum."

"She wanted to serve as an officer on a TERRA capital ship. You know those assignments are restricted," Mortino said.

"Nevertheless, it seems that she may have felt betrayed by being given such a lowly assignment. She had little to lose." Donalds tossed the files on his desk. "Is there any chance that Cadet Roberts can be reasoned with?"

That was an easy question for Mortino to answer. "No. He's always put his personal needs above TERRA. Once he's made up his mind, no one can change it. He has nothing to come back to now except prison."

"Do we have any information on the ship's weaknesses to disable it?" Vespia asked.

"That's already been explored. Admiral Johnson was quite thorough in providing us with misinformation about the ship's capabilities," replied Donalds. "At this point, we can't stop it from leaving the system."

"We're just going to give up?" Vespia said.

"Our goal is to provide information to the public that keeps TERRA in a favorable light and protects our worlds from any retaliation from the Screen," Donalds said. "Superintendent, you will return to the Academy and await delivery of new dossiers on these cadets to replace their existing ones. We need to portray both as less than desirable characters."

"I understand, sir."

"Thank you. Dismissed."

Taken aback by the speed of his dismissal, Mortino looked at Vespia, who only cracked a half-hearted smile. Without another word, the superintendent left.

When the door closed behind Mortino, the two continued their conversation.

"I had my people board the STAR PRINCESS," Vespia said. "We wanted to determine why it strayed into the blackout zone during the supposed thruster test." She pulled a computer chip out of her pocket and tossed it on Donalds's desk. He examined it closely as she continued. "We pulled that out of the ship's navigational computer. It altered the ship's course but displayed false readings to the helmsman, making him think the ship was maintaining its original established course. Essentially, they were tricked into flying toward EXODUS. My guess this was done so civilians could see EXODUS leaving Earth."

"Have you determined who planted the device?"

"No. My people are still interviewing the crew and passengers. I doubt we'll find the perpetrator among them. The device has a transmitter component to it. It could have been installed while the ship was docked and activated remotely from either Earth or

Luna."

Donalds handed the device back to Vespia. "Check our satellites to see if they picked up any unusual transmission heading to the STAR PRINCESS." The security chief nodded. "I also want every member of the EXODUS Project still on Earth found. Use whatever means necessary to get information from those you currently have in custody."

"Regarding that, we had an incident on Earth pursuing a shuttle assigned to the EXODUS Project. My people traced it to a civilian residence in the city of La Habra, California. Security entered the residence, which subsequently exploded. All our officers were killed."

"A trap?" Donalds wondered.

"It would appear so. The security shuttle's self-destruct was activated, and the project shuttle departed."

"Any idea of who did this?"

"No, but I looked up the address of the residence. It's owned by Cadet John Roberts."

The information caught the Admiral's curiosity. "Was anyone living in the home?"

"It doesn't appear so. Cadet Roberts's parents are deceased, and he has a sister who hasn't lived there for years. We're trying to track her down, but it appears she's living off the grid. There's no record of her anywhere on Earth, Luna, or Mars."

"I want that shuttle found." Donalds suspected that Admiral Johnson was the individual who had entrapped and killed the security detail. Since Cadet Roberts had been given command of EXODUS, it would only be fitting for him to offer his home to the admiral to hide from TERRA. "And I want to know how Johnson got the EXODUS off Earth without tipping off security, who should have known about this."

Vespia didn't like the tone of his statement. "Are you implying this is my fault?"

"You're in charge of security. If someone is going to take the fall for this, I can assure you it won't be me."

"I won't be the scapegoat for you, Jeremy. If you try to pin this on me, I'll make sure you go down too."

Her threats meant nothing to him. There were plenty of her subordinates willing to betray and kill her to take her place. Donalds was clever and had his own pawns in all the right positions in case a council member proved difficult. "Then, *Karla,* I'd suggest you get to the bottom of why this happened."

CHAPTER FOURTEEN

"What's the crew's status?" John asked Chief Sandoval as they walked down the corridor. The chief was armed to the hilt with guns and protective gear and made no attempt to conceal his armaments. His ensemble was a little over the top for John's taste. They'd defeated one Screen fighter and the chief appeared ready to take on the entire race.

"All non-essential personnel are either in their quarters or in one of the Central shops," the chief replied in his gruff tone. "Many still refuse to emerge from hiding. Hell, it was only one measly ship!"

John found Sandoval's statement amusing. Yes, it had just been one ship, but the chief was the one walking around like a one-man army.

"What's the next step?" asked Sandoval.

"We're heading toward Pluto. I want to try and make it to the outer rim before we encounter another Screen ship. Hopefully, TERRA has gone to tactical alert to prepare for a potential invasion."

"I don't think they'll need to worry about that," Sandoval said.

"Why do you say that?"

"The Screen would be at a tactical disadvantage to invade now. Doesn't matter how long they've been observing us. No Screen ship has ever engaged a capital ship in an actual fight. They've only taken out small fighters or commercial crafts. They'd be foolish to attempt a large-scale engagement against an enemy they've never fought on a large scale before."

"Even if the enemy is supposedly inferior?"

"Especially if you think the enemy is weaker."

"Point taken," John said as they arrived at the doors outside the medical bay. "I want you to keep your men on full security alert. All sensitive areas are to be guarded twenty-four hours a day."

"For how long?"

"Until we actually jump out of the system. We're not safe until we make that jump."

John hit the panel button to open the medical bay's entry doors. Even though no one on board had been hurt during the attack, medical personnel still raced around the bay, getting ready for potential future casualties. John saw the chief medical officer in the main surgical bay, where he and several of his nurses were attending to the rescued fighter pilot. As John approached the viewing window, the doctor caught a glimpse of him and finished up his treatment of the pilot. He tossed his surgical gloves in the waste bucket as he headed out to confer with the commander.

"How's he doing?" John asked.

"He'll make a full recovery," the doctor replied. "He suffered a few broken ribs, a fractured ankle, and some lacerations."

"Is he awake?"

"I just woke him up a few minutes ago. I haven't told him where he is, and he doesn't appear cognizant of what's happened."

"He deserves to know about his situation."

The doctor nodded. "Try to keep it brief."

"I'll try."

"I must say, Commander, you've performed quite well in our first encounter with the Screen," the doctor said in a congratulatory tone.

"How so?"

"Despite the reputation of the Screen, you maintained control of yourself and kept the ship on course."

"Thank you, Doctor. But I think you need to save your gratitude until after we weather a more formidable attack."

"I have no doubt you'll perform just as well again," Dr. Myers said before leaving John and heading to his office.

Given that the doctor had only met him a few days ago, John was a bit taken aback by his support. It was better than Julie's constant questioning of his abilities, but John didn't believe the doctor's confidence in him was well-placed just yet. He still needed to prove himself to the crew.

John turned and entered the surgical bay. He nodded to the nurses, who left to give him some privacy with the injured pilot.

Despite his injuries, the pilot seemed in good condition. Although his body was pumped full of pain medication, he was wide awake. John looked at his face. He was young, but appeared to be several years older than John.

"Where am I?" he asked, confused, as he spotted John approaching his bed.

"I'm Commander John Roberts." He intentionally avoided answering his question. "How are you feeling?"

The pilot seemed hesitant to answer, so John continued. "The doctor said you sustained some broken bones. You're not in pain, are you?"

The pilot shook his head. "Just a bit sore. Your doctor said I would recover."

John could only muster a weak smile. He imagined being in the pilot's position and how he would react once he learned he was on board the rebel ship.

The pilot looked around at his surroundings. "Am I on the AURORA? This doesn't look like the ship's medical bay and it doesn't look like the medical hospital in Crimson City."

John grabbed a nearby stool and sat down. He sighed heavily before answering. "You're on board the TXS EXODUS, the ship your fighter wing attacked."

The pilot's eyes widened. "You're the terrorists?"

"There are no terrorists on board this ship." John maintained a calm voice, despite the disdain he felt at being called such a derogatory term.

"You going to kill me?" the pilot asked.

John was offended by the question. "What? No! Your ship

clipped our shields and was damaged. You were drifting across the boundary, so we rescued you."

"What do you mean 'across'?" he asked in a panicked voice. "Where are we?"

"Heading to the outer solar system. We crossed the border some time ago."

The pilot tried to sit up but winced in pain. "You're going to get us killed. The Screen will destroy us."

John placed his hand on the pilot's shoulder and gently forced him to lie back down on the bed. He was getting sick of hearing the same old TERRA propaganda. "We already engaged and destroyed the Screen ship that appeared as soon as we crossed."

"I don't believe you. No one can defy the Screen."

"Well, we did, and right now we're passing by Jupiter. If you could walk to the window, you could see us passing the planet yourself."

"Impossible."

"Listen, I know it's difficult to believe what I'm telling you," John said, trying to reassure him. "But if I was in your position I would want to know the truth, no matter how crazy it sounded."

"I want you to return me to Mars."

"We can't do that. We're heading to the outer solar system and intend to jump out into deep space. If the AURORA had chosen to rescue you, then we wouldn't have been forced to bring you on board. I'm afraid you're stuck along for the ride."

"Am I a prisoner?"

"If you want to persist in believing I'm the enemy, then I can't stop you from thinking that. For now, you're a patient in the medical bay. Maybe you'll have a chance to see what we're trying to do here as you recover." John turned and headed out of the surgery ward. There was nothing more he could say that would convince the pilot of his intentions.

The pilot asked one last question. "Why are you doing this?"

John turned and looked at him, not quite sure what he was referring to.

"Why are you trying to take this ship out?" the pilot asked

again.

"Because we should have been out here a long time ago," John said. "Humanity's path shouldn't be dictated by aliens. I don't believe the Screen's a superior force, and we proved that by destroying one of their ships. You'll find that the people on board this vessel share the belief that we can be free."

"Even if it means getting killed?"

John smiled. "We just survived a Screen attack. I'm not really concerned about dying." He turned and left the pilot to his thoughts in the surgical bay. John hoped he wouldn't remain closed-minded. He would hate to have to transfer him to the brig and keep him confined there indefinitely.

CHAPTER FIFTEEN

"This way," David motioned to his friend.

The Blocks' home sat on a thirty-five-acre estate. The grounds included a lake and a small forest. Five bots maintained the grounds and kept it in pristine condition.

David enjoyed the freedom that the size of the estate gave him to escape his father and hide out on the grounds. His mother knew this; it was another reason why she'd refused to move to Mars. Unbeknownst to the rest of his family, David had taken one of the groundskeeper bots and reprogrammed it to dig an underground hideout.

Over the course of nine months, David had installed a range of equipment inside his new hideout. He was adept at communications and had full knowledge of all standard-issue TERRA communication devices. He collected whatever he could get his hands on, which was usually old TERRA equipment he got from the decommissioning junkyard on Mars.

Though Admiral Block wasn't enthused about his son's passion for communications—he wanted David to choose a career track that would lead to command of a capital ship—he nevertheless gave David some standard-issue communications equipment, such as DATs and low range transmitters. David modified these devices and integrated them into the communications hub he'd built in his hideout. He spent hours listening in on TERRA and private sector communications.

If anyone ever discovered what he was listening to, it would have meant serious trouble, so David learned to be covert in his eavesdropping. It was amazing what people were willing to say to one another over an open channel.

The hideout was the perfect spot to listen to John's message. David had installed inhibiting fields around it that blocked outside transmissions from getting through without verification from his computer. He was anxious to hear what John had to say and had to force himself not to run.

"Here we are," David said as they stopped in the middle of the woods.

Billy looked around at their dark surroundings, confused. "We're going to play the message out here?"

"No. In here." David pulled out a remote and clicked its single button.

Billy heard muffled whirling noises and looked down as a piece of the ground slid away. As the hidden door opened, a light brightened inside. Billy could see stairs leading down to an area below.

"Come on," David said as he trotted down the stairs, with Billy following right behind.

When he was halfway down, Billy heard the door slide back over the entrance. He reached the bottom of the stairs and found himself standing in a large underground room, with computer equipment lining the dirt walls and furniture dotted around the room.

"What is this place?" Billy asked in awe.

"It's something I built a while ago. I come here whenever Dad's really laying into me."

"Looks like a bunker," Billy commented as he looked around. "Where'd you get all this stuff?"

David sat on one of the available chairs. "Whenever I'm dragged to Mars, I always stop by the junk depot and see if I can pick up anything of value."

"I'll say. None of this stuff matches at all."

"Yeah, but I've been able to get it all working together. I've been able to listen in on TERRA communications for months."

That surprised Billy. David was skittish by nature, afraid of getting into trouble. To hear that he was covertly listening in on TERRA activities was out of character.

He plopped into the chair next to David. "Since when are you interested in being defiant?"

"Shut up."

"No, I mean it. This isn't like you, David. You're not one to rock the boat. Did John give you the idea?"

"No, but maybe I'm tired of being a wimp. I'm sick of sitting around doing nothing." He had a glimmer of ferocity in his eyes Billy had never seen before. "Maybe I'm sick of Dad telling me why TERRA's the only life for me. Maybe I want to expose some of the dirt on this organization. If you knew some of the things they've done, you'd be disgusted."

"Shit, David. I didn't mean to piss you off. Don't forget I'm on your side here."

"I know. It's you and John that got me thinking like this. You guys do what you want for yourselves. I want to be able to think for myself, too. Everyone at the Academy only wants to live and breathe TERRA's philosophy. They're just a bunch of robots."

"You already think for yourself. Hell, you've proved it by building this place."

"No, I haven't. I've been too scared of my dad to speak up for myself. I shouldn't have to be afraid. I should be able to tell him how I feel."

"I've seen your dad mad. I wouldn't want to deal with him pissed off."

David shrugged. "All I know is, I can't keep going on like this with him. Maybe I don't even want to be in TERRA."

"What?" Billy had never expected to hear this. "I thought you wanted to serve in the fleet."

"No, it's always been his idea. I never had a choice. All his kids must be TERRA officers. Being a Block means serving in the military."

"If you feel this way, I can understand why you wouldn't want to tell your dad. But why didn't you tell John or me?"

David lowered his head. "I didn't know how you'd react. You're my best friends and I didn't want to lose that."

"Hey, we are your best friends, no matter what. You should know by now that you can tell us anything. Look at John. God knows what trouble he's gotten into and he's looking to us for help. TERRA isn't what binds us as friends. You know what I mean?"

Slowly, David nodded. "I think so."

"You don't want to be TERRA? Fine. That's not going to change anything between us."

"I guess I've been so used to hiding how I felt."

Billy patted his friend on the shoulder. "Well, you don't have to feel that way. We like you the way you are, chickenshit and all."

"Thanks." David looked at the message cube Billy was holding. "I guess we should see what John has to say."

"John? Oh shit, that's right." He clicked on the cube and set it on the computer console. An image of John, dressed in a TERRA uniform, appeared.

"This is already weird," David said, seeing his friend in an officer's uniform.

"Billy, David...I hope you heeded my first message and are someplace private. As you may already know, an unidentified vessel lifted off from Earth a while ago. The ship's called EXODUS. Don't ask me, I didn't name it. It's an experimental vessel designed to explore deep space and, more importantly, fight the Screen.

"Both Julie and I have been recruited by Admiral Oliver Johnson to serve on the ship. I know you'll find this hard to believe, but I've been assigned as the ship's commander. Julie's my executive officer. Our mission is to head out of the solar system, find out who the Screen are and what their true intentions are toward humanity.

"Getting through TERRA's defenses won't be a problem. But this ship has never gone against the Screen. No one here is sure if we'll make it through. From what I've seen here, I think we have a good shot at succeeding. If we do make it, TERRA may try to cover up the truth to maintain the belief that the Screen is an unbeatable enemy. I don't want that to happen.

"I was thinking of sending back video and audio logs of our travels through space. I want to prove to people back home that we do belong out here. If the EXODUS is destroyed during the mission, I don't want her story to be lost. But someone needs to receive and distribute the information. You're the only two I can trust. I don't know exactly how to do it. I'm not familiar enough with EXODUS's communications system. But I thought you guys could think of something.

"I know it's a huge risk. You'd be putting your careers on the line and probably go to prison if you're caught. Whatever you decide to do, I'll support. You're my only friends and I don't want to put you in a bind. I hope to talk to you soon. God knows how we'll talk again, but I'll try to figure it out."

"Wow," Billy muttered as the holographic image of John dissipated. The idea of John commanding a starship was hard to swallow—not to mention everything else.

"What do you think?" David asked his friend.

"I think John's gotten into some real serious shit."

"If this is true, he's going to have all of TERRA on him. Is it really possible someone built a ship capable of fighting off the Screen?"

Billy shrugged. "I don't know. It's possible. I believe John when he says it. All I know is our best friend is asking for our help."

"Are you crazy? You know how much trouble we could get into?"

"A moment ago, you were talking about doing something meaningful," Billy said. "John's always said that if a couple people went against the status quo, real change could occur in TERRA. He's out there doing that, risking his own life. He's asking us to choose to make the same sacrifice."

"You'd be willing to throw away a lifetime of work to take this risk?"

"Sometimes the right thing to do is the most difficult thing to do. Maybe the risk is worth it if we can make some sort of difference." Billy picked up the message cube and clenched it. "I'm not surprised John is doing this. No matter what people say of him, you and I know that he's always followed through on what he believes. All he's asking is that people know the truth about what's happening out there. I'm willing to take that chance."

David had never expected to be caught up in something like this. His heart was beating a million times a minute. It was one thing to tell his dad he didn't want a TERRA career. It was another to aid a conspiracy to steal a classified TERRA ship.

But Billy was right. John was willing to put his life on the line for what he believed in. And Billy was willing to stand by his best friend. If John was here, he would tell David that this was the perfect way to get back at his father. He smiled, just thinking of it. The great Admiral Block, with a son branded a traitor by TERRA. A surge of excitement coursed through David's body at the thought.

"Aw hell. If we're going to do this we need to know where the ship's currently located, assuming the Screen hasn't blown it to bits across half the system."

Billy smiled. "You in then?"

"Well, it sure sounds like it. Man, we're going to catch hell for this."

Billy slapped David's back, almost knocking him out of the chair. "You're one of a kind, David. John would be proud." Billy looked at the monitors in front of them. "What do we do first?"

"Hack into the solar system sensor net and locate the ship," David replied as he powered up the monitors in front of him.

"You sound like you've done this before."

"It's not much different than listening in on the comm channels."

"I'll bet," Billy replied, looking at his friend in a different light. David had more balls than he let on.

David wasted no time accessing TERRA systems through security back doors. "Shoot, it looks like something may be going on out there."

"What do you mean?"

"The sensor net's down. TERRA used the emergency mandate to take control and shut it off. I can't get anything from it."

"We should assume EXODUS is still out there and figure out a way to communicate with them without TERRA being aware," Billy said. "John wouldn't have gone on this ship if he didn't think it had a chance of beating the Screen."

"I'm going to need to give you a crash course on spying on TERRA communications," David said as he motioned his friend to the seat next to him. "I can't do this by myself."

Billy smiled. "Sounds like fun. Let's do it. We got a friend out there waiting to hear from us."

——— ——— ———

On the other side of Earth, President Butu entered her office. Sitting on the dark brown leather couch in the middle of the room, she took some deep breaths to relax herself. It was a method her mother had taught her when she was growing up, and she found it very comforting during trying times.

It had been one of the busiest days of her three years in office. She'd received reports of panic reaching unprecedented levels on Earth, and she wanted to calm everyone's fears about the Screen before paranoia ran rampant and extended to the two colonies. She held a brief press conference, in which she only said that the ship was an experimental Earth vessel, had launched for unknown reasons, and TERRA had not established communications with it. She had hoped to receive more detailed information from the command council before the conference, but they'd never contacted her office again after their initial discussions.

Like the general population, the president held TERRA in high regard, but she was becoming increasingly frustrated with the organization. She had received reports from various government agencies about the unfolding EXODUS situation, but TERRA remained silent. They seemed to be holding out on her.

The command council's lack of communication convinced the president there was more going on than what was initially reported to her. But what could prompt them to keep the civilian government out of the loop? Donalds had mentioned the ship was an experiment. What was its purpose? What was the need to build such a large vessel in secret?

A knock on the door broke the president's train of thought. "Come in," she said as she sat up. She tried to take advantage of those rare moments of peace and quiet that came her way, but whenever the office door knocked, she knew she had to put on her political game face.

"Madam President," her chief of staff said as he entered the office. "Your speech seems to have calmed the public's nerves."

"Despite not having much information to rely on," she said ruefully. "It's good to hear their fears have been allayed for now. What do you have for me?"

Charles handed her a large file. "That's everything I was able to get my hands on. TERRA hasn't communicated with any of our constituents or agencies regarding EXODUS. Information from them is in short supply."

"I've made personal requests repeatedly to speak with the council, but they're ignoring me."

Charles continued his brief. "Despite their silence, there's been a lot of activity going on in TERRA. They've sent security detachments all over Earth, and our people confirmed that they have detained several individuals." Charles opened the file in the president's hands. The first page was a list of names. "The individuals they've taken into custody all worked on this EXODUS Project."

Butu looked at the names and the occupational descriptions. They were either scientists or military personnel.

"We haven't been able to ascertain the exact reason why they're being held," Charles said, anticipating the president would ask that question.

"What about the launch site?"

"We've confirmed the ship was launched from the Tormented Valley in the Canadian province. TERRA has cordoned off the area, which further confirms that's where the launch site is located. I had our interior minister try to get to the site and even he was turned away."

Butu got up and paced the office, looking over the files.

"TERRA's determined to keep this quiet if they're willing to go as far as refusing one of my cabinet members entry to the site. It seems to me that this launch of this ship took place without the knowledge or consent of the command council."

"What makes you believe that? My understanding of the council is that they have complete knowledge of what's occurring within their organization. They would have known about the ship."

"Maybe they knew the ship was built, but not that it was being launched. If they knew it was launching, they wouldn't be tracking down these project members and sealing off the launch site. They're trying to get information about what happened quickly while keeping outsiders at arm's length."

Charles didn't question her assumptions. Over the years, he'd told her that he thought she had a keen sense of people's motives that had served her well in her political career. He believed it was what had gotten her elected to office.

"Admiral Oliver Johnson has disappeared," Charles said. "He was the head of the project. We don't know if he's on the ship, but our sources say TERRA believes he's still on the planet."

That caught the president's interest. Why would the head of the EXODUS Project not be on board the ship? There must be a compelling reason why the admiral remained behind, if that was truly the case. "Then we need to find Admiral Johnson before TERRA does."

"We may have a lead on that," said Charles. "There was an incident in California where a house exploded. Our sources say that a large detachment of TERRA security was in the house when it detonated. Witnesses report a TERRA shuttle leaving the scene shortly afterwards."

"Do we have any idea who's on the shuttle?" Butu asked.

Charles shook his head. "No, but there's a connection to the house. It belonged to John Roberts. He's one of the cadets on the ship."

When the president had first heard about two cadets being taken to a classified facility, she did not dwell too much on their involvement. They were just cadets and could provide only a limited role on a spaceship. But this new piece of information piqued her interest. "What do we know about the cadets who were taken to EXODUS?"

"I managed to get a copy of their Academy records through back channels. The superintendent's unaware we have it. Julie Olson's file is typically remarkable for a TERRA cadet. She has excellent grades and is highly regarded by both students and professors. John Roberts's file is a bit more colorful."

The president flipped through John's file and began reading it. "I see what you mean," she remarked as she read the file. She smiled as she read some of the pranks John had been caught perpetrating. The description of his defiant attitude at the Academy read like a good novel. "I can see why they chose to put him in the reserves. He's not an exemplary individual."

"Despite all the animosity he's generated amongst the student body and faculty, the consensus is he's one of the most intelligent individuals to attend the Academy. Oh, and there's one more thing. The cadets were roommates."

"Are there any indications Admiral Johnson knew them?"

"None. We couldn't find any point in their pasts where they would have crossed paths. Olson's father is a farmer in the United States territory of Lexington, Nebraska with no ties to TERRA. Roberts's parents died when he was four. He has an older sister, but she disappeared several years ago."

Butu put the file down and sat at her desk. "It's good information, but we still don't know why the ship was launched or its purpose. Once we know that, we'll have a better understanding of why these people are involved. If Admiral Johnson is still on the planet, we need to find him before TERRA does. Have ES do a thorough but discreet search for him. Let them know that under no circumstance should TERRA know about our search."

ES, or Earth Security, was a separate military entity from TERRA. The organization's main purpose was to provide planetary security for Earth and support regional police forces. "Are our people tracking the shuttle that left the cadet's house?"

"Yes."

"Have them bring in whoever was on board. They may have knowledge of the admiral's whereabouts and may be able to give us some more information about the EXODUS Project."

"Should I have Janice stop making meeting requests with the command council?"

"No, that will draw suspicion. They'll expect me to continue demanding a meeting. Have her keep making the request."

Charles's DAT buzzed on his belt and he activated his wireless earpiece. He put his hand up for a moment to listen to the message coming in. "We need to put on the news."

"ELM channel on," Butu said. A large wall monitor flickered to life and an image of the newscaster appeared.

"Reports have been circulating for hours about a large ship that rose from Earth and headed into space. After numerous eyewitness accounts from people on transport ships and Mars, we have obtained official word from TERRA about the existence of this ship. TERRA has just released a statement about the vessel. According to them, the ship is an experimental vessel called EXODUS that was hijacked by extremists from Earth. Their goal was to take it beyond Mars and initiate a hostile encounter with the Screen.

"TERRA attempted to halt the vessel but was unable to slow its advance without destroying it. The vessel crossed the border and was destroyed by a Screen ship. We have attempted to verify these events; however, the sensor grid that monitors the solar system was damaged when the Screen fired on the EXODUS. We will bring you more information as the day progresses."

"Screen off." Butu turned to her chief of staff. "Confirm that what TERRA is saying is true. This is too convenient and plays into TERRA's hands. I suspect this may be a cover story; otherwise, we would have heard from the command council by now."

"You don't think the ship could have possibly survived an attack by the Screen?"

"It's highly unlikely, but I'm not convinced of anything at this point. The council has already lied to us and we need to verify their statements. See if the Science Bureau has any information about this ship being destroyed. I'm assuming they were monitoring the ship's progress."

"Unless TERRA has taken complete control of the sensor grid. They do have the authority to take control of it and restrict access at any time."

"Then we'll need to go to the public. There has to be an amateur astronomer or star watcher who has equipment that was tracking the ship."

"I'll have our people start looking," Charles said as he headed out of the office.

"One more thing, Charles. We need to hurry on this. I want to have as much information at my disposal as possible before I speak to Admiral Donalds again."

CHAPTER SIXTEEN

On the command deck, John walked down into the pit and joined Julie and Bret at the communications station. Julie had called John while he was down in engineering, going over last-minute details of the hyper-drive system.

John also wanted to meet the infamous Professor Donavin. From what he'd heard from the crew, the professor was a quirky individual, and John discovered they weren't exaggerating. After spending a lengthy time hearing how the military was infringing on engineering operations, John was able to escape the professor when Julie called him to the command deck. She didn't say why he was needed, but her tone of voice clearly indicated it was urgent.

"Commander," Julie said as John approached them. "We've got something."

"What's up?"

"Private Michaels picked up a transmission from ELM regarding us."

"I was able to capture the broadcast over the system-wide sensor network before they shut it down," Bret said.

"They closed down the sensor grid?" John wasn't too surprised. It was the easiest way to keep people in the dark.

Julie nodded. "Apparently they don't want the public to know what's really going on with us. Play the transmission," she instructed Bret.

Bret punched up the transmission he and Julie had just listened to. John's blood boiled as he listened to the news broadcast. TERRA had failed in stopping EXODUS, so now they were going to erase their existence. Just tell everyone that EXODUS had been blown away, and no one would question the almighty TERRA.

"I thought the Science Bureau ran the sensor grid," Bret said.

John nodded. "They do, but TERRA can take it over at any time and shut the bureau and anyone else out. I'm sure when they realized they couldn't stop us from leaving, they instituted that mandate. Tell the people we've been destroyed, and no one would question it."

TERRA's actions were despicable, and they had moved to protect their interests. But John didn't want EXODUS's success to go unnoticed. "Is there a way we could send covert signals to Earth without using the grid?"

Bret thought about it for a moment. "Theoretically, we could send a signal through space disguised as normal background radiation. But the signal would disintegrate the farther it traveled. The contents may be too degraded to recognize by the time it reaches one of the planets. It'd be a tough thing to pull off."

"Work with some of the scientists on board," John said. "See if there's a way to boost the integrity of a signal without increasing the chance of detection."

"Yes sir," Bret said as he got to work on it. John headed over to his command chair.

"Can I speak with you in private for a moment?" Julie said, following behind him. John suspected this was going to be another argument. Reluctantly, he nodded and motioned her toward the office.

"What is it?" John asked in a frustrated tone as they entered the office. Time was limited, and John felt that he had more important things to do than straighten Julie out and put her in her place yet again.

"I don't think now's the time to spend our energy trying to send messages back to Earth. We need to focus our efforts on preparing for another Screen encounter. I would have thought you'd know better, since you're the one so concerned about another attack."

"I am, but we still need to let people know that we're out here."

"Why? They're not going to come running to our aid if we get into trouble. We're on our own. Even if they knew we were alive, they're not going to provide us with any kind of support."

"If we can show that we survived out here, maybe it'll start changing people's ideas that humanity is helpless against the Screen," John said as he sat down behind his desk and knotted his hands behind his head.

"I can appreciate you wanting to spread your ideals to other people. Believe it or not, I share them. But this isn't the time. You've got a ship to command and we need to concentrate on getting past Pluto to jump out of the system."

"We will, but our story needs to be told back home."

Julie was getting fed up with John's stubbornness. She told herself that she had to act as a good executive officer and not fly off the handle. She wasn't going to let John fuel her emotions. "Even if you send a hidden transmission, who back home is even going to look for it?"

John cleared his throat. "Before we left Earth, I sent a message to Billy telling him about our mission and requesting he and David keep an eye out for any transmissions we send."

Julie couldn't believe what she'd just heard. It was like something that would come out of the mouth of a first-year cadet. "What the hell are you thinking, involving them in this?"

"Hey, I'm trying to think ahead here..." John started to explain, but Julie cut him off. She couldn't contain herself any longer. He had finally driven her to the breaking point.

"Damn it, John! You're the commander of this ship. There are 5,000 people here you're responsible for keeping safe. You need to stop putting your wishes above the needs of this ship and crew. You had no right to involve Billy and David in this. You're going to ruin their lives."

"I'm not..." he tried to explain, but he couldn't get a word in edgewise.

"Like hell you're not! You want the respect of being a captain, then start acting like one. These are people's lives you're playing with, and you can't treat them with such a cavalier attitude. What you do affects us, and you need to grow up and start thinking of others instead of yourself. And you can start by not disagreeing with me at every turn."

"Oh, so now I have to go along with all your suggestions? Is that it? I don't respect you?" John threw up his hands and turned his chair around to look out the window.

"We're not cadets back home, debating some school paper. You could have the same viewpoint as I do, and you would still argue just for the sheer pleasure of it. John Roberts has to show how superior he is to everyone. I'm sick of it and sick of you! You're nothing but a spoiled brat! Mortino was right putting you in the reserves. You don't deserve to be an officer."

Julie's words hit John like an ice pick through his heart. He wanted to wrap his hands around her throat and squeeze as tight as possible to silence her. How dare she make such a statement. But he didn't want to give her the satisfaction of knowing that her words had affected him. He just continued to look out the window.

Julie took a few seconds to calm down. She didn't want her emotions to get the better of her again. If she was going to tell John to rise above his deficiencies, she was going to have to rise above her own. But damn it if it wasn't hard for her. She couldn't go on putting up with his behavior.

"Look, we need to start working together if we're going to succeed. We're never going to be friends, but that shouldn't stop us from running an effective command. I'm willing to work with you, but you have to meet me halfway. You have to stop making these rash decisions. You need to think how it's going to affect the rest of us. Millions of people's lives could be on the line."

Damn it. She was right. John did not want to admit it, but for the first time, Julie was right and he was completely wrong. It was an epiphany John did not welcome.

Julie could see John had shut himself off from her. The conversation wasn't going to go much further. For all she knew, he hadn't listened to a word she said. If that was the case, it was a shame. If John was unwilling to accept criticism, then he had already failed as a ship commander.

"We only have a few hours before we reach Pluto," she said. "I'll have a check done on all systems." John didn't reply, and for a long moment there was nothing but silence.

"Have the fighters loaded up in their launch bays and ready to go," John finally said. "We don't want to be caught off guard when we reach Pluto."

Julie nodded, but John wasn't looking at her. She thought about how only a few hours ago, they were worried that they wouldn't survive a Screen attack. They had achieved the impossible, but it had done nothing to eliminate the underlying problems between the two of them.

Admiral Johnson had said that John was vital to the success of this mission. What if he was wrong? What if John was a bigger threat than the Screen? The situation was complicated, and Julie wasn't optimistic that they could get past their differences.

CHAPTER SEVENTEEN

The shuttle flew dangerously close to the ground, dodging rocks, trees, and the occasional hill that littered the landscape. No human could fly a vessel so close to the ground and avoid these obstacles. Luckily for Admiral Johnson, X was in the pilot seat flying the craft.

It had been an interesting journey for the house bot. With increasing frequency, the admiral was uttering phrases that made no sense to the bot. X referenced numerous encyclopedia entries in an attempt to understand his statements and properly converse with him, but the bot could not reliably determine what the admiral's phrases were alluding to. Occasionally, the admiral did utter phrases that X could comprehend, such as, "Are they following us?" or "Hold this knife while I rip out the interface unit" and "I'm not driving anymore, I'm tired."

The admiral had flown the shuttle off the coast of California and away from the North American continent. However, he then changed course and headed eastward toward Mexico, only to change direction again and head south toward South America. When X took control of the shuttle, it repeatedly requested a destination from the admiral. But in response he would only mutter about heaven or fiery brimstone and X could not locate either destination on any of its geographic files for Earth, Luna, or Mars. The bot concluded that these locations must have been recently constructed and not part of its outdated geography software. X made an addendum in its memory bank to download the latest map software at the earliest opportunity.

With no viable direction from the admiral, X flew the shuttle across the ocean to the continent of Africa. Logically, the bot should have returned to its home base, the Roberts residence. But X concluded that returning home was not a viable option. Flying to the other side of the world was in the best interest of protecting the admiral. As X flew the shuttle, it analyzed its mode of logistical thinking, attempting to determine what errors it contained that was causing it to make such erratic decisions.

"It's almost bouncing me," the admiral muttered from behind X. Again, the bot tried to interpret his statements but couldn't come up with anything. Was the admiral talking about a ball? There wasn't one in the cabin. Perhaps there was an underlying medical condition prompting the admiral to make such strange statements. The explosion at the house had initiated a shockwave in the sound spectrum that could have damaged the admiral. Unfortunately, the bot wasn't equipped with medical sensor equipment to conduct deep-level scans.

X slowed the shuttle to a stop and landed it in the middle of the Serengeti. As it turned to walk toward the admiral at the back of the shuttle, one of its legs stepped on his coat. X sensed the cracking of a plastic bottle and immediately went to investigate. It pulled a red bottle out and scanned the label.

"Supraxium," stated X. According to its databank, supraxium was a medicine that treated the most severe cases of dementia. If the admiral was taking it, then it was logical to conclude that he was suffering from dementia. Such a condition would explain his erratic statements.

X evaluated how it would approach the admiral with this new information. The bottle the bot found was empty of any pills. It searched the other jacket pockets and uncovered several more pill bottles. They were also empty.

"Admiral Johnson, your behavior is consistent with an individual suffering from neurological dysfunction. It is necessary to take you to the nearest medical facility so that you may be treated."

"No!" the admiral screamed. "You can't! They'll get me. The devil's everywhere. You can't stop. We must continue. Heaven is too close..."

X placed its claw on the admiral's shoulder to quiet and comfort him. It was a motion X had performed countless times when Nicole was upset, usually after breaking up with her latest boyfriend. The bot could not analyze how such an action could bring so much relief to an individual. The tactile sensation was barely perceptible to the human nervous system. X had dwelled on this unique phenomenon for hours but could not come up with a logical explanation. But since this method always produced a positive effect, the bot continued to use it in its interactions with humans.

As soon as X touched the admiral, he quit his rambling and looked at the bot. He was scared. He tried to focus on the bot, but the voices in his head were too loud. There was no escape from them.

"You won't let them hurt me, will you?" he asked in a desperate tone.

"This unit will ensure no harm will befall you," the bot promised.

The admiral's eyes darted wildly. His hands fumbled as he took in his surroundings. Feeling his gun right behind him, he grabbed it and handed it to X, making sure the bot had a firm grip on the gun.

"You can use this. You can protect me by eliminating our enemies."

X examined the gun for a moment and verified that it was indeed a weapon. The bot had never held a weapon before, and it wanted to process as much information as possible before initiating its next action.

"Admiral, it is against my programming to harm a human being."

"But they're going to kill me!"

"As this unit has stated previously, you are suffering defects in your neurological process. That is most likely causing you to believe that you will be killed by a devil. Treatment at an appropriate medical facility..." X stopped its statement in mid-sentence. Its sensors alerted it to a shuttle landing nearby. Since the admiral had destroyed the interface unit, the bot could not link up with the shuttle's sensors and get a detailed scan of what was unfolding outside. It instead had to rely on its own meager sensors to garner any readings.

"This unit is detecting a shuttle containing multiple human life signs."

The admiral began to panic. "The devil has found me!"

"Silence."

"You need to kill them!"

"Negative." X's sensors picked up the humans exiting their shuttle and swarming around X and Johnson's shuttle. The bot moved to the front and activated the blast shields so that they could not peer into the cabin. It seemed odd to X that it was conducting such actions. Logically, the humans would gain entry into the shuttle and declare their intentions. That would provide much-needed information to X and the admiral. Yet for some reason the bot chose to hide itself and the admiral for as long as possible.

Loud blasts could be heard from outside. The humans who surrounded their shuttlecraft were yelling and screaming. X recalibrated its sensors to determine what had occurred but couldn't pick up anything. Whatever was causing the blasts was interfering with the bot's ability to monitor outside events.

Unable to discern whether the screams were real or in his head, the admiral began crying out. He wanted it all to stop. He craved silence. X detected the agony in his voice and crawled right next to the admiral as it threw the gun to the front of the shuttle. It extended its arms around him in a cradle and rocked the admiral, trying to provide him some comfort. When John was a baby and had nightmares, it had comforted him when X did this. It was the only thing the bot could think of to calm the admiral.

Soon the blasts stopped. However, X's sensors were still scrambled. After a long moment of silence, there was a large thump from outside the shuttle's side door. The bot's upper sphere rotated so its ocular sensors stared straight at the door as a few more thumps sounded.

"Please don't let them kill me," the admiral whimpered.

"This unit will permit no harm to you," replied X.

A few more thumps and then the door opened. The bot saw a gun muzzle pass across the open door.

"Please do not inflict damage on us," X announced. "We are not armed."

The man holding the gun emerged at the entrance. He was dressed in black with guns hanging from his belts. He looked ready to go into a heated battle. He wore dark sunglasses so X could not see his eyes. The man looked at X, then at the admiral.

"He's here," the man called out. He moved toward the admiral, but X blocked his way. Three more individuals came up behind the man.

"This unit has given the admiral its word that no harm would come to him," X stated.

The man seemed taken aback by the bot's behavior. He had never seen a bot act in such a manner. "We're agents with the president's office. We've been ordered to find and bring you in for safekeeping. TERRA has their people all over the planet trying to locate you."

"Lies," the admiral hissed.

X rotated its upper body and could see the admiral in desperate need of help. The bot contemplated what course of action to take. None of its programming offered any assistance in analyzing the situation. It had never been placed in such a predicament. John had told X to do whatever the admiral requested. It was obvious to the bot that the admiral was in no condition to make requests. But could X trust these people? The bot determined it could. After all, none of them had harmed it or the admiral.

The bot handed the man the prescription bottle. "This unit located this medication in the admiral's jacket. He appears to be suffering from significant neurological impairment. It is imperative that he is attended to by a physician."

As the man took the bottle hesitantly from the bot, X turned and took the admiral's hand. "These people are here to help you. It may be difficult; however, you must try to dispel any notion that they will harm you. This unit will stay by your side and ensure you are treated properly."

The four agents couldn't believe how compassionate the bot was acting. It was unheard of for a bot to show any sort of emotional display. They were designed to perform numerous tasks to improve the lives of people. They weren't programmed to act like humans. It was considered a waste of resources to add such programming to them.

X helped the admiral to his feet. "This unit will assist you in transporting Admiral Johnson."

"We've got a shuttle right outside," the agent said. "We're to bring you directly to Sydney." He motioned for the others to clear a path and let the bot and admiral through. They all watched as X patiently helped the admiral out of the shuttle. Although none of them could hear clearly, each thought they could pick up the bot calmly whispering to the admiral as if it were trying to ease his pain.

——— ——— ———

In Virginia, David and Billy worked feverishly on the communications equipment in David's hideout. They had been at it for hours, as David instructed Billy on the fine art of electronic spying. Communications was one of his strong suits at the Academy, and he easily picked up on David's methods.

"Try to route the frequency through the secondary buffer," David instructed as Billy worked the makeshift communications terminal.

"You know," Billy said as he worked the system, "even if we figure out a way of sending a message without alerting the fleet, it'll be difficult for John's ship to detect it. They won't know what to look for."

David was optimistic. "If John wants to communicate with us, he'll find a way." He looked over at Billy's progress. "No, no. You'll lose the signal if you do it like that. Tighten up the gap on the bandwidth."

As Billy followed his friend's instructions, a loud beep went off. Billy put his hands up, thinking he'd done something wrong.

"What'd I do?"

"It's not you." David pulled his DAT out. "Someone's calling me." He looked at the ID signal. "Shit, it's Dad. Turn off the equipment."

As Billy complied, shutting everything down, David fumbled with his DAT and almost dropped it before answering. He hadn't expected his father to be calling now. He figured he'd be busy dealing with the EXODUS situation.

"Dad," David said, trying not to sound guilty.

"Where are you?"

David quickly picked up that his father was in a bad mood. Whenever he came out with a question so forcefully at the start of a conversation, it meant he was ready to go into a tirade. Any little thing would set him off.

"Uh, I'm out at the barn house."

"I'm at the house. Get up here now. Bring Billy with you." Admiral Block shut his DAT off before giving David a chance to respond.

"He sounds pissed. What the hell does he want with me?" Billy wondered.

David looked at his friend nervously. Billy could see he was starting to become stressed out. "Relax, you haven't done anything. He's probably just had a bad day."

But Billy didn't believe his own statement. The admiral must be upset about EXODUS. He couldn't help but worry that perhaps the admiral was already suspicious about what they were up to.

It took only a few minutes for the cadets to get back to the house, mainly because David ran the entire way. Billy tried to get him to slow down, but David wasn't listening to him. All his earlier talk of bravado had gone out the window. He just hoped that David wouldn't completely crack under Admiral Block's interrogation.

The cadets entered the house and looked around for the admiral. He was waiting in the living room and spotted them first.

"In here," he yelled.

David almost lost his footing as he rushed into the living room. Trying to maintain his composure, Billy followed at a slow, deliberate pace.

"Dad? What are you doing home?"

"I want to talk to you about John Roberts. Have you been associating with him?"

"John? Uh, no. I haven't talked to him since you told me not to." That was lie number one.

The admiral got up real close to David. "Don't lie to me. I can find out if you've been lying to me."

Billy couldn't believe how agitated the admiral was. He knew he had to deflect attention away from his friend. "David hasn't talked to John in two years. If you want to know about John, ask me."

"You're still friends with him?"

"Well, yeah. I know you don't think much of John, but he's always been a friend to me."

The admiral moved to face Billy. "Do you know where he's gone for winter break?"

"He's always stayed with a friend in Arizona. That's all he's told me."

"Has he ever talked about Admiral Johnson? Has he ever mentioned meeting him?"

Billy shook his head. "No, never. Why are you so interested in him?"

"Your so-called friend has gotten himself mixed up in a lot of trouble. If you two know anything about him, you better tell me. Has he ever talked about trying to leave the solar system?"

"We don't know anything," David insisted. Admiral Block looked at his son, then to Billy. "Why are you badgering us?"

The admiral ignored his son. "You're a good boy, Billy," the admiral started. His entire demeanor changed, which Billy found creepy. "You've been like a son to me. I hope you know you can always come to me to talk about anything."

"Thank you, sir. And you've been like a father to me." Billy could lay it on just as thick as the admiral. Two could play the same game of bullshit. He knew the admiral was only trying to pump them for information. "I wish I could tell you what you would like to know about John. Even with his friends, John doesn't say much."

"What about Julie Olson? Can you tell me anything about her?"

"Only that she's a dedicated student at the Academy. We've hung out a few times together at NEON."

"And her relationship with John?"

"Oh no, there's no relationship. They hate each other. I think she even tried to move to a new apartment. They can't stand each other."

The admiral was aware of that situation, as it was documented in Julie's file. He wanted to see if Billy would say anything to contradict that information. It seemed he was telling the truth about what he knew of both individuals.

"I want you boys to do me a favor. Do not discuss either cadet with anyone. If you come across anything regarding them, you must come to me. I can't stress that enough."

"Of course, sir," Billy replied, knowing full well he had no intention of keeping that promise.

"Are you staying here for the night?" David asked as he tried to remain calm. He hoped his father was heading back to Mars and wouldn't return home for a while.

"Just for the night. I have to take care of some business before leaving. I'll be gone early tomorrow. I'm afraid I won't be spending any time here while you two are on winter break."

David couldn't have been more pleased to hear that, and Billy wanted to clap his hands to celebrate. He didn't want to be working on trying to communicate with EXODUS with the admiral around.

"When your mother gets in, let her know I'm home. I'll be in the study," the admiral instructed David, who only nodded.

As soon as he exited the room, the cadets huddled together and whispered to each other.

"Let's get back to the hideout and continue working," David said, wanting to escape being under the same roof as his father. He didn't want to risk another confrontation.

"Are you kidding? I'm not going back there with your dad around. Let's just sit tight tonight. As soon as he leaves, we'll get back to work. We just have to act normal until he goes."

Although he didn't relish remaining in the house, David knew his friend was right. They couldn't risk being found out. "I think I can do that."

"You didn't stand up to him, so I think you acted completely normal," Billy said.

CHAPTER EIGHTEEN

The planet Pluto grew more prominent through the windows of the EXODUS as the vessel approached it. The ship began to slow its advance. Officers were at their battle stations, ready with charged weapons, shields, and fighters on standby.

The last few hours had seemed to stretch into an eternity. With the Screen fighter defeated near Mars, many assumed EXODUS would quickly make its way out of the system. Instead, they had received orders from the ship commander to maintain battle alert status. John did not share any information with the crew to ease their apprehension. Nothing had been said about jumping out of the system.

John himself was on pins and needles. He hadn't felt right after defeating the lone alien adversary. His instincts were telling him that a more serious confrontation was awaiting them. He could not fathom that the Screen would allow the EXODUS to leave without engaging the ship with more serious firepower. He was determined not to have a repeat of what had happened to the HORIZON nearly seventy years ago.

Tension on the ship was at an all-time high. Although EXODUS had defied all expectations by just getting to the outer solar system, John's order to have the ship on high alert had placed the crew on edge. Many of them still could not comprehend that there was a real possibility they could make a jump out into deep space.

"We're approaching Pluto," Lieutenant Jacobson reported.

John brought the sensor images up on his command monitor to get a sense of where EXODUS was in relation to the planet.

"Scan the planet for any unusual energy and matter readings," John ordered. Even with the sophisticated system sensor net, accurate scans of Pluto had always been elusive. The theory was that the Screen had some sort of satellite out here that jammed scanning frequencies, but TERRA had never been able to confirm it. John worried that the Screen had set up a small command post on the planet to monitor human activities. If they had, he had every intention of taking it out. He wasn't about to leave any Screen facility intact before EXODUS took off.

"No unusual readings coming from the planet," Alex'sis reported. She remained calm and stoic, and showed no signs of being under pressure. "I'm picking up some metallic debris in high orbit around the planet. Readings are consistent with the hull composition of the HORIZON."

John accessed the ship's sensors and looked at the visual images of what was left of the HORIZON. He could see black scarring on some of the bigger pieces of the hull. He could only imagine the horror the HORIZON crew must have felt when the Screen attacked them. With no weapons or defenses of any kind, the ship was nothing more than a flying target. The Screen must have known the HORIZON was no threat to them, yet they chose to destroy it. It was a cowardly move. Well, they were going to learn the hard way that EXODUS could defend itself.

Julie stepped off the elevator onto the command deck. Since their blowout, she had chosen to give John his space. She visited many of the departments on the ship to go over battle preparations. During her time away, she'd mulled over the idea of replacing John as ship commander.

Julie had always known him to be stubborn. She increasingly felt he would not be able to demonstrate the flexibility required of a ship commander. She began to rehearse the argument for why replacing him was in the best interest of the ship. But it didn't make her feel better. Regardless of what John was to her, she was contemplating stabbing him in the back. Julie was not the type of woman who could do such a thing, even to someone she didn't like.

Julie made her way around the upper perimeter toward John in his command chair. "All departments report ready for jump. Engine controls have been transferred to the command deck. We can move into the prearranged coordinates Lieutenant Jacobson has set up for us whenever you're ready."

John merely nodded. He was still fuming over their argument. He realized everything Julie had said about him was correct. Whatever problems existed between them had to be left behind on Earth. This mission was far more important than their years of bickering. If they were to succeed, they would need to work as one. But John was upset that he couldn't see the changes he needed to make within himself. He prided himself on being insightful about other people. So why couldn't he be insightful about himself?

EXODUS turned away from the planet and began to head out of the system. The crew continued working to make sure the ship was prepared for its first interstellar jump. On the command deck, Kevin checked the navigation calculations he'd made so many years ago. This was his last chance to ensure his numbers were accurate. The ship's computer had all navigational information pre-programmed and the jump itself would yield new data on how it would affect EXODUS and the crew.

"Navigation is ready to go," an anxious Kevin announced. "We can jump once we've reached position in five minutes."

"Bring the engine to full power," John ordered. Julie inputted the command code and transferred power to the main engine, bringing it to full strength.

Satisfied that the ship's jump preparations were going smoothly, John got on the ship's internal communications.

"All hands, this is the commander. Prepare for jump in four minutes, twelve seconds." John couldn't help but feel this moment was more critical than the ship's encounter with the Screen fighter. It would be the first time since the HORIZON that a human-operated ship had attempted to jump out of the solar system.

The proximity alert blared without warning. At the operations table, both Julie and Alex'sis checked what had triggered it. John gripped the arms of his command chair tightly. He'd known leaving the system would not go unchallenged.

Alex'sis was more familiar with the ship's controls than Julie and accessed the information first. "Commander, I'm reading multiple energy signatures four hundred thousand kilometers from the ship. The signatures conform to the Screen."

Multiple energy signatures. Not just one. Damn it! John had known in his gut this was going to happen. Somehow the Screen must have been monitoring their movements. Either that, or the ship they destroyed had managed to send off a distress signal. It was convenient for them to show up just as EXODUS was preparing to jump. He knew this would be the Screen's last attempt at stopping them.

"How many ships?" John asked.

"Twenty-three," Alex'sis replied. "Twenty-one conform to the same Screen type fighter that we've seen before. But two signatures are displaying a significantly higher energy output."

"Larger ships we've never seen before," Julie said in a worried tone. Only a bigger ship would produce a higher reading.

Twenty-one fighters didn't bother John. EXODUS could take them. But two large ships never seen before? It was not a good situation for them to be in. What if the larger ships had more advanced Screen technology?

Maybe they could escape and avoid an engagement. "Can we jump before they reach us?" John asked.

"It's possible," Kevin replied as he checked the sensor data. "I could shave a minute or two off the jump cycle."

Julie wasn't keen on trying to escape. "If we jump now, they may continue toward Mars, or even Earth."

The thought sent a chill up the spines of most of the command deck staff. Many hadn't considered that the Screen could just continue to the inner solar system and initiate an attack on one of their worlds.

The admiral had made it clear that getting EXODUS out of the solar system was their highest priority. Deep space exploration was within John's grasp, but he couldn't abandon his home to the wrath of the Screen. It was something a captain, a good captain, wouldn't do.

"Power down the jump drive," he ordered. "Divert power to shields and weapons. Lieutenant Brandus, tell our fighters to deploy and establish a perimeter around the front of EXODUS. By the time we're done here, there won't be a Screen ship remaining to threaten our planets."

"All right people, let's move it!" Alex'sis yelled to the command deck staff.

Everyone snapped into action. Julie looked up at John and smiled. John looked at her briefly, nodded, and gave her a quick thumbs-up. She nodded in return and got back to work. Now that was what being a ship commander was all about.

The fighter bays opened outside EXODUS. Fighters shot out like bullets and formed into multiple fighter groups in front of the ship. Each fighter had its weapons armed and at the ready, making no effort to disguise their battle readiness from the incoming Screen fleet.

In the medical bay, the recovering fighter pilot noticed the doctors and nurses running around grabbing supplies and equipment. Their frantic pace unnerved the pilot, and he tried to get someone's attention to find out what was going on. No one listened to him. They were too caught up in readying themselves for the expected casualties that would result from this battle.

The pilot got a glimpse of Dr. Myers out of the corner of his eye and yelled out to him. "Hey, doc! What's going on?"

"We're about to go into battle," the doctor replied as he continued to check his medical equipment.

"The Mars defense fleet?" The pilot was hopeful with the thought of TERRA rescuing him.

"No, the Screen. The ship's going to engage their fleet."

The pilot was dumbfounded. Humans engaging a Screen fleet? Had this John Roberts been serious about what he'd said to the pilot earlier? He'd dismissed John's story as some sort of trickery, but maybe the commander had been telling the truth. The pilot had never thought anyone would be crazy enough to try and make a run out of the system. It appeared this crew was bound and determined to succeed—or die trying.

Back on the command deck, officers were at their stations ready to execute their duties. "Do we have a visual of the fleet?" John asked as he monitored EXODUS's systems from his command chair.

"Stand by," Julie said as she reworked the sensors to compensate for the distortion the energy readings were creating. Succeeding, she punched up the images of the Screen fleet as a hologram above the operations table.

As the images came up, the familiar piercing sound preceding a Screen appearance resounded throughout the ship. John jumped down from his seat and joined Julie and Alex'sis at the operations table. Together, they stared at the three-dimensional images of the alien ships. Despite everything, it was a beautiful sight. The triangular ships' familiar bright green hulls shimmered like stars in the blackness of space.

"My god," Julie muttered under her breath. She was hardly able to comprehend the sheer number of ships she was seeing. No one had ever seen a group of Screen ships. Before, only a single ship had attacked. Regardless of EXODUS's advanced technology and size, how could it hope to survive an attack from an alien fleet?

John tried to swallow the lump in his throat. His attention was on the two larger ships accompanying the fighters. They looked the same as their diminutive green and triangular counterparts—just bigger. But their size was intimidating, even if EXODUS was far larger than both craft.

"Analysis of the larger ships," he managed to say without sounding too nervous.

Alex'sis already had the information ready. "The ships are equipped with one primary particle beam weapon. It's supported by four secondary beam weapons, two fore and two aft."

"That's it?"

"With the exception of the four secondary weapons, they're dependent on a single primary weapon. Their offensive make-up is no different from the fighters' weaponry."

Julie was astonished. In comparison, a TERRA fighter and capital ship were heavily armed. Yet the Screen had remained the dominant force all these years using a far simpler arsenal.

"Screen fighters are accelerating toward us," Alex'sis said. "Their weapons are fully charged."

"Notify our fighters not to engage until the enemy has approached within 5,000 kilometers," John ordered. "Activate our pulse guns and target the fighters." The two larger ships were holding back. He assumed they would not engage first to see what effect multiple fighters had against EXODUS. Test the enemy using fighters first rather than engage with a full-frontal assault. It was a smart tactical move on their part.

"Screen fighters on approach," Alex'sis said. "Here they come."

John made no effort to return to his command chair. He was going to handle the fight alongside Julie and Alex'sis at the operations table.

The Screen fighters screamed toward EXODUS and her supporting Interceptors. As soon as they hit 5,000 kilometers, the Interceptors broke formation and attacked. The Interceptors opened fire first. Two Screen fighters were instantly destroyed before they could respond with their own attack. However, none of the Interceptors were hit by weapons fire. Some of the Screen fighters fired at them, but the bulk of the enemy force concentrated their attack on EXODUS. Particle beams repeatedly bombarded the massive ship. The inside of the EXODUS shuddered a little from the strikes.

"Multiple impacts from Screen weapons to our lower hull," Alex'sis reported. "The shields are absorbing the blasts; however, we're already at 80 percent absorption."

The ship's shields could only take in so much energy at a given time. Once they hit 100 percent absorption, the energy could only be deflected, which increased the odds of causing a breach to the shield system.

"The Screen fighters are ignoring our Interceptors and concentrating their attack on us," Julie said. "They're moving faster than before. Our targeting scanners can't get a positive lock on them."

"Adjust targeting scanners to compensate. Try to predict their flight paths," John instructed his xo. "Have our fighters close in. Make them a more serious target for the Screen."

The Interceptors moved quickly to try and disperse the Screen fighters and divert their attention from EXODUS. Although a couple of enemy fighters did counterattack, most were still concentrating their fire on the large starship. The Screen's tactics provided an advantage to the Interceptors. They were having an easier time targeting the Screen fighters and picking them off in quick succession.

"Fifteen enemy fighters destroyed," Alex'sis reported, sounding pleased at the outcome so far.

John was still concerned. The Screen had a plan. He knew it. They wouldn't just send in their fighters to be picked off.

His instincts were correct. As EXODUS was busy battling the fighters, the two larger Screen vessels had crept in closer.

"Commander, the larger Screen ships are powering their primary weapons," Julie reported. She looked up at John in a panic. "They're targeting our lower hull."

John knew instantly what they had planned. The fighters had been sent in to attack one area of the EXODUS. The goal was to weaken her shields in one spot. With the crew concentrating their efforts on destroying the fighters, no one had thought to pay attention to the larger ships. Now that they were in proximity, the larger enemy ships were in a perfect position to attack. How could John have been so stupid?

"Helm, turn us about!" John yelled to Kevin. "Don't let them see our lower front hull!"

Kevin hit the thrusters to try and turn the ship around, but EXODUS was too slow. A single particle beam streamed from both ships and struck the starship's shields, obliterating the remaining Screen fighters and taking out a few Interceptors who weren't quick enough to fly out of the beams' paths. The impact was too much for the shield grid to absorb at once. The shield in the lower hull area breached and the remnants of the particle beams impacted the hull.

The ship rocked violently from the strike. Everyone on the command deck held onto the nearest thing that was bolted down to prevent themselves from being thrown across the deck. John, Julie, and Alex'sis all managed to stay upright by holding onto the operations table. Alarms blared throughout the ship. Damage had been done. John looked down at the table and saw the ships still closing in, ready to finish off EXODUS.

John's mind went blank as fear finally got the better of him. They couldn't fail. They had made it this far. He couldn't falter now...no, he couldn't die. He had too much at stake to let the Screen win. Too many people here and at home were depending on him.

John checked the weapons systems. They were still operational. While Julie and Alex'sis were assessing the damage to the ship, the young commander punched in his command codes. He wasn't taking any chances. It was now or never. He had every weapon—primaries, even the auxiliaries—open fire on the Screen ships at once.

Despite their impressive size, the Screen never had a chance against the full force of EXODUS. The two larger ships managed to hold together for about six seconds before breaking apart under the enormous firepower. And then, as quickly as it started, it was over.

John, weak at the knees at seeing the enemy obliterated, barely managed to shut down the weapons. He looked at the sensor readings and verified that the entire Screen fleet had been destroyed.

"We've got a huge drain to primary power," Alex'sis reported as she assessed the data coming in from all over the ship. Firing all the weapons simultaneously had caused a significant power loss to the ship. It was going to hamper repair efforts.

"I'm routing power from the engine core to compensate," Julie said, looking up at John, who was leaning heavily on the table.

John's heart was beating so fast, he thought he would pass out. "Damage report," he said, as he pulled himself up to a standing position.

"Hull breaches on levels 43 through 47, sections 3 through 7C," Julie replied. "Multiple plasma leaks and fires are being reported. The fire extinguishing system is offline in those areas. Force fields on level 47 have failed, but emergency bulkheads have sealed that area."

John almost didn't hear her. His mind was swirling with so many thoughts that it took him a few moments to process what Julie had said. "Get medical and repair crews down there ASAP," he said as he gathered his thoughts. "What's the status of our shields?"

Alex'sis checked the shields. "The grid is at 85 percent. The shield breach has already sealed."

John simply nodded. He looked over at Julie. "Commander Olson, you have the command deck. Recall all remaining fighters back to the hangar and continue to facilitate repair crews to needed areas. I'll be down there helping out."

"Yes sir," Julie replied. It was strange. John was showing no elation after their victory. She had pictured him gloating over their survival against the Screen and bragging how it was all thanks to his great leadership. Instead, she watched a man walk away who seemed grounded and focused. She got the sense that John felt defeated.

"Commander, what about jumping out of the system?" Kevin asked John as the commander headed to the upper walkway.

"Not until all repairs are complete, everyone is accounted for, and we've had a chance to collect ourselves," John replied in a somber tone. He needed to take stock of their situation. He wasn't sure he had a place on the ship anymore. His behavior during the battle had been appalling. Admiral Johnson had made a huge mistake choosing John to command this ship. TERRA was right, he didn't deserve to be an officer.

The command staff watched John step onto the lift. Kevin looked over at Julie. He too could see the commander was not happy.

Alex'sis shouted and got everyone focused back on their duties. "You heard the man. Let's get to work."

—— —— ——

After sixteen hours of grueling work, John lay on the couch in his office. His face was covered in sweat and he didn't bother to wash it off. He'd worked side by side with the repair crews as they pulled twisted metal and debris from the damaged sections of the ship. He'd assisted the medical teams in reaching those trapped behind or beneath the rubble in the damaged areas.

All throughout the cleanup, people had patted John on the back and congratulated him on a job well done. Despite incurring some casualties, the ship and crew had survived an attack from multiple Screen vessels. Such a feat had been inconceivable a day ago. EXODUS had accomplished what no other human-operated ship had ever done.

But the more people congratulated John, the worse he felt. He couldn't help but feel like a complete fraud. His actions during the battle had been reckless and uncoordinated. It was only dumb luck that they'd prevailed. He was so scared to lose, no, to die that he'd thrown out his military training in a desperate move to achieve victory.

As the crew celebrated surviving the Screen attack, John went over in his mind how he had failed personally and professionally. All he wanted to do was hand over command of EXODUS to Julie, take a mid-range shuttle back to Earth, and face whatever consequences were awaiting him. His dream of commanding a starship felt like nothing more than a heap of smoldering debris.

The door chime rang. John looked over at the door, not in the mood for company, and decided to ignore the ring. Whoever was there would take the hint and leave. But the door chimed again.

"Come in," he said, ready to promptly tell the person to get out. When he saw it was Julie, he sighed. She was the last person he wanted to talk to right now.

"What is it?" he asked, not bothering to sit up on the couch.

She handed him a computer printout. "It's a summary of our casualties and ship repair status," she answered. "The final tally is three people dead, sixteen wounded."

John skimmed the printout. The three dead people were Interceptor pilots whose fighters had been incinerated by the

Screen particle beams that hit the ship.

"Repairs are almost done. We should be ready to jump in less than twelve hours."

"Yeah." That was all John could muster.

Julie could tell that he was upset. "You've been in a funk since the attack. You should be pleased. We'll be out of the solar system in less than a day. Before you know it, we'll be out there exploring the galaxy."

"The ship will, but I won't."

"What? Why? What's wrong?"

John sat up. "What's wrong is I completely fucked up out there. My performance was miserable."

Julie was confused. What the hell was John talking about? "Miserable? We defeated the Screen and took out two of their ships that humans have never encountered before."

"By unloading all our weapons in one attack. Not exactly a move a halfway decent tactician would perform. I panicked and let my emotions get the better of me. I got scared, Julie."

Julie was taken aback. So that's why he was acting so depressed. Boy, after all these years, he still managed to surprise her. How could she have ever thought of replacing him as the ship commander? She plopped down on the couch next to him. Neither looked at the other, only the floor.

Julie couldn't hold it in any longer and started to laugh. "I don't believe it. The great John Roberts admits he's not perfect. If only Billy was here to see this."

John gave her a nasty look. He hadn't expected any sympathy from her. But to kick him while he was down was simply mean. "I'm glad you're savoring the moment."

Julie managed to compose herself. "I'm sorry, really. Listen, I'll admit that what you did was unorthodox."

"Unorthodox? That's the same stunt I'd pull during battle simulations just to get a rise out of the instructors."

"And show them that sometimes the best move is the one least expected." Julie put her hand on John's knee. "And you know what? It worked. We destroyed the Screen and have a ship that's still intact. What matters is that we won. You did good."

"I should have held it together. I've always looked down on people who let fear override their senses. But that's exactly what I did! Those are emotions a commander needs to control."

It was Julie's turn to open up to John. "How do you think I felt? I wanted to crawl into a hole and close my eyes. Just think how the rest of the crew felt. They were scared too. None of us expected to survive.

"You're too hard on yourself John. You did great and I'm proud of you. You should be too. You met all the objectives you set out for us. We made it through the solar system without firing on any TERRA ship, rescued a pilot, and survived two Screen attacks. Everything from here on out is going to be new to us. We're going to make our share of mistakes. But if we lean on each other, we'll get through it. You've already proven yourself to me. I now know I can depend on you."

John nodded slightly.

"I've been approached by people all day telling me what a remarkable job you did. You've earned the crew's respect and not because of Admiral Johnson. You earned it because you're a good leader. Your actions out there demonstrated that. You belong in the command chair."

John looked at Julie and gave her a sincere smile. He thought about what to say but he could only come up with, "So, should we commemorate this moment with a kiss? No tongue, of course."

Julie shoved him away. "And some things never change."

"I'm kidding. Despite how I acted before, I did listen to what you said about me earlier. Thank you." He looked over to his desk and the platinum picture frame on it. There was no picture in it, but two names were engraved on the frame itself.

Julie recognized it from their dorm. "Can I ask you who Princess and Spot-C are?" She had asked him once before, when they first moved to Dorm Row, but John had never answered her or even acknowledged the question. She assumed it had to do with his family. He never discussed them. Julie hardly knew anything about his past.

John got up from the couch and took the picture frame off his desk. He looked at it for a long moment, remembering—then looked at Julie and decided it was time to let someone in. As a gesture, he handed her the frame.

"My parents died when I was little. I had an older sister who took care of me after they were gone. But when I was twelve, she left home and disappeared. I have no idea why she left, and I never saw her again."

"I'm sorry," Julie said sympathetically. No wonder he was such an independent person. Julie had lost her mother and had no memory of her. She couldn't imagine having lost her dad as well. John had not only lost his parents but had a sister walk out on him. To lose so many people close to him must have been hard. "So, who are Princess and Spot-C?"

John just smiled. "My cats."

Julie didn't expect that answer. "Your pets?"

John sat back on the couch. "It was tough when Nicole left. I didn't know what to do. I certainly wasn't going to a foster home, so I stayed home. Our house was situated on a huge lot, so it wasn't hard to maintain the illusion that my sister was still around. But it was hard being there by myself and I got emotional support from the most unlikely of places."

Julie looked at the picture frame again. John was fortunate to have this personal memento with such pleasant memories associated to it.

She handed the frame back to John, who ran his hand over the three names on it. Julie likely assumed the X situated in the lower center of the frame was a just design mark, and John chose not to clarify. "I think they knew how hard it was for me. I could talk to them about anything and they would listen."

"You're lucky to have them."

John nodded. "I lost Princess the year before I came to the Academy. I think she knew I was leaving and couldn't take her with me to New York. It was hard when she died."

"And Spot-C?"

"I took her to a Buddhist sanctuary in Sedona, Arizona when

I left for the Academy. She died two years ago." Tears started to well up in his eyes.

Julie could see how much the cats had meant to John. This man she had hated for four years, he had a heart. She patted him on the back.

"I think they'd be so proud of you right now."

"Yeah." He looked at his executive officer. "Thanks, Julie." He regretted never giving her the chance to befriend him. She wasn't such a bad person after all.

"Sure thing," she replied as the doorbell chimed.

"Come in," John said as he reined in his emotions and wiped the tears from his eyes.

"Commander. Commander," Bret said as he entered. "Do you have a moment?"

"Sure," John replied. "What's up?"

"I finished analyzing our data from our first Screen encounter. I ran the data through a multispectral analyzer and picked up a signal that the fighter sent out of the solar system just before we destroyed it. The signal was faint but had a complex frequency algorithm. That indicates that a significant amount of data was sent in the transmission. My theory is that the fighter sent information about its encounter with us to its compatriots."

"That makes sense," Julie said. "When they knew a fighter couldn't stop us, they sent two larger ships for the second attack."

Bret nodded. "I ran the same analysis of our last fight and picked up the same transmissions being sent out by one of the larger ships."

"Oh shit," John said as he realized the implications. He'd been afraid of something like that happening.

"You're worried?" Julie asked him.

"I fired all of EXODUS's weapons to destroy the larger ships. If they were scanning us during the fight and collected data about the ship's capabilities, it would be valuable information to their superiors. They'll know what this ship is capable of and will adapt for our next encounter. They may not be so easy to defeat next time."

Julie and Bret both realized John had a valid point. The Screen had changed their tactics in their second battle by sending larger vessels. With additional information about EXODUS now in their possession, chances were that the Screen would change their tactics again to defeat the ship. The Screen had been caught off guard twice. They wouldn't make the same mistake a third time.

"They may have more information about us, but we also have more information about them," Julie reminded the two officers. "The intel we gathered from our two encounters should be very helpful in improving our defenses. We'll just have to stay one step ahead of them."

John nodded in agreement. "Bret, was there any chance you were able to track where the signal went?"

"I'm afraid not."

So much for getting an easy trail to a Screen base of operations, or even their homeworld. "Anything else?"

"One more thing. It's about what happened during our second battle with the Screen." Bret handed John a paper with his findings. "Just prior to the fight, I picked up a very small power reading coming from the solar system sensor net. I thought it was a sensor glitch generated from the Screen weapons. But I cross-checked the data and verified the reading was legitimate."

"What's this power spike you detected?" Julie asked.

John handed her the paper. "Someone activated the sensor net."

"I think someone back home was monitoring our activities," Bret speculated.

"We figured TERRA would be monitoring us," Julie said. "That's no surprise."

"The sensor net was reactivated minutes after we picked up the Screen approaching us," Bret said. "How would they know exactly when to reactivate it to monitor the battle? It's too coincidental."

John went from the couch to behind his desk and looked out the window. "What are you saying?"

"With the sensor net out, TERRA would have no idea the Screen had appeared. The only way they would know to activate it at the right time is if the Screen alerted them or someone on this ship told them."

Julie immediately stood up. "You're suggesting that a crewmember somehow sent a message to TERRA and alerted them of our activities?"

"I don't know. It's just a theory."

John pressed him. "But your instincts are telling you that. Otherwise, you wouldn't be saying it."

Bret debated carefully before revealing what he knew. Admiral Johnson had sworn him to secrecy, as this knowledge had the potential to create distrust and dissent within the EXODUS Project.

"A couple years ago there were rumors going around that a spy had infiltrated the project. Admiral Johnson and I investigated it, but we couldn't come up with anything. TERRA never shut down the project and eventually the rumor went away."

"Did Admiral Johnson suspect anyone in particular?" Julie asked.

"He never told me if he did. I'm not even sure how the rumor started. We couldn't even verify if the so-called spy came from TERRA or the government."

"If there was a spy, TERRA would have known of our plan to launch in advance and they would have stopped us," Julie said. "It wouldn't make sense to let us go only to put in all that effort to try and stop us."

"But we can't dismiss the possibility either," John countered. "You're right, it wouldn't make sense. If there is a spy on board, we need to find out who it is and how he or she is contacting TERRA." He looked at Bret. "I want you to start exploring how someone could communicate with TERRA without using the ship's communications systems."

"Yes, Commander."

"I want this to stay between the three of us for now. We don't talk about it to anyone. If there is a spy, I don't want them to get wind of our suspicions."

Julie nodded. "Agreed."

John looked at Bret. "Anything else?"

"That's all, sir," Bret replied.

"Thank you. Dismissed."

Bret nodded and left Julie and John alone in the office.

"Should we let Lieutenant Brandus in on this?" Julie asked. "She's had the most contact with the crew and may be helpful."

John thought about it for a moment. "We'll keep this under wraps for now."

"She won't like that she wasn't included," Julie warned.

"I know, but it's my call. I'll take the brunt of her anger when the time comes."

In this instance, Julie was glad not to be the ship commander. She wouldn't want to be on the receiving end of Alex'sis's wrath when John chose to tell her about this issue.

CHAPTER NINETEEN

"I think you're ready to be checked out," Dr. Myers said as he looked at his patient's bone scans.

The recovering fighter pilot said nothing as he sat on the bed. He had kept quiet since the battle and refused to speak to anyone. Realizing that everything John had told him was true, the pilot wondered what would become of him. As he dwelled on his fate, a familiar voice interrupted his thoughts.

"Good, because I just got quarters assigned to him," John said as he entered the medical bay. He briefly looked at the pilot before walking past him and to Myers, who stood by the surgical control console.

"Commander! Here to see our patient off?"

"Maybe," John said in a low tone, so that the pilot would not hear him. "How is he?"

"Physically, he's fine. He'll still be sore for a few days, but he's recovered."

"And psychologically?"

"He hasn't said a word since the fight. I can't say what it is. It could be fear or uncertainty of what's going to happen to him that's keeping him quiet."

John looked over at the pilot. He knew he would have to talk to him and make one last try at reasoning with him.

Readying himself, John walked over to the bed. "The doctor says you're ready to be discharged."

"You have quarters ready for me?" the pilot asked. "That means you're not sending me back to Mars."

"No, we won't be taking you back. I'm sorry, but it's too great a risk. Our sensors show that TERRA has amassed the bulk of their fleet around Mars. If we went back, they would try to retake the ship. And the longer we stay here, the more likely the Screen will return with a bigger armada."

"I'm trapped."

"I know you never expected this. If I could, I would send you back home. But we both have to make the best of this situation."

"How?"

"For starters, you can become leader of Virgo Fighter Squadron," John offered. "They lost their squad leader in the fight. You have the experience to take over the squad."

"Why would I want to help terrorists?"

"I don't think you look at us as terrorists anymore," John replied. How could he? The ship had gone head to head against the Screen by choice instead of running at the first instance. "If you've been watching what we've been doing, you know that our intentions are not malicious. We're out here because we want better for humanity."

He could tell the pilot was thinking about it, possibly weighing his options. "What exactly are you planning to do?"

"To find out all that we can about the Screen," John replied. "I know this galaxy doesn't consist of just humans and Screen. There have to be other alien civilizations out there that can give us information about the Screen and maybe help us. With luck, we'll be able to locate the Screen homeworld, find out what they have planned for us, and stop them."

"And why should I follow you? You're just a kid."

"Who happens to be the only ship commander in history to defeat the Screen in battle." The response was purely defensive, and John was aware of it as the words flowed from his mouth. He had to stop being so reactive. This wasn't the Academy anymore. There were no professors or superintendents out to get him. He was working with people on a starship and had to be diplomatic if they were to succeed.

John chose his next words carefully. "Everyone here has chosen to follow me. I can't tell you why you should too. All I ask is for you to trust me."

Again, the pilot weighed his options. Whoever this kid was, he had somehow led this crew to victory against the Screen. Since the battle, he had heard people saying how much they respected John. They had confidence in him. He had led them to success, and they were willing to stand behind him.

"Then I guess you have a new squad leader," he answered.

John extended his hand. "Commander John Roberts. Welcome aboard the EXODUS," he said as the two men shook hands.

"Lieutenant Martin Everold."

Dr. Myers looked at them and nodded in satisfaction. He knew Admiral Johnson would be proud to see John right now.

"Commander Roberts, report to the command deck. Repeat, Commander Roberts to the command deck," came the announcement through John's pip. He worried that the ship had picked up a new Screen energy signature, but the absence of the battle siren temporarily abated his concerns.

"The doctor has your room assignment. Get rested for a few days before reporting to the hangar," John said to Lieutenant Everold as he headed out of the medical bay.

John smiled to himself, pleased he had convinced the lieutenant to join their cause. It was one small victory, and much more work needed to be done. EXODUS was going to be the first human-operated starship to explore interstellar space, and John was beginning to realize what an enormous task it would be. The crew had spent years establishing protocols to handle first contact with new alien races, studying and visiting habitable planets. But none of those protocols had been tested. Everything they did from here on out would be a first for everyone.

The lift door opened, and John stepped onto the command deck. "Over here," Julie waved as he walked along the catwalk. She was standing next to Bret at his communications station and John made his way down to the pit to join them. Had something gone awry?

"What is it?" he asked.

Julie smiled, "We got a message from Earth."

"What?" John was confused by her answer. "I hope not from TERRA."

"From us, you blockhead," came a familiar voice from the station speakers. John looked down at the monitor and saw Billy and David. Billy waved to John while David seemed busy checking various monitors..

"I was able to create a logarithmic sequence and send a signal to Earth and disguise it as normal background radiation," Bret said. "I sent it to the comm unit number you gave me and twenty minutes ago got a reply back from Cadets Pedia and Block."

"Twenty minutes?" John asked. "Why'd it take so long?"

David spoke up. "We had to be sure we had the transmission properly concealed before establishing a link."

"There's no indication that anyone from TERRA has detected the signal," Billy announced proudly.

"But this will be the only time we'll be able to communicate in real time," Julie said. "Once we leave the system, we'll only be able to send message packets to Earth."

"You guys don't have communication satellites to deploy?" David asked from behind Billy. If the EXODUS deployed satellite relays, they could continue to communicate in real time, even with the EXODUS hundreds of light years away.

"We have a limited number on board, and I don't want to establish a communication network. The Screen could use it to track our movements. Communicating via message packets will be good enough for what we need." John looked at his friends on the monitor. "Has Bret explained to you what we want done?"

"Don't you worry about it on our end," Billy assured him. "You send videos and reports on your progress and we'll get it out to as many news outlets as possible. We'll make sure that the public knows about what you're doing out there."

David spoke up. "John, TERRA has already reported the ship

was destroyed by the Screen. They've taken full control of the sensor net so no one can confirm their story."

"Undoubtedly, they'll create more propaganda to discount anything we send," Julie said.

"Eventually people will start to question them. They can't keep fooling people forever." John looked at his friends one last time. "Just be careful, you two. If you get caught..."

Billy interrupted him. "We'll be fine. You just keep yourselves alive out there. David and I will take care of things on our end."

"We're rotating toward Luna's trajectory," David told Billy. "We need to disconnect, or risk being picked up by Luna Station."

"Right." Billy looked as his friends one last time. "John, Julie... you two take care."

"You as well," John said as the transmission was cut and the images of his best friends disappeared. He knew it was a real possibility that he would never see them again. Going out into deep space was one thing; coming back to Earth was another.

"There's one more thing." Julie tapped John's shoulder.

The commander looked up from the console and noticed the entire command deck staff standing together behind him. Alex'sis, who was in front of the group, stepped forward.

"It's been discussed with the entire crew and after everything that's happened, we realized we couldn't have the ship led by a commander."

She handed John a small black velvet box, familiar to him from TERRA military ceremonies. When he opened it, he saw a set of gold captain bars.

"I know this is unconventional, but on behalf of the entire crew, we hereby grant you a field promotion to the rank of captain." Alex'sis extended her hand. "Congratulations and thank you for getting us this far."

John took Alex'sis's hand in kind and shook it. The entire command deck crew clapped and cheered in celebration.

CHAPTER TWENTY

President Butu looked out toward the ocean as the sun began to set in Sydney. It was nothing like the sunsets of the mountain region in her home of Ethiopia, but it still provided a calming view that enabled her to clear her thoughts.

The president was waiting for the arrival of Admiral Donalds. She had finally demanded a face-to-face meeting with him after repeated delays by the command council. There had been quite a public stir since the release of footage showing EXODUS was still intact and had defeated several Screen ships. The footage was authenticated, which meant that everything the command council had told the government was a lie. Butu had known the council had not been forthright; still, she was shocked at the extent of their coverup.

The door opened and Butu turned to see her chief of staff walk in alone. "Is the admiral here?" she asked.

Charles said nothing until he was at her desk.

"Admiral Donalds elected not to meet with you in person," he replied in a somber tone. "I communicated the urgency of the meeting, but he was committed in his decision not to come."

Anger welled up in the president. Never in her years in office had she been dismissed in such a manner. TERRA reported directly to the president, but it seemed the command council no longer felt a need to report to her.

"I did manage to convince the admiral to speak with you over communication. He's on the line now."

"Thank you, Charles," she said, concealing her anger. "I'll need some privacy."

Charles nodded. "I'll be heading over to see our guest."

"Let me know how he's doing."

As Charles left, the president turned on her desk monitor and saw the admiral. He looked as smug and arrogant as ever.

"Admiral Donalds, so good to finally speak with you again." She maintained a pleasant composure, even though every bone in her body urged her to show him no mercy.

"And with you as well," he replied in an equally pleasant voice. "My apologies for not keeping in regular contact with you. This whole situation has been most troublesome."

"Oh, I agree. It's quite disturbing what the news has been broadcasting. It contradicts what you've been telling the public and my office."

"Unfortunately, there are those out there who look to discredit TERRA. I hope the public sees this erroneous transmission as the fabrication it is."

"Except it's not a fabrication, is it?" Butu leaned in toward the monitor, her eyes ablaze. "I know the EXODUS wasn't destroyed. Did you think we weren't going to verify the legitimacy of that footage?"

The admiral sat back in his chair and took stock of the situation. "I could deny it. No one in your administration had access to the sensor net."

"Did you really think I was going to sit here and do nothing as you told the world what you wanted them to believe? I know the ship survived two Screen attacks. I know about the dummy dossiers you created on the cadets to discredit them in the eyes of the public."

"Very good, Madam President," the admiral applauded in a mocking tone. "You would do well in TERRA. A shame you will have your hands full confirming our cover story to the public."

"I have no intention of going on with the lies you created."

"You cannot contradict them, either. If you expose our cover story, the people may think you approved of the ship's launch. Some may even think you orchestrated it. It wouldn't be difficult to link the president's office to EXODUS or Admiral Johnson."

"If that's supposed to scare me, then you've threatened the wrong woman."

"Who's the public going to believe? A president who deals with planetary affairs, or us, who have protected humanity from the Screen for generations? TERRA is revered by everyone. We protect the well-being of our territories. It's because of TERRA that the Screen has never attacked Mars, Luna, or Earth."

Unfortunately, Butu knew Donalds had the advantage. A showdown between TERRA and the government would certainly result in the public siding with TERRA. The organization was simply too well respected. Butu's presidency would be consumed by such a fight. She would become a lame duck.

"Don't be too sure about how you're regarded," she said. "Not everyone in TERRA holds the institution in such high esteem. The people on EXODUS have proven that TERRA has its own dissenters."

"That ship is gone and the chance of her surviving in space is negligible."

"She's already survived two Screen encounters. If she could do that, then I believe she'll survive in space. TERRA will have a lot to answer for the day she returns home." Butu was ready to turn the monitor off but had one more comment. "By the way, did you ever locate Admiral Johnson?"

Donalds looked at her with wide eyes. She ended the call before he could respond.

Butu sat back in her seat and took a deep breath. Her relationship with TERRA had permanently changed. She could never trust them again. But she had to be careful. TERRA was the military and could try to exert martial law over Earth, Luna, and Mars if the relationship between the president and the organization degenerated. Not even Earth Security would be enough to repel TERRA if such a scenario occurred.

Her interoffice line beeped. It was her assistant, Janice.

"What is it?" Butu asked.

"The techs just dropped off the bot. It's out here waiting for you."

"Good, send it in alone. Did they find anything wrong with it?"

"According to them, the bot's old but in perfect working order."

Butu saw the door open and the black bot roll in. "Thank you, Janice."

Butu disconnected the line and stood up. She had been given regular updates regarding this house bot who called itself X.

It had taken a lot of convincing from the agents to separate X from Admiral Johnson. Only when the bot saw the admiral was receiving medical care did it agree to leave the hospital. Given its odd behavior, the bot had been thoroughly checked out before being interviewed by the president.

"Hello there," Butu said. X's upper body rotated so its ocular sensors could lock onto her. The bot said nothing and seemed to be gauging the president. "Do you know who I am?"

"Your physical parameters conform to President Mushari Butu, president of the government."

"That's correct," Butu confirmed as she stepped from behind her desk and approached the bot. "Do you know why you're here?"

"It has been stated that you wish to have a private conversation with this unit."

"Is that all right?"

"Are you the one responsible for arranging Admiral Johnson's care?"

Butu found it strange for the bot to ask such a question. They had not even addressed the issue of the admiral, yet the bot had taken it upon itself to inquire about him.

Butu nodded. "I am. I was told the admiral's quite ill."

"Your assessment is correct. This unit is grateful for your assistance with him and will answer any question you may have."

This bot was acting very strange. It seemed to display emotional concern for others. The president had never seen such traits in a bot. It made her uneasy and she wondered if maybe the technicians had missed something in their assessment.

"Do you mind if I sit down?" Butu asked as she sat on the couch.

"I understand you lived at the Roberts residence in California."

X moved around the couch and stood near the president. "Correct. This unit was initially owned by John Senior and Graciella Roberts. When they died, this unit assisted Nicole in raising John."

"She became your owner?"

X looked away from the president for a few moments and contemplated the question. It looked again at her when it replied. "According to law this unit was technically owned by Nicole; however, this arrangement was not reflected in the structuring of the household. Nicole, John, and this unit were a family unit."

This bot intrigued and unnerved Butu at the same time. It seemed to be able to convey some sort of self-awareness. Such a thing was impossible with bots. Research into artificial intelligence was still in its relative infancy. It was still far from making a bot self-aware.

"When Nicole departed, this unit assumed responsibilities for John's care. When John moved to New York, this unit's primary function was relegated to the house's upkeep."

"Why did Admiral Johnson come to the house?"

"John sent an electronic message to this unit stating that Admiral Johnson might reside temporarily at the house and to obey all his instructions."

"Did John tell you anything else?" Butu was hoping the cadet had confided in the bot about EXODUS and their plans.

"John informed this unit that he was leaving the planet and would not return for an extended length of time. He requested this unit continue watching the house in his absence."

The president had learned that the house had been destroyed. "Did you or the admiral blow up the house?"

"Admiral Johnson was the only individual capable of detonating the house with people inside. Since it is against this unit's programming to harm a person, I could not execute such a task."

Butu was relieved to hear that the bot still seemed to have its basic programming parameters intact. "John never told you about where he was or what he was doing?"

"Negative," X replied.

Butu was disappointed to hear this. She was hoping the bot would have yielded some new information.

"May this unit make several inquiries?" X asked.

The question dumbfounded the president. "Of...of course."

"Do you know where John is and when he might return?"

Butu was amazed at the affection the bot seemed to hold for people. She thought about telling it where John was but felt it best to keep the bot in the dark.

"I'm afraid I don't know. I was hoping you had an idea."

X rolled away from the couch and to the window, looking out at the view. Butu was genuinely touched by what she saw. She wasn't sure, but she felt that X was saddened at not having any news about its owner.

"With the house nonexistent, this unit is no longer able to fulfill its functions," X stated. Its ocular sensor rotated back toward the president. "What will become of me?"

"It hasn't been decided," Butu replied. "What would you like to happen?"

"Logically, this unit should be turned over to Robonetrix for refurbishment and upgrade so it may be sold to another family or company. However, a refurbishment would entail a memory wipe and this unit does not wish to have its memory lost."

Butu stood up. "You don't want to lose your identity?"

"This unit has many years of memories of its time with John. It would not want to lose those memories. This unit also made a promise to Admiral Johnson to ensure he is properly cared for."

Butu had seen many things in her life, but nothing could match what she was witnessing. Somehow this bot had made a personal connection with the people in its life. It had transcended its basic programming and was able to formulate thoughts and opinions about others.

Butu approached X and kneeled to face its ocular sensors. "How about you stay here with me? I promise you won't be refurbished, and we can both wait until John returns."

"That is a most agreeable offer," said X. "Why would you agree to take ownership of this unit?"

Butu patted the bot on its dome. "Because it's the right thing to do. Sometimes people do things because it's simply the right thing to do."

"It is logical to assume that John would be satisfied with this arrangement." X turned its sight again toward the window. Butu joined it in watching the night filling the sky.

——— ——— ———

Charles had the presidential car take him to the local hospital. It dropped him off in the back of the building, where two Secret Service agents were guarding the door. He headed inside and down the stairs, making arrangements to have the entire basement level evacuated per orders of the president. The only individuals down here were the president's personal medical staff and Secret Service agents.

Charles knew exactly where he was going. He had personally made all the arrangements. He entered a room and found the president's chief medical doctor and nurse talking. The room was mostly bare, with only medical equipment lining the back wall. In front of the equipment was a bed where Admiral Oliver Johnson rested.

"Doctor," Charles announced himself. He shook hands with the older gentleman and nodded to the nurse. "Have you finished all your tests?"

"I did, and the results are not good," the doctor replied. "The admiral is suffering from severe dementia. It's apparent that he's had this condition for years. Blood tests indicate he was taking medication for it, but his condition has deteriorated severely. He's at the point where his medication can no longer suppress his symptoms."

"Have you tried treating him?"

"We've tried various combinations, but nothing's worked. His body has developed immunities to the medications he was taking and nothing else has proven effective. We'll continue to do what we can for him, but I'm afraid he's beyond help."

Charles knelt by the bed and looked at the admiral, who was tranquilized and asleep. He felt sorry for him. This great man, thought of so highly by everyone, was now reduced to the mental state of a child.

"He's become extremely combative, so it's easier to keep him sedated. Probably easier on him as well," the doctor added.

Charles stood up. "The president wants you to explore every possibility of helping him. Whatever it takes and whatever resources you need. He's the only one who can tell us about the EXODUS."

——— ——— ———

TERRA's head of security walked alone down the corridor of the security wing of TERRA headquarters on Luna. Admiral Vespia was heading to her office after meeting with the command council. She did not want to attend; however, she knew it was prudent to be present for all command meetings if for no other reason than to keep her eye on Admiral Donalds. The situation with EXODUS was precarious, and Vespia wanted to keep tabs on the entire council in case one or more of them tried to make her the scapegoat if things went sour.

The admiral passed through the reception area and went straight to her office. Her assistant had left for the day, which suited Vespia fine. She wanted to be alone. Once inside, she punched a passcode in the door terminal and locked herself in her office.

"Computer, bring up all outgoing transmissions from Luna," she said as she poured herself some tea.

"Working." A computer monitor popped up from the top of the admiral's desk. Vespia grabbed it and activated it.

"Any messages for me?"

"Three messages. One message flagged as VDC-1 priority."

That caught the admiral's attention. She sat down at her large maple desk and looked at the message. It was verbal only.

"Verify authenticity of message."

"Verifying. Authentication of message verified."

"Download message to this station. Then terminate all data

streams coming in and out of this building. Authorization Vespia 2-9-1-7-Alpha-6-9."

"Working."

The admiral sat back in her black leather chair. The plush cushion cooled the back of her neck. She wasn't sure if she would ever receive a message from her operative. It had been years since she'd heard from them.

"Message downloaded," the computer announced. "All data transmissions to and from the facility have ceased."

"Play the message."

"Admiral Vespia." The message was scratchy and distorted.

"Run the message through the filters," Vespia ordered. "Clean up any background noise and enhance vocal patterns."

There was a momentary pause as the computer ran the message through some algorithms. A few seconds later, the message replayed.

"Admiral Vespia." The voice sounded clearer but still distorted. The admiral recognized that a voice modulator had been used to prevent identification of the person speaking. She trained her operatives well.

"As of this message being recorded, I'm on board EXODUS, which is now in the outer solar system. As you may already have concluded, the technologies on this ship have worked successfully under full operation. Admiral Oliver Johnson vacated the ship prior to his launch, and you should be able to locate him somewhere on Earth. He has placed the command of this ship in the hands of cadets John Roberts and Julie Olson. They intend to carry out Admiral Johnson's orders to learn more about the Screen."

Vespia knew Johnson was an idealist and admired him for it. She also knew he was pragmatic and never thought he'd be foolish enough to launch EXODUS.

"I never expected this ship would survive. The Mars cannon should have disabled or destroyed her, but as you already know, that's been proven wrong. Since I haven't had any contact with you since the launch, I assume you'll want me to take whatever means necessary to prevent the ship from completing its mission. Unless I bring the ship under my control, this will be my last communication to you. I suggest any intelligence you have on EXODUS be discarded immediately."

"End of message," the computer announced. Vespia pounded her fist on the desk. She wanted to contact her operative to issue new orders, but she couldn't risk it. She knew Donalds was keeping a close eye on her. Her agent was going to do something she didn't want them to do: destroy EXODUS. The ship was leaving the system and she wanted it to complete its mission.

"Computer, erase all traces of this message. Then access all files regarding EXODUS and destroy them as well."

"Working," the computer replied.

The information she had about EXODUS was valuable. If it was ever discovered that Vespia had been gathering intelligence on the EXODUS Project, Admiral Donalds would certainly use it to brand her a traitor for not coming forward to stop the ship's launch. It was better that the information was destroyed so that she could never be traced back to EXODUS.

"Files erased," the computer announced.

"Good." Vespia opened her desk drawer and pulled out a paper file. It contained information on the agent Vespia had deployed to the project. She took the precaution to never keep information about this agent on the computer server. As far as anyone knew, the agent had never existed.

She flipped through the file. Tonight, it would be going into the fireplace at her home. Her only goal now was to locate Admiral Johnson and bring him in without Donalds finding out. Her plans for Johnson were quite different from TERRA's.

CHAPTER TWENTY-ONE

John was sitting in his office, reading various reports filed by EXODUS personnel over the past twenty years. He wanted to get a sense of the people who made up the crew. He was amazed how much he was learning from these reports.

If John could sum up the crew's attitude in one word, it was that they were passionate. Each person was dedicated to the mission and what their expertise could contribute to help make this journey a success. They had all pledged to support Admiral Johnson during his tenure as project leader. With him gone, they had now pledged to follow John as he led them through uncharted space.

"Captain Roberts, please report to the command deck," Julie said over the ship's speakers. It was time. The ship was now repaired, and the hyper-drive was primed and ready to go.

John stood up and headed out to the command deck. The captain bars rested nicely on his shoulders. He took one quick glance at the platinum picture frame on his desk—the one with no picture, only the words 'Princess, X, and Spot-C' engraved on the frame.

"I did it, you guys. I did it."

He thought about X for a moment. He wished he could have

seen his house bot one last time. During his last few years at home, he had taken the bot for granted. He'd grown distant from it as he focused on his preparations to enter the Academy. Hopefully, X would still be there when he got back.

He turned and left his office, stepping out on the catwalk and heading down into the pit. His senior staff was waiting, including the doctor and chief of security.

"We're ready, Captain," Julie said from the operations table.

John looked around. Everyone was focused on him.

"Open speakers," he instructed his executive officer.

Julie activated the ship-wide speakers so the entire crew would hear what John had to say. She nodded to him that the channel was open.

At first, he couldn't think of what to say. He'd wanted to have some speech ready to give the crew. But as hard as he tried, he couldn't come up with anything. He decided to simply speak from his heart.

"Attention crew, this is the captain. In just a few moments we'll begin a remarkable journey, a journey that humanity tried to start long ago with the HORIZON. Each of you understands the dangers facing us. We have no support from home and face an enemy we know little about. But despite that, we have already prevailed. Some of you are wondering if we're ready for this. I knew we were the moment I watched this crew work together in the face of adversity. You all have been working for years to get to this moment. That preparedness is what will allow us to succeed."

John took a breath before continuing. Julie could not help but admire her former roommate and how much he had grown up these past few days. When Admiral Johnson had told them that John would lead this ship, Julie thought it was a mistake that would only lead to disaster. Now that thought seemed nothing more than a distant memory.

"Admiral Johnson made it clear what the ship's mission objective should be. To seek out the Screen, learn their true intent toward humanity, and find a means to eliminate them as a threat. But that will not be our only mission. The existence of the Screen proves there is life out there. There's a chance that other advanced alien races exist. We'll seek them out. They may have information about the Screen that we need. If we can forge alliances with them, it will increase our chance of success.

"Our journey will be difficult, but there are millions of people back home depending on us, even if they don't know it yet."

John looked at his command deck crew. Alex'sis, Julie, Bret, Joseph, and Kevin all looked back at John with confidence. Satisfied with his speech, he headed to his command chair.

"All decks, prepare for jump," he ordered.

"Aye, Captain." Julie focused on her computer console. "All decks, prepare for jump."

"Navigation ready," Kevin reported. "We're ready to jump to Alpha Centauri at your command."

Julie turned to John. "All decks report ready."

John looked up at the stars through the windows on the upper command deck. He would never get tired of that view. What was waiting for them out there? It was a thought that had excited John back at the Academy and a dream that had finally come true.

"Navigation, engage the hyper-drive. Take us to Alpha Centauri."

The ship headed away from the solar system and out toward space. On the hull, the place where the word EXODUS was once displayed had been blacked out by the ship's repair crews. Instead, a new name was displayed prominently in red: PHOENIX. The ship that had originally been intended to facilitate humanity's escape was now a symbol of rebirth for humanity's journey into the stars.

The hum of the engines grew louder as the energy buildup increased. Then, in an instant, the newly-born PHOENIX flew out of the solar system and disappeared into the unknown.

THE GALAXY AWAITS...

The adventures of the TXS PHOENIX and her crew continues in
Phoenix Among The Stars

NOVELS BY ROBERT STADNIK

EXODUS SERIES
Exodus Of The Phoenix
Phoenix Among The Stars
Phoenix In Chaos
Fury Of The Phoenix
Fractured Alliance

EXODUS UNIVERSE
The Io Effect
The Jumpgate
Infinite Retribution

HEROES & CONSEQUENCES
Tales Of A Former Child Superhero

CPSIA information can be obtained
at www.ICGtesting.com
Printed in the USA
FSHW011613051220
76518FS